Just Like Candy

Kimberly Kaye Terry

D0815422

APHRODISIA
KENSINGTON BOOKS
http://www.kensingtonbooks.com

APHRODISIA BOOKS are published by

Kensington Publishing Corp.
850 Third Avenue
New York, NY 10022

All Kensington Titles, Imprints, and Distributed Lines are available at special quantity discounts for bulk purchases for sales promotions, premiums, fund-raising, and educational or institutional use.

Special book excerpts or customized printings can also be created to fit specific needs. For details, write or phone the office of the Kensington special sales manager: Kensington Publishing Corp., 850 Third Avenue, New York, NY 10022, attn: Special Sales Department, Phone: 1-800-221-2647.

Aphrodisia and the A logo Reg. U.S. Pat & TM Off.

ISBN-13: 978-0-7582-2249-7
ISBN-10: 0-7582-2249-1

First Kensington Trade Paperback Printing: January 2008

10 9 8 7 6 5 4 3 2 1

Printed in the United States of America

This is dedicated to my beautiful daughters. The first two, in heaven, inspired me to begin this journey of writing. The third, whom I'm blessed to have here on earth, continually motivates me to be the best I can be.

To my wonderful husband, Bill: Thanks for putting up with my sometimes diva-like attitude, late nights writing and my many theatrics over the last thirteen years. I love you, Boo.

To my editor Hilary Sares: You rock, mama ;)

Nyame-nti

Imanhan

1

"Please . . . don't stop this time."

The sounds of her groans were loud and harsh in the still of the room as she tossed her head on the pillow. She arched her body up from the bed in sharp response to her lover's latest ministrations.

Oooh, it felt *sooo* good.

When he pressed the heel of his palm in just the right spot—in her special spot—the spot that no other man had ever figured out *did it* for her, she almost came.

She felt the ease of cream as it slid down the inside of her thigh despite her automatic and natural inclination to clench her legs together.

He laughed low and throaty and then she felt his strong, capable hands spread her legs even further apart. He forced her thighs wide, and she was left open and vulnerable as he stared at her naked, bared flesh.

She was forced to close her eyes, the excitement was nearly too much to bear.

She exhaled a long, shaky breath.

In all honesty she didn't care that she was exposed. Not here, not now.

Neither did she feel the slightest bit of embarrassment . . . nothing mattered as long as he gave her what she needed.

And she was more than certain he would.

He knew just what to do to get her wet and ready. Ready for anything and everything he had in store for her.

"Candy, I bet you taste as good as your name, baby, just the way I like it, sweet, sugary . . . and sticky."

He bent his head and inhaled long and deep.

"Ummm. You even smell good," he rumbled in his deep, throaty, "let-me-do-you" voice. The kind of voice that made a woman want to snatch off all her clothes and give in to his every heated, pussy-clenching demand.

Candy felt no shame accepting—no, begging—for his sweet, sweet touch. She was wanton and didn't give a hot damn. As long as he would give her what she wanted, she was one happy woman.

"Do you want it, Candy? Do you want *me*?" he breathed against the inside of her thigh.

Candy nearly came from his low-talking barrage, from the way one of his big hands stroked back and forth over the short, tight hairs covering her mound.

As he spoke, the heel of his other hand kept the pressure steady and direct above her pubic bone. Lord, this man was lethal.

"Ummm. Yes," she moaned.

Candy didn't have the strength to say much more than that. She was helplessly trapped in a sensual web of her own making.

"What do I want to hear? What do you have to say for me to give you what you need, baby?"

If he didn't give her what she wanted soon, didn't just *do* her the way she longed to be done, she was going to lose her ever-lovin' mind.

At the point they'd currently reached, there was nothing she wouldn't say or do to get him to finally finish what he'd started months ago.

"Please," she whispered, barely able to choke the words out, past the tight constriction in her throat. "Please, please . . . give me what I want . . ."

Her shameless plea was cut off mid-beg by a long keen when he licked one finger, gently separated her slick folds and *stroked* her.

"You beg so pretty, Candy. But what else? What else do I want to hear? *Tell me what you want me to do to you.*"

"Please, don't make me say it!" she pleaded. "You know what I want," she said in a low, barely audible voice.

She cried out again when he slid one finger, and then another into her wet slit, working his way inside the tight opening. She squirmed around his thick fingers and clenched the walls of her vagina in response.

"You tell me what I want to hear and I'll give you what we both want," he lifted his head and promised. The look in his light grey eyes was lusty and demanding, before he turned his attention back to her bared pussy.

He stroked a swift, deadly caress with his tongue, separating her vaginal lips. He captured the hood covering her clit between his teeth, ferreted out her tightly drawn bud, and slowly, so slowly . . . released it.

The sudden, unexpected caress forced Candy to cry out in passionate disbelief.

This was as far as he'd ever gone in his lovemaking. She was filled with nervous excitement, hoping this time, at last, he would satisfy her.

Candy would finally get to feel the long hard length of him embedded deep inside her. She lay back down against the pillows with her heart pounding erratically in her chest and knew it was now or never.

It always came to this. This was the point where he'd offer her an ultimatum and she would retreat, unable to give him what he demanded. Afraid.

But not this time.

No. This time, she was ready and beyond tired of being strung out, begging him for the release only he could give her. No other man would do.

She was tired of fear holding her back. This was the man she wanted, and no one else.

No one else *did* it for her. No one created this deep, all-encompassing, yearning . . . this crazy *ache* in her heart, like he did.

She took a deep, determined breath and held it for a fraction of a second, before she slowly released the pent-up air.

This time she would give him the words he demanded. She'd admit to him what he already knew.

"I want you to fuck me."

She knew the words were stark, bold. Didn't leave much to the imagination. But there it was.

"Nice start, Candy," he breathed against her inner thigh and stroked her again with his hot, talented tongue. "But *how* do you want me to fuck you?"

Oh god. This was going to be harder than she thought. To actually say out loud her secret kink, to risk being exposed . . . the thought alone was enough to scare the hell out of her.

She almost backed out, almost.

Taking another deep breath, she allowed the words to trip from her tongue. "Get the binds . . . and the paddle. I'm ready. I want you to . . ."

BZZZ. BZZZ. BZZZ

She uttered a cry of disbelief. Her eyes flew open and she looked down between her legs hoping to see a dark blond head lying between her spread thighs, ready to give her what she needed . . . Lord, what she craved!

The only thing she saw as she glanced down was one of her own hands buried deep inside her creaming opening, the other braced against her thigh.

Well, damn!

At that point, Candy felt like howling out loud in sheer frustration.

"Oh damn . . . not again," she groaned. She reluctantly withdrew her wet fingers from her vagina and sat straight up in bed.

With a sinking heart she realized she'd been dreaming. Reality had reared its ugly head with a vengeance in the form of her alarm clock going off.

She whipped her head around, almost giving herself whiplash as she searched the room.

As though she was trying to see if anyone had witnessed what she'd been doing in bed, under the covers, lights out and all alone, she thought, completely disgusted with herself.

She acknowledged she was a mess. Or better still, as Pauline Rogers, her new assistant at the youth center, would say . . . "a hot mess."

With a sigh of disgust at her unreasonable embarrassment, Candy reached over and slammed a hand on top of the offending apparatus. It was one of those art nouveau, old-fashioned-looking alarm clocks that friends who thought they were funny gave you for Christmas gifts.

The type whose alarm was so shrill and long, it could wake the dead.

With a groan, Candy flopped back down and pulled the comforter up to her chin as she snuggled deeper into the covers.

She'd had another erotic, *wake-up-with-her-panties-wet-and-fingers-smelling-like-her-own-coochie,* unfulfilling dream.

Candy released a heartfelt groan, grabbed her pillow and shoved it over her face as she rolled over in the bed to lie face down.

She stayed in that position for long moments and allowed her heartbeat to return to normal.

Damn it.

Just when she was ready to admit what she wanted. *Just* when she was ready to give her dream lover the words he needed to hear, before he'd give her what *she* wanted—the friggin' alarm had to go off.

"Oh well, guess I wasn't exactly ready to go down that path of discovery anyway. I ought to be ashamed of myself for even wanting to, even in a dream," she mumbled, her lips pressed into the bed.

With forced determination she made herself climb out of the bed and start her day.

She looked around for her slippers. She groaned when she only found the one near her bed and spied the other one clear across the room.

"Doggone it, Rus! Leave my house shoes alone, boy!" she fussed out loud when she spied her tomcat, Russell, laying his big striped head on her slipper as though it were his pillow. The cat had an unnatural love for all things furry.

She grumbled as she put one foot in the available slipper, grabbed the thin robe hanging from the foot rail of her bed and hopped over to retrieve the other slipper, snatching it from under the big cat's head. She rolled her eyes at his indignant cry of anger.

"Sorry, sugah, but Mama's tootsies get cold on these hard wood floors. Especially this time of the year."

With affection she patted the top of his large head on her way out of the bedroom after she placed the matching slipper on her foot.

Yawning deeply, Candy walked into the small bathroom at

the end of the narrow hallway. She stood before the vanity and stared at her reflection.

"Ummm. Girlfriend, you need a man. This dream lover stuff is seriously not cutting it."

She reached a slender arm up and opened the medicine cabinet to withdraw her toothbrush and toothpaste and began her morning ritual.

"I mean, it's not as though you can't *find* a man, right?" she asked herself around a mouthful of white paste.

As she brushed her teeth, she carefully examined her face. Without conceit, Candice knew she was attractive enough. Her smooth, oval, mocha-colored face was clear and free of blemishes.

Her teeth, despite her never having had braces as a child, were fairly straight. She had a small space between her front two teeth that even if she had been able to afford to have straightened as a child, or as an adult, she wouldn't have.

Her father had the same gap and said it was a Cain family trait. He said it added character to her face.

As Candy had never met any other Cain family members besides her father and her older brother, Corey, she could only take his word.

When she was a child, other children had teased her because of the gap between her teeth, among other things.

She remembered her father telling her the small imperfection was something to be proud of, not ashamed of. It was a part of who she was, and no matter what, she was never to be ashamed of who she was.

As usual, his words had helped ease the sting of their cruelty.

She smiled in remembrance and the deep dimples she'd also inherited from her father flashed in the mirror as she did so.

She missed her dad. It had been too long since his last visit. Too long since he'd breezed into town and made her couch his bed.

But she knew it was only a matter of time before he'd come around. When he grew bored with his current job or he got fired. Either way, she knew she'd see him soon.

It wasn't that he wasn't a hard worker. It was just . . . hard for him to stay in one place for too long. As a child she'd seen it all as one big adventure, she remembered with a melancholy smile.

She grabbed the washcloth from the bar attached to the wicker shelf and ran warm water over it. She added a bar of her favorite homemade rosemary-scented castile soap and got a good lather going. She gently wiped her face clean. The warm water and pleasant smell helped to invigorate her, fully waking her up.

After she finished, she draped the washcloth over the side of her vintage, cream-colored porcelain pedestal sink in order to tackle her hair.

She deftly unbraided the thick French braid and allowed her kinky mass of hair free rein. She eased her fingers into the thick tresses and massaged her scalp and moaned.

It always felt good when she unbraided her hair and allowed it to *breathe.*

Candy loved wearing her hair natural and chemical-free. She enjoyed the sense of completeness, of wholeness, she'd gotten when she'd kicked her creamy crack pusher, formerly known as the relaxer, to the curb.

Within moments her hair was a wild mass of riotous kinks and curls all over her head. Candy laughed at the image in the mirror.

She opened the door to the small, old-fashioned mirrored cabinet mounted on the wall and removed a few of her favorite natural hair oils.

She poured a quarter-sized dollop into her palm, rubbed her hands together and began to massage the fragrant oils into her hair and scalp.

Candy had learned how to make her own soaps and oils during the course of one summer, as a young girl, from an older women who'd babysat her as her father worked.

The woman hadn't had much money and the small change her father had been able to give the old woman to watch Candy had been needed and appreciated.

The skills the older woman had willingly passed on to Candy, she'd not forgotten.

It was a skill that came in handy when she began to create her own concoctions as a young teenager and sell them, often helping to make ends meet.

She was more than happy to share that talent with the girls at the youth center where she was the director, knowing many of them came from poor backgrounds.

Since wearing hair natural and using natural hair and skin products was the latest cool "nouveau culture" thing to do, she could teach them a useful skill. Also, they wouldn't be made fun of by others because they couldn't afford store-bought products.

Instead it was seen as cool to make something uniquely designed. Candy chuckled out loud about the change in times.

She continued to stare at her reflection, the smile sliding from her lips as she kept on massaging her scalp. She noticed how the movements of her hands on her hair caused her small breasts to rise and gently slap against each other.

Her gaze hesitantly dropped to her plum-colored nipples. They were beaded and stood stiff and proud, right in the middle of her dark areolas.

Slowly she dropped her hands and allowed them to brush over the small mounds, before she cupped their light weight in her hands. She imagined that was just how *he* would do it.

He'd never actually touched her breasts in real life. But in her dreams, he'd come close.

Deliciously so.

In fact, he'd come close to doing more than caressing her breasts this last time.

But not in real life. In real life her dream lover was a man who saw her as little more than an irritant. Someone he was *forced* to have dealings with. At least it was the impression Candy always got from him.

Whatever. His loss.

She forced negative thoughts away. She didn't feel like treading down that path of no fulfillment from her dream lover, or his real life counterpart.

It was time to get ready for work anyway. No time for thoughts along those lines or she'd have to turn to Big Billy.

However, of late, Billy had provided her with little or no relief as she craved something more than what the plastic toy, no matter how many vibrating levels it boasted, could provide.

After she'd taken her shower, Candy grabbed the thick cotton towel and dried herself. She pulled out a small, lidded crock that sat in one of her baskets near her bathtub.

After she opened the lid to the crock, she scooped out a generous portion of the cocoa butter/shea butter blended smoothie she'd made herself.

The dry weather would ash her skin to death if she didn't keep it moisturized, and her own homemade products kept it nice and supple, better than anything she could find over the counter.

She loved how the blended creams felt sliding over her skin as she anointed her arms, torso and legs, before recapping the crock and returning it to the basket.

She rewrapped the thick towel around her oiled body and walked back to her bedroom and toward her closet.

Candy stared at the contents of her closet for long moments, just trying to figure out what she'd wear for the day.

It wasn't like she had *that* many choices. Her closet was

filled with all very similar clothes. The main differences were the pattern and color.

The closet was filled with an assortment of long, loose-fitting dresses, a few pairs of jeans she'd had forever, what looked like a hundred T-shirts and tons of various colored and textured fabric.

Just fabric.

She wore her various fabrics most often. She'd stand with her legs spread apart so when she finished wrapping it, the fabric would swing natural and loose on her body. Holding both ends of the fabric in each fist, she'd then start wrapping the cloth around her body and end when the tips met, and knot it.

She'd first started wearing fabric in college, after sharing a room with an exchange student from Ghana, but had soon loved the style so much she adopted it as her own.

Candy had grown so used to wrapping herself, as her father once put it, that she never gave it much thought. Throw on a T-shirt, some chunky jewelry and she was good to go.

As the director of a girls' recreation center, thankfully, formality in dress wasn't a job requirement, or she'd be in trouble.

Growing up with a free-spirited parent, one who drifted from job to job, toting his small family with him, Candy had never given fancy clothes or designer labels much in the way of consideration.

Often as a child, she'd had little more than the clothes on her back and a few other garments stowed in her knapsack when they moved on to the next job, the next town . . . the next opportunity.

Today she opted to wear her luxury for the month: a new pair of jeans. She removed the jeans from the shelf in the closet and with near reverence ran a caressing hand over the material.

She rarely bought anything new and when she did, it generated a feeling of guilty pleasure. But this time she ignored the guilt and focused on the thrill of the purchase.

She grew tired of her self-inflicted guilt whenever she would buy some new thing or other, but old habits died hard.

She carefully removed the price tag from the waistband of the jeans, not wanting to rip a hole in the soft material. She set the jeans aside and reached back in the closet to withdraw one of her favorite T-shirts and donned it.

Before she eased the jeans up her legs and fastened the buttons on the low-riding waist, she tried to place the ends of the shirt inside but the ends didn't quite make it and the gemstone in her belly ring showed.

She caught enough grief about her lack of conventionality without showing off one of her piercings, so she reluctantly removed the shirt and reached for another.

After putting on the second shirt, she nodded her head in self-approval. This one, although only fractionally longer, would do. It should stay in place, at least enough to cover her ring.

A loud purr and strong push against her legs made her look down. Russell was twining his large body around her legs.

"Are you hungry, big boy? Okay, okay, let Mama get her shoes and we can get us both something to eat, all right?" she both promised and asked.

She rooted around the closet for her Birkenstocks. Once she located them, at the back of her closet, she slid the comfortable shoes on her feet.

She turned and hefted the loudly purring cat into her arms and left the bedroom.

"And maybe you can convince Mama all she needs is a good man, a *real* man, and all her nocturnal longings will be a thing of the past. Hmm? What do you think, boy?"

The only answer the cat gave was to leap agilely from her arms, despite his massive size, and land gracefully at her feet. He quickly walked ahead of her toward the kitchen and breakfast, mewing so loudly he sounded more like a lion than a domesticated cat.

"Men are all the same. One thing on their mind, and unfortunately, it doesn't seem to be me. Dang it," she muttered to the empty room at large, before, with a self-pitying sigh, she followed the cat into the kitchen.

2

"Are you going to let me do it this time?"

He waited with his breath held, waiting to see if she'd find his desires kinky and tell him to go straight to hell.

She didn't say anything, only looked at him from the corners of her big brown eyes, and he knew better than to rush her. The last time he had, she'd done exactly what he was afraid she'd do this time. She'd told him to go straight to hell. It was all a part of the game.

"Do you think you're ready for that, Davis? Are you ready for me?" she asked from behind the large desk, across the room from him.

He stood and slowly walked over to her and looked down at himself as he did so. Judging from the raging hard-on he had, he'd say that was a definite yes. He took the base of his penis in one hand and stroked down to the end of its his bulbous, cum-filled tip and lifted his eyes to watch her as he did so.

The quick breath she inhaled, coupled with the swipe of her tongue against her lush bottom lip, showed Davis that she liked what she saw and was ready for him.

She sat behind her desk, wearing one of those wraps of fabric she loved to wear, one leg planted on the floor, the other over the arm of the chair, swinging back and forth, pendulum style.

As he stood within a foot of her, he was surprised to see her skirt was much shorter than what she normally wore. It was so short in fact, he could see the dark, tight, curly thatch of hair surrounding her glistening pussy as it played peek-a-boo with every swing of her leg.

She loved to tease him. Loved to see how far he'd allow her to take it, before he lost it and demanded she give him what was his. He knew it, but played the game anyway.

She was ready.

Davis could tell from the way her small breasts heaved, the look in her pretty brown eyes . . . and the glistening of cream easing down the inside of her smooth brown thigh. He bent his head, leaned in and inhaled.

Damn.

The scent of her pussy was a pungent combination of hot chocolate and peppermint. Heady and sweet, just like her. He reluctantly lifted his head.

"You're always ready for me," she purred. "Physically."

When she amended her statement, he felt the first stirrings of unease.

The uneasiness turned into a more demanding churning in his gut with her rebuttal.

"But what about Gail?"

"Damn it! She has nothing to do with this. *With us!* This is between you and me, and my wife has nothing to do with it!" He pressed her unresisting body down onto the desk.

With a determination born out of frustrated desire, he pulled her short skirt higher. Grabbing the backs of her thighs, Davis lifted them over his arms. He leaned into her mound and stroked her, deeply, with his tongue.

In satisfaction he watched as she nearly bucked him off her small body with the first touch of his mouth against her silken folds.

"Oh god, Davis . . . what are you doing to me?" she panted.

"It's not what I'm doing to you, but what I have planned to do to you, that you have to worry about. What we both have to be worried about," he promised grimly and leaned back in, prepared to give her what she'd been wanting, what *he'd* been craving, for nine long months.

Ringgg. Ringgg.

Davis was jerked awake when the jarring sound of his Black-Berry rang. He wanted to roar in anger and frustration with the interruption. Fuck! Even though it had been a dream, he'd been so damn close he could smell her distinct scent in the aftermath of the dream.

He reached over and picked the cell phone up from the nightstand and stabbed the talk button viciously.

"Hello." His voice was scratchy from sleep and his dick was hard as a damn rock due to the familiar, erotic dream he'd been snatched out of reluctantly.

"Davis? Are you okay?" a soft feminine voice asked hesitantly.

"Yeah, I'm fine. Just was asleep is all. What's up, Mil?" he grumbled.

"I didn't interrupt anything, did I?"

He heard the doubt in his sister's voice. He was so predictable, it never crossed Milly's mind he might actually have a living, breathing woman in his bed.

By all rights, he should have one lying beneath him, limp and fully satisfied, instead of the dream lover he'd bedded. And even in his dreams, he'd only gotten a small sample, Davis thought in disgust.

"No, it's fine. I needed to get up anyway." He looked over at the alarm, surprised it was already seven a.m.

"I can give you a call back, once you're awake," Milly volunteered.

"Just give me a few—make that fifteen—minutes so I can shower."

"You're not running? Things change since I've been gone?"

Milly had only recently returned from an extended time away from both the town of Stanton and Strong Construction, the family business.

"No, I don't have time today. I need to get out to the site in a couple of hours. We break ground today and Rodney can't make it," he said, mentioning his operations manager.

Usually Davis ran three miles every morning without fail, but the dream had kept him enthralled so strongly his internal alarm hadn't gone off.

"Okay, I'll give you a call back in a bit," she agreed and they hung up.

When Davis disengaged the phone, he reluctantly got out of bed and made his way, barefoot, to the adjoining bathroom. After adjusting the showerhead, he allowed the water to heat before he stepped inside the steaming, black-tiled, roomy stall. He turned his body fully into the hot, stinging spray and rubbed both hands over his face.

He'd had the dream again. This time, he'd almost gotten a real taste of her, this time he had been determined to shut his brain off and allow his libido to take over.

No thinking about the past, present or future. No thinking about Gail, his late wife.

Not this time.

This time he was going to fulfill the desires he and his dream lover had been flirting around with for the last nine months. This time he wasn't going to think, even if it was just a dream, about anything but the pleasure two willing bodies could give each other.

He turned his face upward, allowing the invigorating spray to wash over his face, and thought about the woman who played the starring role in his dreams.

Candice Cain.

The kids called her Miss Candy. Her name alone was silly and immature.

He had no damn business thinking of the young woman constantly, not to mention the wet dreams where she'd been cast in the starring role. Dreams reminding him of his adolescence they were so graphic. Hot and so damn real he woke up hard as hell, dick in hand, with cum splashed against his thigh.

Shit.

He was too old for her. He was almost forty years old and Candice couldn't be any older than her early twenties. Not only that, but she appeared to be the exact opposite of Gail.

He'd always been careful, sexually, with his wife. Before she'd been sick, she'd been the same way. When they'd made love, Davis had always been forced to hold back.

And it had been damn hard to do.

He was a man with a strong sex drive. After one disastrous time when he'd been less than . . . *gentle,* Gail had made him feel like a pile of shit. From that time on, he'd refrained from deviating from the norm with her, the sex had been done straight missionary style, and once he came, Gail quickly eased her body away from his.

He definitely never thought to ask her to do some of the freaky shit he'd had on his mind of late, when he saw or thought of Candy.

Damn, it was getting worse and worse every day. With everything going on with his daughter, it was a complication he didn't need.

He didn't know what had come over his Aunt Mildred

when she'd suggested to the board to hire Candy as the center's director.

Candice Cain had come barreling into his life nine months ago and things hadn't been the same since.

Aunt Mildred had been in the process of turning the reins of the business over to him and his sister, Milly. She'd told him she'd found the perfect replacement for the previous center's director, who'd retired.

Girls Unlimited had been one of Mildred's projects and she'd held a position on the board for years. The board members respected her, just as they appreciated her sizable donations to the center. Therefore, when she'd found a replacement they'd eagerly accepted the young woman without hesitation.

But Davis had enough reservations for them all. There was something about Candy, besides her youthful appearance, that made him question his aunt's judgment.

She was an intelligent young woman—she had a bachelor's as well as a master's degree in psychology and early childhood development. The girls seemed to like her and she'd made some noticeable improvements already in the time she'd been the director.

Still. He wasn't going to bring Candice into the picture and ask for her help with his daughter. To do so would be a set-up for disaster. He had enough problems with Angelica without adding the complications of Candice.

"I don't know what the hell is going on with Angel, Milly. What would you do? I'm at a loss. I freely admit it."

Davis held the receiver propped between his ear and the top of his shoulder as he searched the fridge for something decent to eat.

His housekeeper was on vacation and he hadn't bothered to go shopping for groceries since his daughter, Angelica, had been spending the last few days with her great-aunt Mildred, after her latest bout of trouble.

With pure disgust, he noticed the refrigerator was all but bare. There was nothing in its hollow caverns but a quart of milk, butter, a half-dozen or so eggs, juice and a carton of vanilla yogurt. He needed to eat something more substantial than yogurt, so he opted for the eggs, milk and butter and hunted for bread.

"French toast will work," he mumbled after scanning the refrigerator.

"What? Who are you talking to?" his sister asked.

"No one. Who else would be here other than me anyway? Anne's on vacation and Angel is with Aunt Mildred. It's just me, myself and I."

"And I thought *I* had no sex life." Although she spoke low, in an aside, Davis heard the comment.

"What's that supposed to mean?" As he spoke, he deftly cracked the eggs into the Pyrex bowl and added milk.

He moved to the center of the kitchen and removed the pan hanging above the butcher-block island counter, placed it on the stove and added the half-stick of butter.

"Damn . . . I'm out of real vanilla!" he scoured the cabinet, looking for the spice.

"And I suppose you don't have any of the fake variety, like a normal man would, huh?"

"Fresh is best. Doesn't taste right, otherwise. I think I have some nutmeg, that'll have to work." He added the powdered spice to his mixture.

He brought out the wire whisk and beat the eggs, milk and spice to a frothy blend before he dunked the thick bread slices into the mix and carefully placed them into the sizzling pan.

"I can smell it through the phone. Just what me and my hips need," Milly groaned.

"Thanks . . . but don't think I forgot your little comment."

"What comment?"

"About my sex life . . . or lack of one," he mumbled and sucked his thumb when he burned it after flipping the French toast over by hand.

The hot butter popped from the sizzling skillet, landing on his bared chest. Uttering a low curse, he jumped away from the stove.

If Milly could see him using his hands and not a spatula, she'd probably revise her opinion about how "uptight" he was.

He knew the impression he gave, to his sister, along with his daughter: that he was conservative, uptight and, if Angelica was right, a stick-in-the-mud.

But what the hell else would any nine-year-old say after she'd been busted skipping school and her father wasn't jumping up and down cheering over the fact?

He'd done the exact opposite and had gone off in nine different directions, beyond angry she'd done something so stupid.

It made him wonder if he was doing a good enough job with her. Maybe what Anita Watson, her school principal, intimated, was true. Maybe she needed a stronger female presence in her life.

Then again, he knew damn well Angelica's well-being was not the reason for Anita Watson's concern.

"My sex life isn't up for discussion, Mil. Angelica's behavior is what's paramount on my mind right now."

"I know. It's what's on mine as well."

"Did Angelica tell you why she did it?"

"We didn't talk about it when I spoke with her. I didn't think it's was a good idea to talk about it at the time. I think she's been punished enough."

"I disagree. I don't know what the hell to do. She's skipping school and her entire attitude is changing. It's like I have a different child, and I don't like it, Milly. Gail is probably turning over in her grave," he said and flipped the French toast onto his waiting plate.

"Davis, you're doing fine. You've got to expect this. Most kids go through a rebellious stage; don't beat yourself up. And Gail isn't turning in her grave. I don't think Angel's behavior has anything to do with her mother being dead. I think if Gail were alive, it would be something else."

"Yes, I know. You're probably right, Mil, but lately, I keep remembering what Gail asked me, before she died."

"That you make sure Angel has a black female role model?"

"Yes, I think maybe she was right." He thoughtfully chewed the French toast. "Until now, I never gave it much thought. She has you and Aunt Mildred as good role models, so it's not as though she doesn't have any females in her life. But when you left, she didn't have anyone. She lacked a mother figure to talk to and I think it was hard for her. She's not as close to Aunt Mildred as she is to you."

"God, I'm sorry, Davis. I didn't realize the impact on Angel when I left. I was being selfish," Milly replied, sadness in her voice, and Davis instantly wanted to retrieve his words.

He still wasn't clear on the reasons Milly had decided, several months ago, to take a hiatus from Strong Construction. She'd left Stanton to visit friends on the west coast for an extended visit, saying that she needed to get away. She'd only recently returned and they hadn't talked about her reasons for leaving.

"No, Mil, that's not what I'm saying. It wasn't your fault. You and I both know Angel started behaving differently before you left Stanton. Besides, you needed to get away," he replied. "But maybe it's time for her to have someone around her who can help her with things you and I can't."

"Davis, I never thought about that, honestly. Not until Gail said the same thing to me before she died."

"I didn't know she had."

"Yes, she did. She thought it was important for Angel to have a black woman in her life. I agree with her."

"Why?"

"It's important. There are some things she's going to need help with. Things you or I won't be able to help her with. Life is harsh, Davis; you know that. And the reality is there are some people who aren't color-blind, and can be cruel. Just like there are people who treat people with disabilities differently."

Although Milly spoke from experience, because of her own disability, Davis remained silent. More than anything, Milly despised sympathy.

"Someone who was a good role model, maybe even worked with young girls. Maybe Angel would feel free to open up to her. But who? Who do we know that fits those criteria?" When her last few words sunk in, Davis grew wary.

"Don't even try it, Mil. I know what, or who, you're referring to."

Davis felt the clench in his gut, the same reaction he had whenever the woman his sister was none-too-subtly referring to was mentioned or in his general vicinity.

The same woman who he'd convinced himself over the last nine months of their acquaintance was not an ideal woman to supervise the girls at the center.

The same woman who flitted through his mind with irritating regularity from since the first moment he'd laid eyes on her.

The one who'd been the cause of and starred in more wet dreams than he'd had since he was a randy seventeen-year-old adolescent.

He wasn't a kid anymore. He was a grown man with responsibilities. And one of those responsibilities was to raise his daughter the best way he could. This meant having reservations about her being around someone who threw convention to the wind in her manner, dress and overall . . . presence.

"What do you have against Candice, Davis? Really. What is it?"

He damn sure couldn't tell her he found Candice to be the wrong choice as the director of the center. She was way too free-spirited to guide and counsel a slew of impressionable young girls, his daughter included. But he still wanted to fuck the woman so badly it was all he could do not to howl at the moon in frustration.

Self-imposed frustration.

Because although she was very subtle, he knew the instant-lust attraction he'd felt for Candice was reciprocated. Yet, he had no intention of letting her know that. It was hard enough keeping himself in check when he was around her. If she knew what thoughts were in his mind, and she was game to follow up, they'd end up screwing like bunnies for a solid week, without coming up for air once.

Or at least that's what *he'd* want to happen. Whether she would be game or not, he didn't know. In his fantasies, she was a willing participant.

No, it was better little Miss Candice thought he found her anything but attractive. Coupled with his desire, he felt guilt about it. His wife had been dead for seven years and their marriage had been anything but perfect, but the guilt was there.

He and Gail had known one another for years, had flitted in and out of each other's lives from the time her grandfather had worked for Strong Construction when she was a young girl. Upon her return on break from university, no one had been surprised when they'd gotten together.

She'd always had a quiet way about her, always seemed to hold her emotional cards close. They'd flirted back and forth, yet Davis was surprised when she returned from school during her summer break and immediately insisted they take their relationship to the next level.

When she'd shown up on his doorstep, slightly intoxicated,

he'd invited her in. He'd initially resisted, hadn't wanted to take advantage of her inebriated state, but had eventually caved in and made love to her.

Six weeks later she'd told him she was pregnant, and they'd gotten married.

She'd never shown him as much desire, had never been so determined to make love to him, as she had during that time. Davis wouldn't know for several months later why.

Once he learned the reason, he shut down his emotions around her. He'd kept his feelings tightly in check. Tried to make the best of it for Angelica's sake.

"I promised Gail I would make sure Angel had a black woman in her life. And more importantly, I think Angel could benefit from it. And I will find one. A positive, nurturing, *mature* woman. But it won't be Candice," he stated, emphatically.

"What?! Oh come on! What are you going to do? Put an ad in the newspaper? '*Help Wanted: Black woman who is positive and nurturing to be my daughter's friend?*'"

"Whatever I do, it won't be to approach Ms. Cain. End of subject."

Candy Cain. *Just like candy, I can see it when you walk, even when you talk, it takes hold of me . . .* he hadn't been able to get the old '80s song out of his mind from the moment he first laid eyes on her.

"I don't know what I'll do, but I'll figure something out. Now when are you coming back to work? The place isn't the same without you," he quickly changed the subject.

There was a pregnant pause and he prompted her. "Mil? What's going on? Is there something behind you leaving the company and Stanton besides you needing a break?"

"It's nothing I can't handle, Davis."

"Are you sure? I've been so caught up in Angel and her theatrics I think I'm missing something with you."

"It's nothing I can't handle, Davis," she repeated. "You

know I'm a big girl now. I don't need for you to jump in and fight my battles for me," she replied, her voice nonchalant.

Davis held back his desire to probe deeper, knowing his sister was stubborn as hell and wouldn't listen to him.

Just as all the women in his life seemed to be, he thought and munched moodily on his cold French toast.

3

"Is it me, or does my ass look like the back side of a very large caboose in these jeans?" Candy mumbled out loud, to no one in particular. It was becoming an eccentric habit of hers, she thought. Talking to empty rooms.

Candy twisted her body this way and that, glaring at her hind end at every conceivable angle. She reached behind and tugged at the waistband of her new jeans, where material and skin met. She blew out a frustrated breath of air. There was enough space between for her to insert her entire hand inside!

The hip/waist ratio thing was a serious pain whenever she bought a new pair of jeans. Too tight in the hips and it was perfect for her waist. Too loose in the waist and they fit to a T in the thighs and butt.

With her eyes still trained on her butt, she knew she'd have to whip out her sewing machine and do some serious alterations to make these babies work.

She had given up finding a pair of jeans that would fit. The best she could do was to make sure they worked for thighs and butt and alter the waistline.

It would be nice if at least *one* designer would get it right for women with her body type, she thought. It wasn't like all women were a perfect size-eight body. All they'd have to do was take a look around at the general population of everyday women, take a poll, *something,* she mentally griped.

Candice blew out a disgusted puff of air.

She should have altered them before deciding to wear them for the first time, she thought.

"Do you want me to answer that question, or are you just talking out loud to hear yourself speak?"

Candice nearly jumped out of her skin when the deep voice answered. She spun around and tripped, catching herself before she fell on the floor in an undignified heap.

Her eyes widened. Davis Strong stood in her doorway, a deep frown settling across his handsome face.

She stumbled again. Before she could right herself, he had crossed the room, his warm palm cupping her beneath her elbow. "Whoa—be careful."

Her reaction to the contact was immediate. The feel of his big, warm palm on her skin caused a direct zing of electric heat to sizzle between them.

She glanced up, heart pounding. "Thank you," she murmured and cleared her throat.

"No problem."

Candy tried to pull away. When he held on, she turned back toward him and their gazes locked. His eyes were trained on her mouth and seemed to darken when her tongue swiped along her full bottom lip.

Her gaze traveled over his face, cataloging features that were already burned into her memory.

He'd recently returned from Florida, and had gained a light olive tan. The color contrasted vividly against his light-gray eyes.

Although he wasn't handsome in the typical model, *GQ*

way—no, his harsh good looks were beyond anything so tame as model perfection—he exuded raw masculine appeal that drew her in like a magnet every time she was anywhere in his vicinity.

Davis Strong had the ability, no matter how put together she thought she was, to make Candy feel like a ten-year-old naughty schoolgirl.

Although the feelings he stirred in her whenever she was in his presence weren't the feelings a young girl would, or should, be having.

Naughty or otherwise.

Not that she wouldn't mind playing the naughty little girl for him, if ever he was so inclined.

Despite her wayward dreams of late, where she'd cast him as the unsuspecting male lead in her very own porn flick, he had yet to ask in real life.

But heaven help her if he did. Or help him, as she knew exactly what she wanted from him.

Despite the disapproving looks he would cast her way, she knew he was attracted to her, no matter how he pretended otherwise.

But he'd yet to act on it. And she damn sure wasn't so desperate for attention to be the one to initiate anything. No matter *how* fine he was, she told herself, clenching her thighs together when her body taunted her, quickly responding to his simple touch.

When he finally released her and moved away, she released a sigh, not realizing she'd been holding her breath. "I need to talk to you about Angelica," he said, bringing her mind back to the reason he had sought her out.

"Please, have a seat."

When he turned his head from her, his eyes surveying her messy office, she refrained from rushing into an explanation that she'd come in early to clean.

As he sat in one of the few chairs in the cluttered office not filled with papers, Candy's gaze wandered over his big body, subtly, from the corner of her eye.

The gray T-shirt he wore clung to his broad chest. It looked as though it had been washed a thousand times at least, it was so soft-looking. The light gray color of the T-shirt was the same color as his eyes, but didn't come close to matching the intensity.

His long legs were encased in worn jeans, his hard thighs bunching against the material as he sat.

Yet, for all his good looks, Candy was drawn to him for reasons beyond the physical. Reasons such as his love for his daughter, along with the way he treated the kids who frequented the center.

He took time out to laugh and talk with them whenever he was there. He was real with them, no pretense.

Candy longed to get to know the real Davis, the one he presented to the kids, when he thought no one was watching. She wanted to be the one responsible for making the deep slashes in his lean cheeks appear whenever he smiled or laughed at one of their jokes.

The Davis she saw was one who closed up around her, a scowl on his handsome face as he broodingly watched her, when he thought *she* wasn't looking.

The Davis he presented to her made her wonder what in hell she'd done to make him so surly around her, yet gave off enough sexual sparks to cause a brush fire.

To make matters worse, whenever she was within a five-mile radius of *him,* she turned into a blushing, gauche, tongue-tied woman who was about as sophisticated as one of the teen girls who attended the center.

"Sorry to barge in like this. Your assistant told me you were in," he said, after settling his large frame in the small chair.

"It's fine. I came in early to clean."

"Is this what you normally wear to clean?"

Candy noticed his gaze centered on her midsection, and glanced down at herself.

He *would* have to come today, when she'd dressed even more casually than normal.

Her plan had been to clean, not entertain one of her girls' parents. Even if said parent was incredibly fine and sported hard chiseled muscles outlined to perfection beneath his T-shirt.

She tried to discreetly tug the skimpy top she was wearing, emblazoned with the phrase *taste like butta,* into the waistband of her jeans when she saw him staring at the small gemstone she wore in her belly.

Candy refused to admit, even to herself, how his attention to her body jewelry affected her. His gaze then traveled from her belly button, up the length of her body, his gaze hot and direct when he met her stare.

The intensity in his light-colored eyes caused her pulse to quicken, her breath to catch in her throat, as their gazes locked.

She folded her arms over her breasts, to hide her nipples' reaction. After walking to her desk, she sat down. It was that, or embarrass herself and fall down.

"I'm here because of Angelica."

When he mentioned his daughter, his somber tone made her forget her irrational, unrequited and silly obsession with him for the moment.

"Is everything okay with her? She's not hurt, is she?"

"No, nothing like that. She's been cutting school. Her principal called me into the office yesterday to tell me. Seems like she's been doing it for a while," he admitted, and ran a hand through his short, dark-blond hair in frustration.

"I'm sorry to hear that, Mr. Strong."

"Please, Ms. Cain, call me Davis. We've known each other long enough to dispense with formalities," he offered.

Candy was thrown off guard. He'd never extended the offer for her to call him by his first name.

"Thank you, Davis. And please, feel free to call me Candy," she offered in return. "That's my nickname. The girls like to call me that. They think it's funny my last name is Cain."

"Candy Cain, huh? I once wondered if that was your real name or not."

She quickly glanced over his expression, to gauge his intent. The look in his eyes seemed more curious than condescending and Candy relaxed.

"No, I understand about unconventionality. My Aunt Mildred raised my sister and me, and, as you know, Aunt Mildred isn't a conformist in the least," he laughed huskily.

Mildred Davis had been one of the first women to own and operate a large construction and architectural firm in the city of Stanton. She'd also been the first female millionaire in the city.

"What's going on with Angelica?" She guided the conversation back to the reason Davis had sought her out.

"Angel cut school on Thursday and gave the teacher a forged permission slip from me. And it wasn't the first time it happened." Once again, he raked a hand through his hair in frustration.

"It wasn't the first time she skipped school, or forged a note?" Candy asked.

"Both, unfortunately. This is her second time skipping and forging a note with my signature. She had a substitute teacher the first time and the second time around she timed her absence when she knew Mrs. Douglas, her regular teacher, would be gone."

"She missed the day Mrs. Douglas was teaching, and the day the substitute came, she returned to school?" Candy asked, seeking clarification.

"Yes."

"At least she's creative in her manipulation."

The laugh he uttered was more like a snort, and his expression was sheepish at best. He reached around and rubbed the back of his neck.

"Yes, she is. She knew the sub wouldn't know my signature and was counting on the fact the woman wouldn't call her out about it. But what she failed to understand was the notes were kept. Mrs. Douglas would eventually see it."

"Why wasn't she caught the first time?"

"The sub misplaced the note but documented she'd seen it and that was it."

"Angelica thought she'd gotten away with it and they'd been fooled by the signature and decided to try again?" Candy hazarded a guess.

"How did you guess that?" He looked at her with what she saw as suspicion, and their tentative camaraderie evaporated as though it never had been.

"I work with her age group all the time, Mr. Strong. You don't believe I had anything to do with this, do you?"

Candy began gathering strewn paperwork on her desk, the need to keep her hands busy paramount.

It was that or jump across the desk and slap him into the middle of next week for insinuating she'd had anything to do with Angel's truancy.

Damn, the man brought out either the need to jump his bones, or the need to throttle him.

"Yes, I know this is your area of expertise. I wasn't trying to imply anything else, Ms. Cain. I'm at a loss and on edge."

Davis sighed.

He was coming across as an ass to Candy. He knew it.

He hadn't come to antagonize her. He'd come to ask for her help.

But every time they were within two feet of each other, sparks flew. He knew he was the one to blame.

It wasn't her fault he couldn't keep his thoughts where they should be, whenever he was around her. And her wearing that tight little top with her smooth brown belly showing, her small tits pushing against the thin material so that he could see them bead when he'd touched her, hadn't helped matters.

The minute his hand made contact with her soft skin, the sexual tension between them, hovering beneath the surface most times, had burst free.

He'd wanted to capture her small pink tongue when it'd snaked out to lick the bottom rim of her full lips. To suckle on those lush lips of hers was a fantasy he'd had for nine long months.

Davis adjusted himself in his seat. He mentally begged his cock not to thicken any more than it already had inside the tight confines of his Levi's.

He had to focus on his reason for coming to her, and ignore his raging lust for her. Milly had been right, he needed her help.

She was so damn *young*. Seemingly too young to give advice about life to teenage girls.

He was disgusted with himself. She wasn't jailbait, but couldn't be much older than twenty-four or twenty-five years old at the oldest. Definitely too young for his thirty-seven years.

His eye roved over her lush ass when she stood up from her chair, walked over to her trash can and placed the balled-up paper inside. He followed her movement as she picked up a watering can and sprinkled a plant on her desk.

She had a nice ATW—ass-to-waist—ratio. His friend and project manager, Rodney Adams, had said that about a woman he was dating, and Davis knew exactly what he meant.

Her waist was small and showed off her rounded hips, thighs, and ass. She didn't have much in the way of breasts, but she had enough to be a nice mouthful.

As she watered the plant, her small, obviously unbound breasts jiggled inside her top. The hem had eased out of the waistband of her jeans. Davis caught the flash of what looked like a wing in red and black ink that spanned her lower spine.

Damn, it figured. A tattoo went with the rest of the package. Davis stifled a groan.

"How old are you?" He blurted the question and wished he could retract it. The words sounded as lame said out loud as they did in his thoughts.

She turned and faced him and her pretty, light-brown eyes widened. When she'd turned, her long, thick braid had whipped around and now lay nestled between her plump breasts.

Her eyes were tilted in the corners and her eyelashes were thick and dark, just like her eyebrows. Although her skin was the color of smooth milk chocolate with only a hint of cream, he could see a smattering of freckles across the bridge of her short nose.

Her lips weren't overly full, but lush enough. His imagination ran wild with thoughts of taking her full bottom lip between his lips and sucking it.

Or imagining the feel of her mouth wrapped around his cock as she slowly glided her tongue over his entire length.

She was definitely too young for him to have the thoughts he'd had lately with irritating and increasing frequency.

Thoughts about what he'd like to do to her.

Lascivious, dirty, *come sit in my lap* thoughts.

The type of thoughts where they were butt naked in a bed playing some twisted version of Barbie and Ken.

The way she dressed further fueled the flame of his lust.

If she wasn't wearing jeans and an itty-bitty top, she was wearing what looked like fabric wrapped around her body.

No seams, button or zippers, just a wrap of cloth around her hot little body, coupled with a T-shirt. He imagined how it would feel to *start unwrapping her.*

"I'm thirty-four . . . why?" She finally answered, and faced him.

"No particular reason. I assumed you were—"

"Younger?" she finished for him and placed the watering can down, near the plant. She walked back to her desk to sit down. "People usually do. If they'd look beyond the outer trappings, maybe they wouldn't make assumptions," she said with a small bite in her tone.

"I'd think that would be a compliment. To be thought younger."

"Maybe to some. For me, I have no problem with my age," she sat back behind her desk. "I don't think you came here to talk about my age, Mr. Strong. You came here to discuss Angelica." She effectively ended that line of conversation.

"Yes, I did. Sorry I asked you a personal question. It won't happen again, Ms. Cain," he promised, and felt a small tic twitch in the corner of his mouth.

Davis Strong thought she was younger than she was. That shouldn't be a surprise to her, yet a strange excitement pooled in her belly. She sat back down and looked across the desk at him.

He sat in her faux leather chair and appeared more relaxed in her presence than he'd ever seemed to be.

That was, until she'd snapped at him. Now his features had tightened, and his body lost his relaxed appearance.

"Angel thought she was *too* smart and when she tried it again, Mrs. Douglas realized right away it wasn't my handwriting."

"What are they going to do about it?"

"The truancy coupled with her behavior at school—it's not looking good for either one of us."

"What do you mean by that?"

"I've raised Angelica alone for most of her life."

"Yes, I do know a bit of your and Angelica's history."

Candy knew more than a "bit." She knew his wife had died years ago when Angel wasn't much older than a baby and Davis had taken care of her, alone, with only the help of his aunt and sister.

She also knew Angelica wasn't his biological child. It was no secret; everyone knew, and Davis never tried to pretend otherwise.

"I got the distinct feeling the principal—the school—hadn't exactly looked on me favorably as a single father raising a little girl alone, before this happened," he said.

"You're a great father, Davis. Why would they look at you in any negative light?"

"It's the way the system works. You know that. Typically, when a man either has custody of a child, or is raising a child alone, he has to go through a bunch of crap to prove he's 'worthy' enough to raise his child by himself."

The system wasn't always fair; she'd had firsthand experience with her own father as he'd fought to raise her and her brother Micah by himself.

"Is there anything I can do to help?" she asked instead.

"Actually, there is. Angelica looks up to you, Candy. She talks about you a lot around the house and—"

"Angelica looks up to me? What do you mean she talks about me 'a lot around the house'?" Candy interrupted.

The little girl was all attitude when she had any interactions with Candy at the center. So much so, Candy had determined she would need to speak with Davis soon. His coming to her saved her the phone call.

"She's constantly telling me what Ms. Cain says a young girl should or shouldn't say, or how funny you are, how pretty you are," he allowed the sentence to trail off.

"She says how pretty I am?"

"Yes. You are pretty, but you know that already."

She was slammed back into awareness of him as a man she wanted, and not the father of a truant child, with the compliment. The heat of his stare all but caught fire as his gaze roamed over her face. Candy's nipples once again pearled beneath her top.

"I suppose I'm just a little surprised, that's all."

"Surprised?"

"Angel's behavior and interactions with me leave a lot to be desired at times."

It had gotten so bad that Candy resorted to threatening to tell her father. Angelica's standard response to Candy had been "my daddy won't care!" and rolling her head so hard on her little neck that Candy thought it would break off.

"I have no idea why she acts that way with you, when she clearly idolizes you."

"Maybe she's hearing something at home that makes her think it's okay to do that."

"What are you saying?"

"I think you know."

Angelica had once repeated a conversation her father had with his sister—one obviously not meant for a child to hear—as Candy had been reprimanding her for a misdemeanor.

"Candy, I've apologized for that. I had no idea Angel would overhear my conversation with my sister," he apologized, sheepishly. "You and I haven't always agreed or seen eye-to-eye on things in the past, but, as I said, I didn't mean for Angel to overhear my conversation. Am I forgiven?"

"Yes. It's over. Let's just go on," she agreed magnanimously and could have sworn she saw his mouth quirk. "The question now is, what do you want from me, Davis?"

4

Davis focused on Candy's question, and not her hot little body wrapped in ass-hugging jeans.

"Angelica . . . what about her?" she asked, snapping him out of his thoughts and forcing him to remember the reason he came to her. It wasn't to check out her ass, no matter how perfect it was. It was because he was worried about his child.

"Angelica and I need you. Whatever I'm doing obviously isn't working. I'm afraid they're going to try and take my child from me," he admitted and felt the crush of fear weigh heavily on his heart.

"What do you mean? They can't take Angel from you . . . she's your daughter. Anyone can see how much you love her." Davis heard the surprise and outrage in her voice, but it did little to stave off the crushing sense of failure that had been looming over his head for the last few months.

"Sometimes love isn't enough. If someone feels she's not being raised correctly, getting into trouble and she's only nine . . . I'm at my wits' end," he admitted.

"I've been working in this industry—child welfare—for

over ten years. Before I came to the center I worked with child services with the state. Davis, I know it takes a lot more than truancy for a child to be taken from a parent who takes as good care of his child as you do of Angelica."

She rose from her seat and perched her plush bottom on the edge of her desk, her voice and the look in her eyes earnest.

"Thank you. It's good to know you feel that way, that not everyone doubts my ability to raise Angel."

"There's no way that I'm the only one who thinks this way," she chided, lightly. When she gave him a lopsided grin Davis swallowed, hard.

"No, you're right. I'm just wallowing in self-doubt lately," he replied. He rubbed his hands over his hair in frustration.

"That's understandable."

"If it was just the truancy, I wouldn't be so worried. But it's more than that."

He took a deep breath, trying to gauge how much he should tell her, how much he wanted to disclose to a woman who had him hard one minute and confused about his feelings for her the next. But there was more at stake than his own tangled emotions.

Frown lines were etched deeply across his forehead.

Candy wanted to reach out and smooth them away with the tips of her fingers.

"It's complicated," he began, only to stop short. "Angelica isn't my biological child." Candy nodded her head in acknowledgment.

"Yeah, it's no secret," he gave a small shrug. "But I've always thought of her as my own child. DNA has nothing to do with that."

Although she made no comment, didn't ask for clarification, she was more than curious about the circumstances surrounding Angelica's birth, or better yet her conception. Her curiosity must have shown on her face.

"Gail had just ended a relationship before we got together. I didn't know this at the time. When she found out she was pregnant two months later, there were questions about who the biological father was."

"And you were okay with that?"

He ran a hand through his hair, a gesture she was coming to understand meant he was either in deep thought or agitated.

"To be honest with you, I didn't know this until after Angel was born."

When he didn't disclose more, and his expression closed, his mask of neutrality slipping over his handsome face, Candy felt a sharp pang of disappointment.

"Gail wanted Angelica to have good influences in her life. Strong women to help guide her. She made me promise I'd make sure it happened."

"It *is* important. And your aunt and sister are wonderful influences."

"They are, and they love Angelica nearly as much as I do. When Milly left, Angel was missing that. Mil was the main female influence in her life. I think her leaving reminded me of my promise to Gail."

He looked away and Candy's curiosity was piqued.

"What did she want, specifically?" she asked when it looked as though he might not continue.

"She wanted me to make sure a black woman was a part of Angel's life." His face flushed.

Candy carefully considered her words before she spoke. She didn't want to offend Davis, his deceased wife or her request. It wasn't for her to make any judgment on what the woman wanted for her child.

"I can see where that would be important for her. Particularly if she knew she wouldn't be there for Angelica, as she grew up," she said as gently as she could.

"She did know. That was the hardest part. For Angelica." She heard the sadness in his voice, although his face was carefully blank. "She had very specific things she wanted for Angelica. A lot of those suggestions came from her grandmother."

His square jaw tightened. He stood from the chair and walked over to her large window, staring out into the outdoor basketball court.

"Does Angelica have close contact with family members on her mother's side?"

"No," he said abruptly. "It's complicated." He continued staring out the window for long moments, before he turned back to face her. "Like I said, Gail was pregnant when we met, although she says she didn't know it at the time." Candy kept her face neutral, although she caught his slip.

"Gail was raised by her grandmother. She was a strict old woman. Her grandmother cautioned her about me raising Angel alone when she knew of her cancer. 'That man has no business raising Angel alone' was how it was put by a few well-meaning friends. Yet none of those well meaning *friends* stepped up to help raise her. Not that I wanted any of their help."

"And her grandmother . . . ?" she allowed the sentence to dangle.

Davis returned to his chair and sat. "Her grandmother is elderly. She doesn't see Angel often."

When he said nothing more, Candy dropped the subject. She was surprised he'd told her as much as he had.

"I have to meet with her principal, her teacher and the school social worker this coming Tuesday . . . and I don't want to do this alone."

"Can your sister or your aunt go with you to the school?"

"They could and would, but I think I want to go another route with this."

"What do you have planned?"

He squinted his eyes and rubbed the back of his neck, his eyes never leaving hers. Candy sensed his unease.

"Would you consider coming with me? I think it would help the situation, if you were to be there."

Her surprise, she knew, showed on her face. Davis mistook her shock for reluctance.

"Look, I'm sorry. This probably wasn't a good idea. I told Milly—" he started, rising from his chair.

"No, wait. I didn't say I wouldn't do it—you spoke about this with your sister?" she stopped her explanation to ask.

"She thought it would be a good idea to ask you if you'd consider helping—look, I know this isn't your problem. I shouldn't have involved you in this."

"No, it's not that. I don't mind helping. It just surprised me that you asked. That's all. I consider it a part of my job to help any child or parent in need. You, Angel, and your family are important to Girls Unlimited. So anything I can do to help your family, I am happy to do."

"Thank you. It means a lot." He sat back down.

"Anything I can do to help, I will. The well-being of my girls at the center is important to me."

"I appreciate it, Candice. I know you take your job seriously, as well as the girls, here. I admire you for that." His steady regard roamed over her face, looking for what, she didn't know.

Whatever it was he must have been satisfied. His once-taut features relaxed and he sat back more easily into his chair.

"It sounds like an interdisciplinary team approach to the problem."

"What is that?" he asked.

"Nothing major, just the way most schools and social agencies work to help resolve an issue. You said her teacher as well as her principal and social worker are coming to this meeting?"

"Yes," he confirmed.

"Then it seems as though this has gone to the next step. Which isn't a bad thing," she quickly interjected when she saw the instant look of worry cross his handsome face.

"You don't have to try and make me feel better. I know it's not a good thing when you have to meet with your child's entire school network," he laughed humorlessly. "Maybe with you there they'll see I'm trying to correct the problem." He glanced down at his watch.

"What time is the meeting and when do you want me there?"

When he smiled widely and the slashes appeared on either side of his cheeks, Candy's heart lurched in response.

"Tuesday after school, around three o'clock . . . can you make that?"

"Of course. I just hired a new assistant, Pauline Rogers. Sister Pauline is what most of us call her," she laughed lightly, thinking of her eccentric new assistant. "She'll be here to help the other staff. It shouldn't be a problem."

"That sounds great. Thank you, Candice."

"Call me Candy. Most of the kids do."

"I wondered if that was your real name or not. You don't mind the kids calling you by your first name?"

"Not really. Most of them call me Miss Candy Cain, which sounds even sillier," she laughed with self-deprecating humor.

Davis laughed a low husky laugh that sent goose bumps racing down her arms. She knew she was beyond help when even a laugh from him gave her the shivers.

"I'd better go," he said after glancing down at his watch again. "I didn't know it had gotten so late."

At the same time he stood from his chair, Candy jumped down from her perched position on the desk. She lost her balance enough so that she fell against his hard body.

Their touch caused an instant electric static, which made her jump, and she fell back against her desk, laughing nervously.

"This is getting to be a habit," he said as he steadied her.

"I'm fine. Sometimes I can be a bit clumsy. Thank you," she answered, embarrassed.

For a while there she'd been professional and had her act together . . . and then she'd had to blow it and fall all over the man. He probably thought she was a basket case, despite his avowal that he saw her as a professional.

"Please . . . I'm fine," she insisted when it didn't look as though he was going to let her go. "I just tripped again," she grimaced as she looked up.

With her usual nervous gesture, her tongue snaked out and wet her lips, as she returned his stare, unable to look away. One of his hands moved from her shoulder to gently run the rough pad of his thumb over her chin.

"I think I may have misjudged you, Miss Cain. I'm sorry."

She knew he wanted to kiss her and her body tensed; her mouth grew dry as he stared at her mouth when she spoke. Candy didn't look away. She couldn't.

Even as his head descended, one hand lightly cupping her cheek as the other rested on her hip, she still couldn't . . . *wouldn't* move away.

Her heart thudded against her breasts, as his lips met hers, soft but firm.

His hand remained on the side of her cheek. One callused thumb caressed the corner of her mouth while he brushed his lips against hers softly. When his tongue snaked out and licked the seam of her lips, Candy released a small groan.

Back and forth he ran his tongue along the length of her lips. When her senses cataloged the sensation, it was gone, forcing her to lean closer, in an attempt to capture his elusive caresses.

He dragged her tight against his body, her body slamming against his. He stopped the light teasing and drew her fuller bottom lip between his teeth. He tugged it completely into his mouth. The kiss deepened and Candy's body melted into his.

Her breasts tingled and her nipples hardened, pressed so tightly against the hard wall of his chest. They tightened even more as her mound crushed against his hard, thick cock, straining against his rough-feeling jeans.

He deepened the kiss by plunging his hot tongue into the warm, wet recesses of her mouth, searching for hers. When the two connected in a hot, sensual tangle she heard Davis groan harshly.

The hand resting on her hip eased down, traveled lower, and cupped her ass. He forced her warm juncture in tight alignment with his dick. She felt the cream ease from her pussy and saturate the lining of her panties.

Candy moaned when he rained biting kisses down the side of her neck.

His hand remained on her ass, while the other cupped the nape of her neck, slanting her head, angling her for better access to her lips.

With a harsh-sounding grunt, he shoved her against the wall, crushing her between the hard plaster and his unyielding frame.

Releasing her neck, he pulled her hips against his groin and ground his cock against her.

"Damn, you taste good!" He released his suction hold on her mouth long enough to grunt out the words.

"Don't stop," Candy begged, her breath coming out in gasps. She wrapped her arms around his neck and pulled him back down toward her aching mouth.

With a gruff laugh he obeyed and captured her mouth, again. He ate, nibbled, suckled and *devoured* her lips while bumping his thick cock against her mound. She frantically clutched at his wide shoulders, crying and whimpering against his lips, grinding herself against the thick ridge behind his jeans.

He shoved her top up. Cupping her warm breasts in his

palms, he thumbed and toyed with her stiffened nipples in perfect orchestration, until she broke.

His mouth swallowed her mewling cry of release, the orgasm sudden and fierce in its intensity.

When she came back to awareness, it was to feel his cool, peppermint breath against her forehead, before he moved away and rested his forehead against hers.

For long moments they stayed in that position, until her heartbeat gradually calmed.

Candy brought her arms down from their position around his neck, and allowed them to rest between them.

Her arms and legs felt like wet noodles, they trembled so. She'd have fallen straight on her butt if he hadn't held on to her.

Davis pulled away from her, his breathing harsh and loud as he looked down into her face.

"God! I'm so sorry," his voice broke. He cleared his throat before continuing. "I didn't mean for that to happen."

"Please, don't—" Candy was interrupted by a loud knock on the door.

They barely had time to spring apart when the door was flung open, and Pauline Rogers, a.k.a. Sister Pauline, waltzed into the office like she owned it.

They had only a few seconds to adjust their clothing between the time she knocked and when she walked in.

"Time for your session with the girls, Miz Candy!"

Candy turned frantic eyes toward the clock on the wall. Time had flown by. She had less than five minutes for her session with her girls.

Candy felt the heat flush her skin when the older woman turned her scrutinizing eyes toward the two of them.

It *would* have to be Sister Pauline to walk in and catch them going at each other like two dogs in heat, Candy thought with an inward groan.

As soon as Pauline had burst in, Davis had shoved her behind him, shielding her from the older woman's eyes, while tugging his T-shirt down, lower, over his jeans.

Before she stepped around Davis, Candy peeked around his big body and saw the telling wet spot smack in the middle of his zipper.

She straightened her back, and looked at Pauline, plastering what she hoped was a nonchalant *I haven't been dry-humping a parent in my office, and having the best orgasm I've had in a long time* look on her face.

"Uh, well, yes, Sister Pauline. I, uh, I'll be out there as soon as I can."

Her hopes were dashed when she noticed the sly look on Pauline's face.

Candy glanced up at Davis and saw a matching flush steal across his lean cheeks.

Pauline peered over the top of the bifocals set low on her wide nose at them, adjusting the curly gray wig on her head as though it was a hat.

Candy bit the insides of her cheek to force herself not to squirm under the older woman's penetrating stare.

"Umm-hmm," Pauline hummed when no one said anything.

"Would you mind getting the session started for me? I need to conclude my, uh, meeting with Mr. Strong," Candy asked as she tried, unobtrusively, to pull her top back down and tuck it into the waistband of her jeans.

Maybe asking her to start the session would throw Sister Pauline off the scent and the woman wouldn't say anything guaranteed to embarrass her and Davis.

When the other woman's ample bosom puffed out in pride at the request, Candy released a sigh of relief. She'd sidetracked her for the moment.

"Don't worry about it. Sister Pauline *got* this, baby! Now you finish up in here and get down to session as soon as you can, you hear?" She immediately focused her stare on Davis. "Aren't you that Angelica's daddy?"

"Yes ma'am. Angelica is my daughter," he said in a respectful tone, no doubt taking his cue from the way Candy spoke to the woman.

"Hmm. She a little hellion, that one. You might want to have Miss Thang hang around Miz Candy. Miz Candy is a good woman. She can teach your little bad as—behind,"—she caught herself when Candy coughed—"chile some manners."

"Yes, ma'am. I'm in total agreement."

Pauline narrowed her eyes even more when he docilely agreed. Candy gave him major kudos for not squirming under the old woman's piercing stare.

With a satisfied look she nodded her head.

"I'll get the girls rounded up ready for you, Miz Candy. But don't be too long finishing up here."

Pauline popped her tongue against the roof of her mouth and gave Candy the *look*. Whenever Pauline did that, Candy felt like one of the young girls she mentored, all of ten years old.

"You might want to lock the door if you plan on having any more in-depth meetings. Understand?"

"Yes, ma'am," Candy and Davis replied in unison.

Pauline withdrew the whistle she kept buried deeply in her bosom, and left the room, firmly closing the door behind her.

Seconds later they heard the shrill whistle and Sister Pauline's booming voice. "Time for session! Don't make me have to find y'all! You *don't* want me to come and hunt your little narrow behinds down, trust Sister Pauline on that! If you're in this session, saddle up, it's time to roll!" Her heavy footsteps faded away as she stomped down the hallway.

"Who was that?" Davis' voice was hushed as though he was afraid Pauline would overhear him and return.

"Um . . . that's Mrs. Rogers, she's my assistant."

"Your assistant?" His deep voice held a discernible squeak. "Didn't you call her Sister Pauline? Is she a nun?" he asked, horror in his voice, forcing a laugh from Candy despite the tension in the air.

"No. We all grew up calling her that. She's one of the mattrons at the local church. It's a sign of respect to call her Sister," she explained. "Sometimes she's a little gruff, has a tendency to quote biblical passages in one breath and well, say a *mild* curse word—or two—in the next. But she has a heart of gold." Candy straightened her clothes and moved toward her desk, gathering what she needed for the session.

There was a strained moment before Davis spoke again.

"Look, I don't know what came over me. I didn't plan for that to happen," he said, running his hands through his hair. "I'm sorry—"

"Please, don't." Candy held up a hand, forestalling him from continuing.

She didn't know what to think, much less what to say, in reaction to what had just happened between the two of them. What she *didn't* want was for him to apologize.

To tell her it was something he regretted wasn't what she wanted to hear.

"I wasn't exactly pushing you away." She straightened her back and looked him in the face.

Davis's eyes blazed before his expression shut down.

"I don't know what came over me. I'm sorry that happened. It won't happen again. I'd better go," was his stiff reply.

His next words banished any desire she had for him to pick up where they left off before Pauline's interruption.

"In case you get busy or lose track of time, I'll have my secretary call you."

Without waiting for a reply, he turned and left her office, closing the door quietly behind him.

Candy didn't know whether to laugh, cry or throw something at her closed door.

Damn.

Just like that, he'd brought back to mind why one minute she wanted to jump his bones and strip off her clothes, and the next she wanted to hurt him. Badly.

After the intimacy of what they shared, she didn't know what she expected to happen.

That odd exchange had *not* been it.

One minute he ran hot for her, giving her what she'd been dreaming of for longer than she wanted to admit, and the next, he insulted her by suggesting she was so feeble-minded she'd forget something that was so important.

They both were a crazy mess of contradictions, she thought, and gathered her things, preparing for the session with her girls.

Her mind was a chaotic jumble. Angrily, Candy threw her notebook into her bag, tossed it over her shoulder and left her office.

5

"Hey Davis, I just got the specs back on the Henson project. Everything looks good. We have the approvals we need and should be able to start on schedule."

Davis glanced away from his computer monitor and removed his glasses when his project manager entered his office.

"That's great, Rod. What about the men? You have your team assembled for this project?"

Rodney was his right hand man. They'd been friends since their freshman year in college, both majoring in architecture. When he'd needed a project manager, Rodney was the first one he'd asked, and Rodney had gladly accepted the position.

Rodney had been at Strong Construction nearly as long as Davis had, and was as invaluable to Davis as Milly was. Or as Milly had been, before she'd taken a hiatus from the company.

"Yeah, I have a strong crew for this one. I was thinking of using Griffins as the foreman for this job."

"He did a damn good job on the school expansion project last summer, but that was a small job. You think he'll be able to handle one this size?"

"Yeah, it's a bigger job, but I'm sure he can handle it. He's a good man, and hell of a crew chief. The men look up to him. He's ready for the next step."

Davis nodded his head in agreement. He trusted Rodney completely and knew he had his finger on the pulse of the men who they employed to work the sites.

"What about the crew?"

"There's Rosalina Cruz, the new worker we hired. I was thinking of putting her on this job. Her resume is tight."

"Did you speak with her last foreman?"

Rodney ran a hand over his short dark hair and grimaced. "Well, the jury is still out on that one. Something about the man irritates the hell out of me. . . . I don't trust his ass. He says Cruz had some problems adjusting to working with a crew that was mostly men."

"What was the problem?"

"That was it. He couldn't say what it was, just alluded to a bunch of shit. I don't buy it. She's been working construction for over five years and has a solid resume; previous employer never said anything about her having problems with her crew. I'm going to go on my instincts and give her a shot."

"I trust you can handle this, Rodney. I have enough on my plate without dealing with another defiant female," he murmured.

Davis massaged his temples. He glanced over his console, his attention divided between the spreadsheet he'd been creating, the upcoming construction project and Angelica. And Candy.

"Milly giving you problems?" Rodney settled his large frame in one of the oversized leather chairs facing Davis.

"Milly? My sister? Why would you think it's Milly giving me grief?" he asked curiously.

Rodney looked uncomfortable. Had Davis not known him better he'd have sworn he saw a faint blush across his friend's dark brown skin.

"Or did you mean Aunt Mildred?" Davis took pity on his friend and gave him an out.

"No, actually I meant Milly," he said and Davis was even further surprised. "I just thought with her taking a break from the business and all, you two may be having problems."

"No, Mil and I are fine. I may not have understood her reasons, but I didn't have a problem with her taking a break. It was hard on Angel when she left town. I'm glad she's back home," he finished.

Milly had not only taken a hiatus from Davis Construction, she'd also left Stanton for six months to stay with a college friend in New York. Davis had felt the impact of her leaving the business, although they'd hired an assistant to help in the interim.

"I was even happier when she told me she's coming back to work soon."

"She is? When? No one told me." Rodney's dark eyes widened and the look on his face was so comical Davis wanted to laugh.

"She mentioned it to me last week. I didn't think to tell you about it. She wasn't sure she was coming back, for sure. Besides, you have Letty to help you, isn't she working out?" Davis mentioned the new admin assistant they'd hired.

Milly was not only a partner in the firm with Davis, but she'd occasionally worked alongside Rodney on various projects, aiding him in coordinating the jobs as well as choosing the crew.

When she'd decided to leave Davis had made the decision to hire Rodney his own assistant to help ease his workload.

"Letty is doing fine. She's no Milly, but who is?" he asked and he and Davis shared a laugh.

Milly, although she didn't have their aunt's ballsy, dominant demeanor, was a force to be reckoned with whenever she was on a project.

She rarely went to the actual sites, as their aunt had, claiming she preferred to work behind the scenes. Yet, she made sure projects ran smoothly and jobs were completed on time.

Davis worried about her, whenever she *would* go on the sites. As a child, Milly had been in the same accident that had killed their parents. Milly had survived, but the injuries to her legs had been severe. So much so, the doctors thought she would never walk again.

Several operations later, and with the gritty determination she'd inherited from their aunt, Milly had regained the use of her legs, although she required a cane.

"How's Milly doing, anyway?" Rodney asked, nonchalantly. Davis picked up on the undercurrent lying beneath the casual query.

Davis thought back over his conversation with Milly the previous week, when they'd been discussing Angelica's truancy. He remembered Milly had the same tense undercurrents in her voice when Rodney's name had come up in the conversation.

He'd been so wrapped up in worry over Angel he hadn't dwelled on it.

"Mil's fine. Angel has been spending time with her since she returned," he replied just as casually.

"Good to hear." Rodney nodded. "So, if the problem isn't with Milly, it must be Angelica." Rodney changed the subject.

"Yeah, it's Angel. She skipped school."

"Again?"

"Again," Davis nodded his head in agreement. "This time they've requested a parent meeting between me and the whole damn interdisciplinary team," he said and ran his hand through his hair in frustration.

"Interdisciplinary?"

Rodney was unmarried, and he had no children. Therefore he had no need to know about things like interdisciplinary teams.

Davis felt a pang of jealousy.

"It's a meeting with her teacher, school counselor and principal."

"I don't suppose this was Anita Watson's idea, was it?"

Davis snorted. Rodney knew of his odd relationship with Angelica's principal. She and his wife had been friends growing up as well as college classmates.

When she'd returned to town, just months before his and Gail's wedding, Anita had come on to him. Hard.

He'd played it off in the beginning, but even after the wedding it hadn't stopped. When it became obvious Gail was pregnant, Anita had made it a point to drop by when she knew Gail wasn't around. She told him in no uncertain terms if Gail wasn't satisfying him sexually, she would be more than happy to pick up the slack. At the time, he'd marveled at her gall until he'd overheard a conversation between her and Gail.

His wife had been telling Anita of her dislike for making love, particularly the further along she was in her pregnancy. He'd always known Gail wasn't particularly passionate, and although it had been hell trying to keep his strong libido in check, he'd honored his marriage vows and hadn't taken Anita up on her frequent offers of no-commitment sex.

One evening Gail had gone to visit her grandmother and Anita dropped by. Instead of leaving when she learned Gail wasn't home, she'd come on to him so hard, he'd had to physically push her clinging body away. After hurling insults his way and belittling his masculinity, Anita had stormed out of his home.

She hadn't approached him again until Gail passed. In a final attempt she'd tried, again, to seduce him. He'd coldly rebuffed her and told her not to ever come by his house again. She'd turned on him, promising him he'd need to wear earmuffs in hell before he ever got a chance to get with her.

Davis hoped hell maintained a constant boiling temperature.

She'd never gotten over his rejection. And neither had she ever forgotten.

"Who else but Anita?" he answered Rodney's original question.

"Damn, that woman needs to find a man. She's still got it for you, man. Shit! Why'd you put Angel in that school anyway?" Rodney asked.

"It's the best school in the city. And I promised—"

"Gail. I know. You promised Gail. But still . . ."

"Yeah, I know." Davis agreed wearily, "maybe she'll go easy on me, on us, at the meeting."

Rodney leveled a look his way, without saying a word.

"Yeah, I'm fucked," Davis agreed.

6

"Hear that? Told you we shouldn't have agreed and let those bad tail boys in here with our girls, Miss Candy!" Pauline Rogers tsked as she and Candy walked toward the game room.

The noise from the rec room had reached decibels so loud Candy had been forced to come out of her office and investigate, with Sister Pauline hot on her heels.

Before they made it to the door, the noise was pounding past the walls and Candy massaged her temples in an effort to ward off the headache she felt hovering.

She and Sister Pauline entered the room to see it was teeming with music, adolescent girls and roughhousing teen boys.

With no supervision.

A potentially lethal combination.

So this was where her older girls were, Candy thought as she and Pauline walked further inside.

Candy had made arrangements with the director of Young Men on the Move, the rec center for boys, for them to be able to use the services at Girls Unlimited as their center underwent renovations.

Unfortunately, with the increased number of youths in the

center, Candy was in dire need of additional staff and her extra hands hadn't arrived.

Two of her favorite volunteers, Karina Woodson and Liza Toulson were available on the weekends only so she'd asked Sister Pauline to help fill in the gap until the extra staff arrived.

"Boys you need to play a little less . . . wild with the girls. Remember, this is a co-ed *foosball* tournament. Not Monday Night Football!" Candy shouted over the loud noise in the game room. "And can we turn the music down a tad? I can't even hear myself think in here!"

"You can forget tryin' to convince their little rough asses to act right *that* way, Miss Candy. Uh uh . . . no, these knuckleheads need something more direct. Honey, the Bible say spare the rod, spoil the child, and I'm 'bout ready to get to roddin' up in *here*!"

With that pronouncement, Pauline Rogers withdrew her ever-handy whistle buried deep in the V of her ample bosom and blew. The sharp, shrill sound reverberated against the walls of the game room and the room began to quiet down.

"Listen up, y'all heard Miss Candy, don't act like you didn't. Come on now! These is young ladies you little hoodlums—"

"Ms. Rogers! Don't call them hoodlums . . ." Candy hissed. Out of respect Candy kept her voice low; she didn't want the kids to hear her reprimand the older woman. Although with all the loud noise, she doubted they could hear a semitruck run through the center at full speed.

"Did y'all hear what I *said*? I told your little narrow as—"

"*Sister Pauline!* Don't refer to them as narrow asses either!" Candy cut in before Pauline could finish the word.

Candy had raised her voice to be heard *just* as the noise level died down to a low rumble and was mortified when the last of her sentence echoed in the near silence of the room.

She was so ashamed she could have crawled in a pit when twenty pair of eyes, all varying shades of brown, stared at her in open-mouthed astonishment and snickered.

She wanted to then cover her body with the dirt from the same pit when she looked into the doorway and saw Davis Strong staring at her. The look on his face mirrored the kids' look of astonishment. But where she saw laughter lurking in the kids' eyes, there was nothing even *remotely* amused in Davis's penetrating gaze.

The silence was ominous in the room as Candy and Davis simply stared at one another for what felt like eons to Candy. The kids looked from Candy to Davis, back and forth, waiting to see who would speak first.

"Ms. Cain, could I speak with you outside for a moment?" There wasn't anything humorous sounding in the tone of his deep voice either.

Candy turned to Pauline Rogers and smiled weakly.

"Ms. Rogers, could you stay and supervise the kids? I need to go and speak with Mr. Strong. I'll return shortly."

"Umm hmmm, baby, don't worry 'bout it," the older woman said and made a popping sound with her tongue against the roof of her mouth. "I'll stay. Just go on and handle your business. Sister Pauline *got* this."

Candy didn't care for the inflection Sister Pauline gave to the word "got," but for the time, she had more pressing matters to attend to.

Besides, some things were better left unknown.

With a final glance in Pauline's direction, Candy followed Davis out of the room. She kept her shoulders erect, her posture tight. She didn't want the kids to pick up on her embarrassment or dismay at being called out by a parent.

Davis didn't know who was more surprised, he or she when their eyes connected after she yelled out to her assistant not to call the kids asses. The look on her creamy brown, flushed face was so comical he was tempted to laugh outright.

But he held his laughter in check. He reminded himself it wasn't funny and she was a grown woman who should know better. Even if she was reprimanding the old woman and not actually calling the kids asses *herself,* it was the principle of the matter.

Davis had searched the center for Candy, although he'd already picked Angelica up. She was outside playing with two of her friends and he'd made the excuse that he needed to speak to Ms. Cain and told her to remain put.

He told himself he was only coming to remind her of the meeting the next day, and nothing more. His subconscious called him a bald-faced liar. The truth was he simply wanted—needed—to see Candice again.

Particularly after what happened on Saturday. He hadn't been able to chase the memory of their hot exchange, or the woman, out of his mind.

Damn. He hadn't dry humped a woman since he was a kid, which had resulted in yet another adolescent-type wet dream, starring none other than Ms. Candice Cain.

As she approached him, his brooding glance slid over her body.

She was wearing one of her more typical wraps. She wore a long-sleeved T-shirt beneath, and although the colorful fabric molded her small breasts, it hung loose to her calves.

Davis could make out her rounded curves as the fabric swayed around her, gently following the motion of her curves.

"I came by to remind you of the meeting tomorrow with Angelica's school," he said as soon as she reached his side.

"There's an empty classroom right over here." Candy indicated a room a few feet down the hallway.

She allowed him to lightly grasp her elbow and guide her further into the hallway. The small touch sent a sizzle of electricity from her skin to his. He removed his hand, allowing her elbow to drop to her side.

"I wouldn't forget. I know how important this is for both you and Angelica," she replied, looking up at him with an unreadable expression on her face.

"Good. I wouldn't want to give them any more ammunition against me by announcing I have you on board to help with Angelica, and you forget to show."

"Did you come by to insult me, or remind me of the meeting? Because frankly, Davis, I don't understand the purpose of the visit."

After he guided her inside the room, he closed the door behind them, and braced his back against it.

"No, I didn't come here to insult you. I came by to see if you would like for me to pick you up for the meeting." He crossed his arms over his chest and glared at her.

"I can make it myself, Davis. I have an appointment scheduled for another student, so I'll be out of the center for the afternoon. And come to think of it, I don't think I like the implication you've made, not once, but *twice,* that I need to be reminded of this meeting. As though my mind is so damn feeble—" but she was cut off mid-rant.

Davis hauled her close, pulled her tight against his chest with one hand gripping the flesh of her hip, the other grasping the back of her head. He leaned down, slanted his mouth over hers, and covered her lips.

His sensual, full lips pressed against hers and delivered feathering strokes, caresses designed to force her to open her mouth for him. Once she did, his slick tongue quickly invaded her mouth, hot and exploring.

With a groan she raised her arms and wrapped them around his neck as her tongue swept against his, matching his heated strokes. They explored each other, both greedy as they engaged in a sensual battle of tongues and lips until Davis tugged at her lower lip with his teeth, and bit down gently, before suckling it.

Hunger for him rose sharp and immediate. When one of his hands moved down her body, past the curve of her waist and grasped one of her rounded butt cheeks and squeezed, Candy moaned deeply into his mouth.

Her hands slid from his shoulders, roaming down the broad

expanse of his back, down to the narrow expanse of his waist until her hands rubbed over his taut, muscled ass.

Their bodies were pressed so closely together, Candy felt his responding groan rumble deep in his chest.

Her nipples tightened and spiked more sharply beneath the T-shirt she wore the longer they kissed, along with the increase of moisture at the apex of her thighs.

"God, I love your mouth," he groaned, lifting away and resting his forehead against hers.

Candy inhaled deep breaths until her heartbeat returned to normal, and she was able to speak. One glance at him from beneath her lashes and she could see the way he fought to bring his breath under control. His chest heaved with the effort, his nostrils flaring.

"And Candy, if you wear one of these wraps of yours, make sure it covers you, completely." Candy was stunned when he picked up the conversation as though the last few minutes of tongue-curling kisses hadn't happened.

But she knew he was as affected as she by their heated exchange. The hoarseness in his voice and the tremor she felt from his hands when he eased her away from his laboring chest told the story.

He eased one of his hands back inside the top waistband where her wrap started, in the space where flesh and fabric met.

"It might even be better if you wore something more ... traditional. I want to make the best impression possible. That wouldn't happen if this showed," he finished.

His fingers circled around until they reached her belly ring, nestled firmly inside her navel. Although his words made her see red, the feel of his thick fingers toying with her body jewelry gave her a direct zing from her ring to her clit.

She reached out in front of her body and plucked his hand from her waist.

"What you see is what you get with me, Mr. Strong. If

you're looking for someone more . . . traditional, then I'm not the woman for you," she issued the challenge coolly, and saw from the slight lift of his eyebrow that he caught her double meaning.

"There's no backing out now. You're exactly what I'm looking for," he replied, easily moving away from her. He gave her one final glance before he opened the door. "Just make sure you're there on time, Ms. Cain."

After he closed the door behind him, Candy pushed herself away from the wall she'd been leaning on and headed toward the door.

She hadn't missed the way he'd told her she was his, or that she was exactly what he'd been looking for, but his hot and cold vibes were really, *really* starting to work her third nerve. And as Sister Pauline would say . . . she only had two.

Despite her irritation with Davis, Candy laughed out loud at her mental—stolen—quip as she straightened her clothes and headed out of the door.

7

"Mr. Strong, I can only wait so long before we start the meeting. And I wish you had informed me Ms.—" Anita Watson waved a hand, silently asking Davis to fill in the last name.

"Cain."

"Yes. I wasn't aware you'd invited Ms. Cain to this meeting. It was only to be a team meeting with the staff and parent, not outsiders."

Her overall irritableness over the surprise was evident in her tone and twisted facial expression.

"I apologize for not informing you, Ms. Watson. Yet I wish you would have informed me of the change, as well. Had I known it was only to be you and me at this meeting, I would have made other arrangements." Her features twisted even more with his response.

"Well, if she isn't here soon, we'll have to start without her. I do have other appointments."

Anita Watson pointedly glared at her wrist and the slim black watch she wore and Davis bit back a curse.

"I know you're busy. I asked Ms. Cain to take part in this meeting because I thought she would be beneficial in helping my daughter. I'm sure she'll be here soon," Davis glanced down at his watch, and noted that although Candy wasn't late yet, she was damn close.

He'd been expecting the social worker as well as Angel's teacher, but when he'd arrived Anita Watson had blithely informed him of her change of plan. He'd silently thanked God he'd asked Candy to accompany him. He had no desire to be in close quarters with this barracuda of a woman.

"I think a one-on-one meeting would have been more effective, Davis. That's all. My concern is for Angelica and Angelica alone," she insisted.

More effective his ass.

Davis had bitten back telling the woman what he thought of her fake concern. With disgust he realized Anita was using the circumstances for her own twisted reasons.

He glanced down at his watch, again. Where in hell was Candy? he thought. Damn! He should have driven to the center and picked her up himself, but hadn't.

He didn't want her to get ticked off and think he didn't believe she'd make it without his assistance. She'd accused him of that yesterday, when he'd dropped by the center.

The second reason he'd chosen not to go to her was less noble. He didn't know if he could handle being closed up in the same car with her.

He'd also refrained from calling her earlier in the day, although it had been hard to do.

The last time he'd spoken to her he'd told her what to do, how to dress and act when she showed up for the meeting.

He didn't know what came over him whenever he was around Candy. He couldn't manage to keep it together for more than five consecutive minutes whenever he was. He always managed to come off sounding like a dictatorial ass.

That or he would grab her and assault that sweet, lush mouth of hers.

"Well, I think we need to go ahead and start the meeting, Mr. Davis." When the principal spoke, Davis reluctantly turned his attention to her.

There was a soft knock on the door before it opened and Candy rushed inside with an apologetic smile crossing her face. A rush of relief washed over Davis and unbidden, a grin tugged at his lips.

"I'm sorry I'm late. I was with another student in a school across town, traffic was crazy—" she stopped and smiled, her deep dimples flashing. "Forgive me," she finished, her gaze settling on Davis first before she turned to Anita.

Davis felt the familiar tightening in his gut return, the same feeling he got whenever he was within ten feet of Candice Cain.

Candy rushed inside the office, knowing she was beyond late, but it couldn't be helped.

"I presume this is Ms. Cain? Please, have a seat, Ms. Cain and we can begin."

"Thank you," Candy murmured as she took the offered seat.

Although a small tight smile of welcome graced the woman's face, Candy saw her dark close-set eyes size her up, in one all-encompassing gaze.

Candy had carefully dressed for work today because of the two meetings she had scheduled for her girls, Theresa and Angelica. Although she made it a point never to judge anyone by their outer trappings, and taught her girls the same thing, she knew not everyone felt the same way.

The principal wasn't the only one who tended to judge. Davis Strong held the same propensity.

After his parting comment yesterday, she wanted to tell him what he could do with his advice on appropriate attire.

Candy instead chose to keep in mind the sole purpose of the

meeting, which was how to help Angelica, and not about her and Davis.

She mouthed an apology as she settled herself, placing her large bag near the leg of the chair.

His only response was a slight nod before he turned back to face the frowning principal.

Candy ran a quick, assessing eye over the room. The principal's office was spacious and airy. There were no personal touches added to the decor; it was expensively furnished in cool—albeit bland—colors of grey and black, with oversized leather chairs scattered strategically. The dark grey leather chair Anita sat in, behind the large cherrywood desk, was as opulent as the rest of the furnishing.

Abstract art—no doubt acquired from one of the upscale, downtown art galleries—adorning the walls, along with abundant ferns set in the corners near her desk, completed the picture of sophisticated elegance.

Candy smiled, thinking of her own messy office splattered with various "art" she'd acquired from her youngest center members, and held her grin.

Yet for all its cool elegance, the office was impersonal. Beautiful, but impersonal. Despite the warm air blowing from one of the large vents, Candy resisted the urge to rub her hands over her arms to ward off a sudden chill.

Neither did much personality shine through the conservative two-piece, navy blue suit Anita Watson wore, along with the matching mid-heel pumps Candy saw planted close together, beneath the oversized desk. She appeared to be all business, yet, as Candy observed, the gleam in her eye as she watched Davis was anything but.

She filed that bit of information away mentally to revisit later.

"Well, now that Ms. Cain has deigned to join us, shall we begin?" the woman asked and a small, tight insincere smile graced her pinched features.

"Again, I'm sorry I'm late," Candy offered the apology with a polite smile and settled back into her seat. "Are you waiting for the others to join us as well?" Although the question was directed at the principal, Candy looked to Davis.

"There was a change of plans, it seems. Ms. Watson thought it would be best if she and I had a private meeting. Fortunately, with you joining us, I'm sure we'll be able to come up with a better plan, in order to resolve this matter with Angelica."

"Yes, well . . . the reason for this meeting is to discuss Angelica. It has come to my attention Angelica has committed a series of grievous offenses at St. Monica's and I am unable to continue to turn a blind eye to them."

Anita Watson reached a hand over and lifted a pair of square-framed glasses from the top of a manila folder and placed them on the thin bridge of her nose.

She opened the folder and pursed her lips as she scanned the contents. After a brief perusal of the documents, she placed the folder to the side and released a long breath, shaking her head. She then began to speak, verbally outlining the changes in Angelica's behavior along with her truancy.

As she spoke, her eyes stayed glued on Davis. The rare times she glanced Candy's way, Candy noted a distinct chill enter the woman's dark gaze, and a sour look cross her face, her mouth turned downward. If Candy happened to catch her, Anita Watson would check herself and rearrange her thin lips into a façade of a smile.

Candy saw through the woman. She didn't know what history, if any, she and Davis shared, but whatever it was, it wasn't resolved. At least not on Anita Watson's part.

By the close of the meeting, as far as Angelica was concerned, Candy wasn't impressed with Ms. Watson's concern for the child. In her opinion, the principal was acting a bit theatrical, just a tad over the top with all the breath-blowing and sighs of feigned concern. And Candy was certain that's all it was: an act. She was adept at reading people, a skill she'd developed as a child when she and her father moved from home to home, job to job, and she'd cultivated the ability as an adult.

Not that Candy condoned what Angelica had done, skipping school and mouthing off to her teachers, but there was more than concern for Angelica going on.

It was confirmed when Anita suggested Angelica needed counseling, and perhaps *she* be the one to provide it. After school, one-on-one . . . and Davis was invited to attend the meetings.

"Perhaps something *more* is needed. Something she isn't receiving at home," she said and cast her gaze in Davis' direction.

"What do you mean by that, Ms. Watson?" Davis crossed his big arms over his chest, his expression closed.

"I do have degrees in child development and education," she said, waving a manicured hand toward one of the built-in shelves where several framed diplomas were set.

"And?" he asked and Candice was surprised at the blunt, almost rude tone of his voice.

"And—" she dragged the word out. "I'm offering to provide counseling for our little Angelica," she finished, her tone that of a queen lowering herself to provide for one of her servants.

Little Angelica she'd called her. Yes, this woman had issues and Candy wanted to help Davis and Angelica more than ever.

"No worries, Ms. Watson, Davis and Angel are going to be just fine. How wonderful that you would sacrifice your time in this way, to help one of your students," Candy began and smiled widely.

She glanced from the corner of her eye over at Davis and noted that although he remained relaxed in the chair, he was suddenly more alert.

"You're not going to have to worry about going to that extreme! *We* wouldn't dare dream of you doing that," she said and her emphasis on the word "we" didn't go by unnoticed, from the narrowing of the woman's eyes.

Candy ignored Davis' sudden coughing fit.

"Angelica isn't going to need the deep one-on-one counseling. They've got me, now," Candy replied and turned her attention toward Davis.

"Isn't that right, Davis?"

Davis' lips twitched, trying to hold back a smile. He nodded his head before answering.

"Yes, we do. I think you're going to see some changes from here out, Ms. Watson," Davis replied to the woman, yet his eyes were fixed on Candy's.

It was as though Anita Watson was no longer in the room, the way he looked at her. Candy shivered and rubbed her hands over her arms as goosebumps peppered her flesh.

They both silently acknowledged in that moment the connection they'd mutually felt from the first time they'd laid eyes on one other.

They also acknowledged the instant leap in evolution of their relationship.

8

"Well, I overheard Ms. Watson talking on the phone and she said your mama didn't even know who your daddy was! She said your mama lied to your father and said it was him, just so he'd marry her!" Chandra said, hand on hip, laughing at Angelica.

"You did not hear that, you big liar! Take it back!" Angelica yelled.

"I ain't either lying! I heard her say it. Everybody knows that ain't your real daddy anyway!" Chandra yelled back and crossed her bony little arms over her non-existent chest.

"He is too my daddy! Now take that back, before I knock your dumb ass teeth down your throat!"

When the little girl openly laughed, Angelica hauled back a clenched fist and was within two seconds from laying one on the child.

Candy ran up, just in time, and caught Angelica's raised fist in one of her hands, before she made connection with the other girl's nose.

"That's enough! Angelica! Girls—what is going on?" Candy asked, separating the two before the fight could ensue.

"Miss Candy, I wasn't doing nothing! I was just talking to Angel, and she got all mad at me and tried to hit me and cursed at me! I swear I didn't do nothing to her!" Chandra wailed, instantly turning from the teasing troublemaker back to a nine-year-old afraid of getting in trouble.

"We're late for session, so we'll have to talk about this later, Chandra. But you know I don't allow fighting. Fighting won't be tolerated any more than hurtful teasing," Candy leveled a direct stare at Chandra.

"Yes, ma'am," she murmured.

"And you have one more fight and you're suspended from the center, young lady. If I were you, I'd slow my roll. Think about how your parents would feel if I had to tell them you were on suspension, Chandra," she warned. "I'd also think about how your parents would react if they suspected you were eavesdropping on adult conversations," Candy finished.

Chandra's parents worked hard to be able to pay for her to go to the private school she attended along with Angelica. They loved her, but were tough on discipline. The mere suggestion that Candy would tell Chandra's parents of her behavior would be enough to have her rethink her teasing and eavesdropping in the future.

"It's time for our session, why don't you go ahead, Chandra, so you're not late," Candy told the chastened young girl. Before she took off running, she turned back to Candy.

"Miz Cain, you won't tell my parents . . . will you?" she asked hesitantly and chewed her bottom lip.

"No, not this time, Chandra. But understand you have to be accountable for your actions. If I see a repeat of this, I won't be so lenient the next time."

"Yes ma'am," she said and with a more upbeat look she turned and ran away.

Angelica turned to run off as well. Candy quickly caught

her by the back of her shirt, before she could make good on her escape.

"What? You let Chandra go! I'm going to the same session, Miss Candy, can't I go too?" she pleaded.

"Yes, Angelica, you can. In a minute. First I want to know what happened between you two."

Candy knew Angelica would rather be anywhere but where she was, but she waited patiently for her to answer. When she remained quiet, Candy sighed.

"Angelica, I heard what she said. And I know that hurt. But honey, fighting isn't the answer."

She placed her hand over Angelica's shoulder. Candy was surprised when she didn't shrug her away, although she had been, over the course of the last two weeks, much more receptive to Candy.

Candy couldn't say she'd unearthed the reasons for Angelica's recent behavior, but she had a few ideas. One of which was a surprise to her.

Angelica had recently asked Candy, out of the clear blue, if she'd known her mother. Candy had gently told her she hadn't lived in Stanton during the time her mother was living, and she hadn't known her.

Angelica had feigned nonchalance and shrugged her thin shoulders, telling Candy it was no big deal.

But Candy caught the look of vulnerability in her dark eyes before she could hide it. She wondered why Angelica had asked the question, but after the exchange she just witnessed, she wondered exactly how much the child had known about her mother, wondering if her lack of knowledge was at the root of some of her recent acting-out episodes.

As well as the daily interactions with Angelica, she'd already been given two progress reports from the school. Both had been without incident and Candy had given a sigh of relief.

She remembered Anita Watson's look of disdain when Candy

promised she would be helping Davis. Candy would do everything in her power to prevent seeing the superior look cross her face! Ever.

Since the team meeting with her school, Candy had also been in daily conversation with Davis, mostly over the phone.

She wasn't sure wanted to see him face-to-face and deal with the sexual tension between them.

The few times she and Davis had met in person, the tension had been there, no matter how hard either one of them tried to ignore it. Ignoring it wasn't about to make it go away; all it did was intensify the attraction.

For whatever reason, Davis not only tried his best to ignore what was there between them, *right there*, hovering. In fact he seemed to break his neck trying to avoid being alone with her in the same room.

But she knew their last kiss had affected him just as much as it had her, and no amount of avoiding could negate that.

The way he'd hustled her inside the empty classroom at the center the last time they'd been alone together, his big hands feeling her up, backing her up against the door and kissing her . . . she forced her thoughts away as she felt her body's instant response.

Now wasn't the time to take a trip down memory lane. With her new role in Angelica's life, Candy was glad for the reprieve from Davis.

She glanced down at Angelica.

"We'll talk about this after the session, Angelica," she said, sternly. Candy was careful not to allow any of her feelings of understanding to show. Angelica had to account for her actions as well as her language.

"Okay," Angelica replied and released a deep, heartfelt sigh. "I guess I may as well get ready for Daddy to lock me up and throw away the key. I know you're gonna tell him I cursed. He's gonna be so mad at me," she whispered. "It's not fair,

Ms. Cain, *she* started it," Angelica said, her bottom lip quivering.

With a dejected look of impending doom, Angelica turned and walked ahead of Candy, shoulders hunched down low, lips poked out.

Candy suppressed an unexpected smile at the drama only a nine-year-old could create.

9

"Okay girls, we need to wrap this up, session is almost over and everyone hasn't had the opportunity to speak yet," Candy said as the young girls spoke over each other, their voices animated.

"But Ms. Candy, you didn't answer my question," one of the girls spoke loudly over the others.

"I'm sorry, Shante, I didn't hear you over the others. Could you speak up please, sweetheart, so everyone can hear your question?" Candice asked and help up a hand when the other girls continued to speak. "Remember girls, we need to respect one another and when one has the baton, we have to allow her to speak," Candy reminded them.

She'd implemented the "baton" rule when she'd had her first session with the younger girls, as they all seemed to want to talk at the same time.

After Candy had gotten the others to quiet down, she gave Shante her full attention. When it didn't look as though she was going to speak, Candy encouraged her, "Go on, Shante, can you please repeat your question?"

Shante squared her thin shoulders and pushed her small wire-framed glasses further up the short bridge of her nose. She self-consciously glanced around at the other girls before speaking again.

"What do you do if a boy wants you to . . . you know . . . do it?" She finally spit out her question and Candy suppressed a sigh.

It was a hard fact of life, that although these girls were barely out of early childhood, a few of them had been introduced to the concept of male/female relationships. For some, this introduction had gone beyond an innocent peck on the cheek.

As she prepared to answer Shante's question, out of the corner of her eye she caught Angelica's intent stare.

She was probably thinking about the trouble she would be in with her father, among other things.

With caution, she proceeded to answer the question.

"Shante, what have I told you, as well as all the girls here?" Candy began.

Her gaze encompassed all the girls gathered in the semi-circle around her.

"It's our body and nobody else's."

"What else?" she prompted the girl with a smile. "Do we allow anyone to tell us what we should do with our bodies?" she asked.

"No ma'am, we don't," they chorused.

"Good, so why don't we talk about what we do, when we do feel pressure," Candy said.

The rest of the session Candy encouraged the girls to share their experiences; she was pleased when the girls reiterated what she'd been teaching them for the last nine months.

"Okay, that's it for today girls." Candy clapped her hands together at the close of the session. "It's Friday and I won't see some of you until Monday, so have a great weekend! For those of you coming to the center's party tomorrow night, I'll see you then. And . . ." she laughed when they collectively groaned. "And . . . for those of you who so nicely volunteered to help set up—Angelica and Chandra?—I'll see you both an hour before the party, at five o'clock!"

"What?!" both girls chorused.

"I don't want to volunteer, Miss Cain! I was coming later to the dance, with some friends," Chandra wailed and Candy gave her a stern, meaningful glare.

"You *will* be there, or we can discuss this with your parents. You pick."

"What did you say, young lady?" she asked when Chandra mumbled something beneath her breath.

"Nothing, Miss Cain. I'll be there," she said and she and Angelica exchanged mutually evil looks at one another, before she raced out the door.

"I didn't sign up to volunteer! No way am I doing that, Ms. Candy! I'm going to be spending the night and tomorrow with my Aunt Milly!" Angelica stomped her foot in frustration.

"Angelica, we can talk about it in my office. I need to speak to you anyway. Could you please wait for me?" Candy wanted to make sure she got Angel's attention before she could try and run out the door, so she spoke loudly over the sound of the girls laughing and chairs scraping as they left the room.

"This is the last session for today, so girls, please place the chairs against the wall . . . and pick those chairs up off the floor! That's brand new carpet!" she groaned as several of the girls dragged the chairs across the floor before lifting them to stack against the wall.

"Ms. Candy, can I talk to you for a sec?"

"Sure Tasha, what's on your mind?" she smiled at the young girl as she stood hesitantly in front of her, shuffling her weight from foot to foot.

"Everything going well with your new mural?" she asked.

Tasha was in the process of finishing her latest mural in the girls' locker room.

"Oh yeah, it's all good. I think I'll have the new scene done in no time," she said, shuffling from foot to foot, and Candy waited.

"I wanted to know if it's okay if I still can come to the party tomorrow even if I don't have the permission slip signed from my foster mother."

"Sweetheart, I'm sorry, but without the permission slip I can't. Has your foster parent said it's okay?"

"She said I could go, but she forgot to sign the slip."

"Well, if you can bring the slip tomorrow, it's not too late. Just make sure you bring it to me before the party starts, okay?"

"Yes ma'am. I will."

When the girl made no move to go, Candy knew there was something else on her mind. "Is there something else, Tasha?"

"The other day, Sister Pauline was talking to me about responsibility and all that stuff."

"Yes," Candy prompted her, waiting for her to continue.

"She started quoting something I never heard of before. She told me I had a purpose to my life . . . called to be something more, and fulfilling my destiny of greatness . . . Don't know exactly what she was trying to say." Tasha's voice trailed off and then a faint blush stained her sienna-colored cheeks. "Sister Pauline is a trip," she laughed.

"Yes, she can be." Candy gave the young girl a smile. "But her heart is good. She wants the best for you, for all of us, I think. Sometimes her delivery is a bit odd," Candy laughed lightly. "But she's a good woman. And a wise one, as well."

"What did she mean, though? About all that destiny stuff."

"Tasha, you were destined for great things in your life. Don't shortchange yourself by allowing others to dictate who or what you should be. You've had some hard breaks, but it doesn't have to define who you are. Sister Pauline was trying to encourage you. You are intelligent, beautiful inside and out and destined for greatness, sweetheart."

When Tasha turned her face away and rolled her eyes, Candy forced her to turn back around.

"But *you* have to believe that." Candy lightly ran her hand over Tasha's long, corn-rowed hair. "If you do, then it doesn't matter what others think. You're the one in charge of your destiny."

"Since my mama died, I've learned to take care of myself. My foster mother sure isn't going to do that for me. But that's cool, I don't need her, I'm almost grown."

"I know you're almost grown up, Tasha. But still, I'm always here if you need me, okay?" Candy wanted to instantly reject the girl's statement with a screaming denial, as the young girl was barely out of childhood, but knew better. To do so would be seen as a rejection of her burgeoning womanhood.

With a half smile which didn't quite reach her dark eyes, Tasha picked up her backpack. She pulled her arms through the straps and turned and walked toward the door. She said goodbye to Angelica, who was hovering nearby, before she left.

Candy gathered her things and allowed the girls to talk to each other briefly, before she walked over to join Angelica.

"Ready to go?" she asked and turned off the light in the room.

"Go where?" Although she said it with a bit of an attitude, Candy felt her nervousness.

"I thought you and I could have a talk in my office, as we wait for your aunt to pick you up," Candy replied after locking the door to the room.

"I guess so," she mumbled, her enthusiasm dim.

"Come on, Angelica, it won't be that bad!" Candy replied lightly. Angelica slumped her shoulders forward and dragged her feet as though preparing for the guillotine.

10

As they walked down the long hallway, Candy smiled at the few girls they encountered. The center normally closed at seven o'clock, but tonight they were closing an hour early so the night crew could clean the entire center, top to bottom. It was within thirty minutes of closing time and most of the kids were heading home.

"Aunt Milly is going to be here any minute. I told her I'd wait out front for her," Angelica told her as she walked alongside Candy. "Some of the other girls are waiting for their parents to pick them up so we're going to sit out front together."

"After I lock up I'll wait outside with you. Would that be okay?"

Candy knew Milly and Davis both were adamant about picking Angelica up inside the center. There was no way on God's green earth they would allow her to wait outside for them to pick her up, as late as it was.

"Hmmm. I guess so," Angelica grudgingly agreed.

Candy hid a smile. More than likely one of the girls had asked Angelica to come outside and talk. Rather than say she couldn't, she'd agreed. Candy's suggestion let her stay inside without losing face.

"What did you need to talk to me about, anyway? You're going to tell my dad I almost got into a fight, aren't you?"

"No, I won't tell your dad. As long as you hold up your part and come and volunteer early for the dance, you and I are cool." She winked at the girl and instantly saw Angelica's thin shoulders sag in relief. "I just thought maybe you and I could have a chat. Nothing major. Maybe we can talk about school, how you're doing in class."

"Okay. I guess so."

As they walked down the corridor toward her office, Candy saw Angelica looking at the murals on the wall.

"Those sure are pretty. Tasha is good at art. I wish I could do something like that," she said, in a hushed tone of voice.

"Yes, Tasha did a beautiful job, didn't she?" Candy admired the way the murals were all coming together wonderfully. "You'd be surprised what talents you have, Angelica,"

"I couldn't do something like this," she scoffed.

"Maybe not this. This is Tasha's talent. Doesn't mean you don't have another talent all your own. You just have to search for it, or it could be there just waiting for you to discover yourself. That's usually how it works."

Several months ago she'd come in very early one Saturday and had caught a young girl spray painting on the side of the building and was furious. With the money from Mildred Strong's latest fundraising efforts, Candy had been able to hire a crew to power wash the outside of the building and it looked better than it had in years.

And when she saw a dark hooded figure outside, spray paint in hand, poised and ready to deface, she saw nothing but red. At the time she'd wanted to strangle the offender.

With a primal yell, Candy had run up on the delinquent and

snatched the hood off his head and ripped the spray can right out of his vandalizing hand, spinning him around to face her.

Surprised wasn't the word when two long ponytails tumbled from beneath the hood, and a defiant, but very feminine and very familiar young face stared up at her belligerently.

It was Tasha, one of her girls from the center.

Candy had asked Tasha why she was defacing their building, gently grabbed her by the shoulders and forced her to turn around and face the damage she'd done.

And when Candy had turned to face the building along with her, she'd been stunned.

Although the girl had been defacing the property, had no right to do what she did . . . the art was beautiful.

She'd been in the process of drawing a trio of angels. One was an older-looking black woman, one was middle-aged, and the last one was young, maybe in her early twenties. All three were smiling down at a small child jumping rope. There was something about the picture that pulled at Candy's heart.

She'd looked down at Tasha and saw the belligerent stamp of anger on her face. But more than anything, she saw the sadness lurking in the back of her dark eyes and didn't ask any questions about what the scene represented.

She already knew.

She hadn't had the opportunity to get to know all the girls then, or go over all of their files in depth, but she'd familiarized herself with Tasha's story. Tasha had recently lost her mother when the woman had overdosed. She was now living in foster care.

Candy's first reaction had been to punish Tasha. The girl needed to pay for her actions. But instead of the normal route of reporting what she'd done to her caregivers and banning her from the center for a determined time, she thought of a much more suitable "punishment." She'd commissioned her to recreate the same mural, along with others, inside the center.

Candy could still recall the look of surprise and hidden delight on the girl's face when she'd given her "punishment."

But, Candy didn't allow her little behind to get away with what she'd done to the building. Additionally, Tasha had to help clean the building for the next four Saturdays to make up for her transgression.

In the end, the center, as well as Tasha, benefited from her trip into delinquency.

When Candy and Angelica reached the door to her office, Candy opened it and allowed Angelica to enter before she did.

"Why don't you have a seat while I gather my things together for the night? It won't take long." Candy then invited Angelica to sit down in one of the chairs scattered around the cluttered office. "If one of the chairs you want to sit in has something on it, just place it on the floor neatly, next to it, 'kay?" she turned back around and started to gather her things together.

"Suuure thing, Ms. Candy," Angelica drew out the word, and Candy glanced over at her and saw her brows were knitted together. "It's a little messy in here, Ms. Candy. How do you ever find anything?"

Candy laughed out loud.

She'd tried to keep it neat, but it always seemed to find its way back to the typical organized chaos she normally operated with.

"I have a system," was all Candy said.

"Hey, that's what my dad always says!"

"Your dad has a messy desk?" She found it hard to believe Davis could function in an unstructured environment.

"Yes, and Aunt Milly said it the same way you just did! She doesn't believe me either!" Angelica laughed and Candy could see the small dimples appear in her round cheeks.

Candy smiled at her resemblance to Davis. Although they weren't biologically related, they shared an eerily familiar smile, complete with deep, slashing dimples. The only difference was Angelica's dimples were in both cheeks, and her daddy had one, which only served to make him more enticing to Candy.

Everything on the man was enticing to her, Candy thought. Who was she trying to fool?

She listened to Angelica prattle on about her father, obviously one of her favorite topics.

"He never lets anyone in there, though," she chattered, as she began to walk around the office. " 'Cept me, of course."

Candy noticed how she stuck out her little chest, proud she was the only one her father allowed inside his hallowed grounds.

"That's good. Obviously your father trusts you. I bet he doesn't let just anyone in there."

"Nope. Just me. He won't even let Aunt Milly go in there!"

"Wow . . . now that *is* special. Just goes to show how much he trusts you," Candy replied and watered her plants nonchalantly.

She was carefully watching Angelica out of the corner of her eye as she wandered about her office. Her small face was a study in concentration.

"Things going okay between you and your father, Angelica?"

Candy spoke casually. She didn't want Angelica to know she was on a fishing expedition. She was a bright child; if she had an inkling Candy was now working with her school and her father, Angelica would clam up, unwilling to talk to her.

Candy placed the watering can to the side. She bent down to scoop up the wadded-up pieces of paper littering the area near her trash can, where she'd missed several hook shots. Her fantasy of being the first five-foot three-inch, female NBA player was a dream she needed to just let go of.

She glanced over and saw Angelica holding the small framed photo from the bookshelf. The picture was of Candy and her father when she was not much older than Angelica.

Candy smiled and placed the last of the trash inside the can. She dusted her hands over her skirt and walked over to where Angelica stood, fingering the small, faded picture.

"Is this *your* father?" Angelica asked her as she turned with the picture in her hand.

"Yes, this is my dad—how could you tell?" She stood next to Angelica and smiled, remembering the day the picture had been taken.

11

_____

It had been taken during one of the few trips her father had taken with her to an amusement park. A rare treat for her, she remembered.

"I don't know. You two kind of look alike, I guess." Angelica shrugged her thin shoulders.

"You think so?" Candy asked. She glanced down at the picture and smiled. "I suppose we do. I look a lot more like my mother than I do my father, though. I think because my father passed along this," she lightly tapped the small gap between my two teeth. "*And* we have the same big ole forehead." Angelica uttered a startled laugh at Candy's self-deprecating humor. "But if you saw a picture of me with my mom, you'd probably think I look more like her," she finished.

Angelica nodded her head and placed the picture of Candy and her father back on the shelf, in the exact spot she removed it from. She kept her hands close to the frame, and when she looked up at Candy, she could see the curiosity shining in her dark eyes.

"Do you have a picture of your mother?" she asked, her face a study of feigned nonchalance.

"I do. But not here."

"I don't have pictures of me and my mother, either."

She sighed deeply, her small shoulders slightly slumped, and returned her attention to the picture of Candy and her father.

"You don't have any pictures at all?" Candy asked, prompting her.

"No, not really. I have a few baby pictures of the two of us. But none of me and my mom and dad together though. And then she died when I was little, so—" she allowed the sentence to trail off and shrugged.

"Yes, I know. I'm sorry, Angelica." Candy laid a consoling hand on her shoulder.

"It's no big deal, I guess. I mean I don't even know what she was like. People say I looked like her, though. From looking at the pictures, I kind of think I do." She shyly looked at Candy. She pointed to her small round forehead and finished, "She and I both have the same big ole forehead too." They shared a laugh, although Candy detected a hint of sadness lurking in Angelica's eyes.

"Were you living here when she was still living?"

Candy perched on the edge of her desk and smiled at her, gently. "No, sweetheart. I didn't know your mother. I don't think she and I moved in the same social circles."

"Mama wasn't always rich, you know," Angelica said almost eagerly, as though wanting to put Candy and her mother on equal social footing. "Before she and daddy got married, she used to live in North Stanton, too," she referred to the section of town where the center was located, as well as some of the less-affluent neighborhoods.

"I was at the University during the time your mother lived here, I believe. After I graduated, I lived in a city not far from Stanton before I was hired as the director and moved back. I didn't know your mother."

"Daddy never tells me anything about her, you know. When

I ask about what she was like, how they met, stuff like that, he won't say anything."

The unexpected comment took Candy by surprise. She didn't show her shock, but instead remained silent, allowing Angelica to speak freely.

"What does he do, when you ask?"

"Well, whenever I ask anything about my mother, anything about what she was like, he says the same thing. She was nice, smart and she loved me, a lot. Then he smiles in that way grown-ups do, when they really aren't happy. Kind of like this."

Had the subject matter not been so serious, Candy would have laughed out loud at the way Angelica stretched her lips in a parody of a smile. The little girl completely captured the strained smiles adults gave, trying to smile when it was the last thing they wanted to do.

Candy was easily able to envision Davis giving such a smile.

"I know I shouldn't have said what I did to Chandra, Miss Candy. But I don't know what to say when people say mean stuff about my mama."

"This isn't the first time someone said something like that to you, about your mother, Angelica?"

"No." Angelica ducked her head. "And I can't stick up for her, either, because I don't know anything about her!"

Although she valiantly fought against it, one fat teardrop eased down Angelica's round cheek, landing in the corner of her full, quivering lips.

"It makes it hard, you know?" she turned completely away from Candy, wiping her wet face with the sleeve of her shirt and sniffing.

Candy walked over to Angelica and enveloped her in a hug. Angelica's arms tightened around her waist, briefly returning the embrace before she moved out of her arms.

"I'm sorry this has happened to you, Angelica. I am. Have you spoken with your father about it?"

"That some kids make fun of me and whisper about me not having a real family? That me and my daddy aren't even real family? No," she finished angrily swiping an arm over her eyes again, wiping away her wash of tears.

"Listen, Angelica, it isn't true and you know it. You and your father *are* family. Just as much as any other family. And you know how much he loves you. And how much he loved your mother."

"If he loves me so much, if he loved her so much, why won't he talk about her? Is what Chandra said true? Did my mama trick him into marrying her?"

Candy was at a loss. She didn't know what to say to the child. She had no idea what the story was behind Davis and his wife. Over the course of the last weeks, he hadn't spoken about her, although she'd asked him once, during a conversation. He'd quickly led the conversation in other directions and Candy didn't press for details.

"I'm sure it didn't happen at all, Angelica. Sometimes it's painful for us to talk about loved ones who aren't with us anymore. It doesn't mean your daddy didn't love your mother, sweetheart."

"I guess," she allowed, and walked away, returning to the shelf where Candy's pictures and knickknacks were placed. Candy leaned against her desk, her worried gaze following Angelica.

"Why don't you have a picture of your mother up, but you have one of your father?" Angelica returned to her earlier question, lightly tracing her fingers over the smiling picture of Candy and her father.

With her simple, direct question, Candy no longer felt as though she was the one in control, steering the conversation in the direction she wanted it to go, in order to get to the root of Angelica's problems.

"Don't you *want* to have her picture in your office? You

said you had a few, why can't you put one here?" Angelica turned and followed Candy back to her desk.

"As I said, I don't have very many. So the few I do have, I leave at my house," she replied. "I've chosen not to do so, and that's all there is to it. Nothing more, okay?" Candy answered calmly, although she wanted to snap at Angelica and tell the child it was none of her business.

Candy took a deep breath.

She'd had no idea how to answer her, and that's what troubled her more than the question. She felt ashamed. She wondered how she expected to help a child who had questions about her mother, was trying to come to an understanding of who she was, when Candy hadn't resolved her particular issues about her own mother and her desertion of Candy as a child.

Clearly it wasn't something she was over yet. Clinically, Candy knew what was going on with herself.

Clinically. But she was a hell of a long way from having any sort of closure.

"Fine! I just asked. Whatever, it doesn't matter to me, any ole way," Angelica mumbled.

The sullen look had returned and Candy felt like kicking her own butt over the way she'd handled the question.

She and Angelica had been making real progress, and she'd allowed her own feelings to get in the way and ruined the moment. She'd actually gotten a glimpse at a totally different child, one who let her guard down enough for Candy to finally see past the mask she normally wore, of pure attitude.

"Angel, sweetheart, I'm sorry. I didn't mean—"

"Only my daddy and mommy can call me that. And since I don't have a mommy anymore, only my daddy can!"

Candy opened her mouth to apologize, and they both turned when they heard the loud knock on the door. Moments later Davis Strong's big body filled the doorway. Candy wasn't sure which one of them was more relieved, Angelica or herself.

"Hey, Angel eyes, I've been looking all over for you! I didn't know you were in here with Ms. Cain," Davis said as soon as he entered Candice's office.

A grin of delight spread across Angelica's face. She ran over and hugged him around the waist.

"Daddy! I didn't think you were going to pick me up! Where is Aunt Milly? Isn't she coming?" She asked, peeking around his body to see if her aunt was behind him or not.

12

The moment Davis had walked in the door, his eyes had been drawn to Candy, despite the way his daughter was wrapping her arms around him like a king cobra.

Candy looked so damn gorgeous, perched on the edge of her desk wearing one of her wraps, her kinky curls unbound and falling mid-back. Her pretty face was devoid of any make-up, but appealing to him in ways no woman had ever been. In ways he wasn't ready to deal with, at least not until he got Angelica's life back in order.

He hadn't been in her presence alone for over two weeks, and for good reason. He didn't know how much longer he could keep himself in check around her.

The last time he had been alone with her, two weeks ago in the deserted classroom, he'd probably scared the shit out of her, with the way he'd slammed her against the door and felt her up like a damn randy teenaged boy copping his first feel, he thought in disgust. Not to mention their first intimacy, when he'd all but stripped her clothes and made love to her on the floor of her office.

Davis looked down at his daughter and ran a hand down over her two French-braided ponytails.

He'd sat outside the door and shamelessly eavesdropped on Angel and Candy. He'd had no intention of eavesdropping but he'd heard Angel's question to Candy about her mother and had been curious. He'd paused, fist raised, ready to knock on the door, but wanted to hear Candy's response.

Rather than allow his very inquisitive child to continue, he'd quickly knocked and entered.

The tension was thick as he leaned down and hugged his daughter.

"She sure is, Angel girl," he answered Angelica on the whereabouts of Milly. "She's outside waiting for us in the car. Why don't you go sit with her and I'll be out in a minute, okay?"

"Sure, Daddy."

Angelica turned and faced Candy. "Goodbye, Ms. Candy," she said, without making eye contact.

"Goodbye Angelica. I'll see you tomorrow, at five-thirty, right?"

"Yes, ma'am. I'll be here," she replied and glanced at Davis, quickly.

Davis noticed right away the smile Angelica gave to Candy looked strained and unnatural. When she turned back to face him, it seemed as though she was relieved to go.

"I'll wait for you in the car, Daddy. But hurry! Tonight is the UNO tournament. Aunt Milly said we were going to spank your butt this time!" she giggled, the strained look easing from her face, replaced by a wide grin.

"We'll see who'll be spanking who! You and your aunt are always trying to scam me with UNO. I know you two are cheating!" He gave her a mock glare and light swat to her bottom. She giggled, again, before she skipped out the door.

As soon as she left, he turned and faced Candy.

"I'm sorry we're late picking up Angelica. Today was Milly's first day back at the company and time got away from us." As he spoke he slowly walked toward her, where she was stuffing items into an oversized bag from her desk.

Davis gave her a slow appraisal, from the top of her curly hair to the bottom of her Birkenstock-clad feet.

Today she was wearing one of her wraps of a fabric she favored.

This one was a brightly patterned cloth, the same cloth as the satchel she was carrying. Starting under her armpits, it was tightly wound around her small, round breasts, and fell more loosely from there, wrapping the length of her entire body, ending near the calves of her legs.

The fit was snug, showcasing her generous curves—her full hips, nipped-in waist and small breasts—yet she moved with ease. Beneath the fabric wrap, she wore a dark, long-sleeved, scoop-neck T-shirt.

"No problem. The center closed early so I was able to have some time to talk to Angel—Angelica," she corrected herself and continued. "The last few weeks have been going well. Today we had a good conversation, and I'm beginning to gain insights into what's going on with her."

By the time she'd finished her formal litany, Davis was standing less than two feet away from her desk, ready to help her gather her belongings.

"Anything you can share with me, now?"

"It seems as though Angelica has been getting teased by a few of the girls, here at the center, as well as at school."

"About?"

"Something to do with her mother, I believe. I didn't want to probe too deeply," she said.

He carefully scrutinized Candy's expression. "Is there anything you're not telling me?" he asked.

Candy pulled her lower lip into her mouth with her top

teeth, her eyes looking worried. She released her lip, distracted, and his eyes followed her tongue as she licked the reddened rim.

"She did tell me she wished she knew more about her mother, but that's all, so far. I think she's starting to feel comfortable around me. She's starting to open up more, at least."

"That's good. Maybe she'll feel like sharing more with you the more she talks to you. Hell, I know I haven't told her much about her mother. Not sure I know how."

"Is there any reason why? Why you don't discuss her mother with her?"

"It's not an easy topic. There are—things—I'm unsure how to begin to discuss with her."

Candy reached out and lightly touched his arm. "I don't know the situation, and I'm not asking you to tell me. But it's important you look at this from Angelica's point of view. If you have something to tell her about her mother, information others know and she doesn't, she needs to hear it from *you,* rather than someone else. I'm not suggesting anything bad about her mother; could be the children are just being kids. They sometimes blow things out of proportion. Or it's just plain gossip, learning from their parents."

"What did the child say to Angelica?"

"Something about you having to marry her mother, that you're not her real father."

Davis wanted to punch the nearest wall in anger.

"Again, Davis, it's no secret you're not her biological father, but sometimes words hurt worse than a blow. Even coming from a child," she murmured, concern etched deeply into her face.

Davis ran a hand through his hair, frustrated, and blew out a long breath of air. "Yeah, maybe it's time Angelica and I had a talk. God only knows it's long overdue. I'll think about it." He forced a smile on his face. "All ready to go?"

She opened her mouth but clamped it back shut, giving a small shake of her head. Instead of speaking, she threw him a tight smile.

"Sure, I just need to pack a few more things in my bag," she murmured.

After she packed it with a few folders, she carefully placed them all inside the multicolored bag and turned her face up to his and smiled.

"I need to grab my jacket and lock up, and I'm ready. I didn't drive today; my car is in the shop, so one of my grad students is going to give me a ride home."

"I can give you a ride," he replied as she began pulling the straps of the large satchel over her back.

"I couldn't take you out of your way; it's no problem for Nate. He lives in the apartment complex near my house here on the North side. Besides, I'm sure Milly and Angelica are waiting for you."

"Nate? Here, let me help," Davis murmured and helped her ease the straps of the bag over her back, and she murmured a thank you.

She'd worn her hair down, and so she pulled it up and away as he helped her with her coat, and his fingers brushed against the back of her bare neck. He felt her flinch in response. The tiny bumps sprang across her smooth brown skin in reaction to his touch. He reluctantly withdrew his fingers, but not before he allowed them to linger a fraction longer, caressing the smooth, soft skin of her neck.

"Thank you," she murmured in response to his help with her bag.

When she glanced at him from the corners of her almond-shaped eyes and licked the lush rim of her lower lip, his dick thumped against the suddenly tight restriction of his slacks.

"No problem. So, will you allow us to take you home?" He took a deep breath and moved away.

"I don't want to take you out of your way. I don't want to be an imposition—"

"It's not an imposition." His concentration was purely focused on her lush mouth.

The only thing on his mind was parting her lips, devouring her.

A hint of a flush stained her pretty face, either from the warmth of her office, or maybe something else, he didn't know. He preferred to think it was because of him. *He* wanted to be the reason for her rosy cheeks.

13

The need, the desire, to kiss her was written all over his face and she wanted to feel his hard chiseled mouth against her lips *just* as badly.

She'd quickly gotten addicted to his kisses. His making love to her mouth and handling her in a way she longed to be handled had left her aching for more.

Particularly after nine months of erotic dreams, along with their recent sexual explorations.

She moved her eyes past the small dimple in the corner of his sensual lips, past his high cheekbones and settled on his light grey eyes. Beautiful eyes staring down at her like he wanted to gobble her up.

Candy didn't dwell on the change in him, the way he no longer seemed to try and hide his feelings. She didn't analyze the whys of it. She only wanted to feel. Feel his smooth lips, his hard body, pressed tightly against the softness of hers.

When he brought his thumb up to caress her chin, and pulled her into his arms, she willingly went. The first touch of his lips on hers was gentle, until she opened her mouth, inviting him inside.

That was all the encouragement he seemed to need.

He pulled her even tighter against his hard body, one hand on the back of her head, near the base of her neck, the other on her ass. The kiss began with a soft melding of lips, exploring, light, sweet touches.

When his tongue snaked out and licked the corner of her lips, Candy opened her mouth and allowed her tongue to softly stroke his.

He groaned harshly and pulled her lower lip into his mouth, sucked and pulled on it, laving it relentlessly until he slowly released it. Immediately, he shoved his hot tongue inside, and gave a full, sensual lick around the circumference of her mouth.

Candy shivered from the hot invasion of his marauding tongue.

"You taste as good as your name, Candy," he groaned as he centered himself in the middle of her heat. She could feel the hard surge of his erection beneath the zipper of his slacks.

"Ummm, you taste just as good," she agreed, her breath coming out in pants, her chest heaving.

He dragged her mouth back to his. Nothing was heard but harsh moans and sensual sighs as he ground her sex against his cock and made love to her mouth.

The effect of his kisses, his touches, the way he was working her body, fully clothed, had her senses reeling, head pounding so hard it was as though someone was in there knocking inside her head.

"Someone is knocking on the door, Candy," Davis pulled back and whispered against the corner of her mouth.

The loud banging finally penetrated the sensual cocoon she was wrapped within and with her breath coming out in gasps she reluctantly pulled herself away from Davis' hold.

His expression was carefully neutral, but the deep breaths and heaving chest said he was as affected by the kiss they shared as she.

"Oh God, that must be Nate!" Candy cried.

She pulled away and nearly fell, her legs were so wobbly. Davis grasped her beneath the elbow and helped to steady her as she tottered on her feet. She extricated her body from his, swaying. She straightened her back and opened the door.

"Miss Candy, is everything okay?" Nate asked, concern heavily stamped on his handsome, young face. "I've been knocking for a few minutes and I was worried."

Candy had an overwhelming need to close the door in his face, knowing good and well she looked as crazy as she felt.

Candy rearranged her fabric wrap on her body, and straightened out the skirt. She smiled at him and self-consciously patted her hair into place, tucking an errant curl or two behind both ears.

"I'm sorry, Nate. Everything is fine!" She smiled nervously. "I was having a session with a parent." So that was a bit of a stretch, she thought with a grimace. Technically, she *was* having a session, just not the type she normally had with a parent. This was beginning to be an ugly habit, she thought. "I'm sorry I didn't hear you."

"That's okay. I came to pick you up. Whenever you're ready, Miss Candy, we can roll out." He quickly assured her and trying, discreetly, to look around her, to see who she was having a "session" with.

She blocked the door with her body, although since she was barely five three, compared to Nate's nearly six feet, she didn't think she was all that effective.

She definitely wasn't hiding a thing, when she *felt* the parent she was having "session" stand behind her, his big body hovering close, his hands resting on the top of her shoulders.

"Candy won't need a ride from you tonight, or any other night, son."

Davis' hands drifted from the tops of her shoulders, slowly, stroking down the length of her arms before he released her.

His male posturing was unnecessary . . . even if it *did* give her an inappropriate thrill.

"You can go on back to your dorm, son," Davis finished.

"I don't live in the dorms, sir." Nate darted his dark gaze away from Candy and focused on Davis. He folded his arms over his muscular, broad chest, his eyes hardening. "Like *I* said, it won't be a problem to help Miss Candy out. I look forward to the ride," he finished with a cocky grin spreading across his handsome face.

Davis circled her wrist with his hands, casually linking their fingers. There was a certain amount of obvious possessiveness, a casual intimacy with his touch.

Maybe it was her, but all of a sudden Candy got the distinct impression that neither man was talking about giving her a ride home.

"Is that true, Miss Candy? You won't need a ride from me? We live so close to one another, it would be too bad to take Mr. Strong out of his way. I'm sure he doesn't live on *our* side of town. In fact, I hoped you would join me for dinner if you haven't eaten."

"Nate—" she began, not sure what to say. She was saved from replying when Davis interrupted, again.

"No, she doesn't need a ride home, Nate. Nor does she need you to feed her. She's having dinner with me. In fact, I think it's time we got a move on . . . Candy?" he murmured, moving to the side of her, his hand on the door as though to close it in Nate's face.

Candy was confused, but decided rather than to pull Nate into her suddenly crazy world, she'd play along with Davis, for the moment.

She turned up the wattage on the smile she gave Nate. "Thanks, Nate. I'm sorry I didn't tell you sooner," she replied casting a side glance at Davis. "It was all a bit . . . unexpected."

"No problem, Miss Candy." He said it casually, but Candy saw his disappointment in his expression.

"I'll see you tomorrow at the dance?" he asked around the door closing in his face. Candy grabbed the edge of the door before it could slam shut and shot Davis a nasty, sidelong look.

"Yes, Nate. I'll see you then!" she managed to say, barely, before the door completely closed.

"What was that all about?" she demanded, spinning around, and found herself back in Davis's loose embrace. She tried unsuccessfully to push out of his arms.

"What are you talking about? I simply told the young man his services weren't needed. I thought you would be interested in having dinner with Angelica, my sister and me. That is, if you're hungry?"

Candy was two seconds away from refusing his offer, when her stomach growled and she promptly shut her mouth. She hadn't eaten all day. Hell, she was hungry.

Besides hunger as a motivating factor, Candy didn't want the chance to spend time with Angelica to go to waste, even if Davis had been a total ass to Nate.

Candy turned to move out of his arms, but he didn't allow it. He tilted her face up to his, his thumb resting beneath her chin.

"Don't you want to come home with me, Candy?" he asked again. Saying more than his words.

"Yes." She croaked the words after only a brief hesitation.

"Good," he responded, his deep voice husky and soft. "Good, let's go." He finally released her, allowing her to break out of his arms.

With a deep, shaky breath, she turned away from him and turned out the light. With his hand resting lightly in the indentation of her waist, he ushered her out of the office.

"I'm ready."

What she was ready for, even Candy wasn't sure.

14

The invitation to dinner had been impromptu and he'd been surprised when she went along with it when he'd issued it in front of the grad student.

Shit, he'd surprised himself as well.

He'd wanted to knock the boy's teeth down his damn throat, the way he had been eyeing Candy. The kid damn sure had more on his mind than giving her a ride home. When he'd touched her, Davis had wanted to rip his hands off of Candy's smooth skin.

Who the hell did he think he was, touching her like that?

Davis knew he had no right to feel any sort of possessiveness that way; he'd given her the cold shoulder enough times that he had no rights at all . . . but damn if he wasn't asserting his rights, rights he'd given himself.

As the wind kicked up a few notches, they briskly picked up their pace toward his vehicle. As he neared the SUV he saw Milly had gotten into the backseat with Angel. Angel usually begged Milly to ride in back with her.

"Is this going to be okay with them?"

"You coming for dinner?"

"Yes, I don't want to intrude on family time," Candy replied.

"There's no intrusion. Milly won't mind at all."

"And Angelica?"

"She'll be fine, don't worry," he replied firmly, his hand on her waist.

Davis opened the door to the passenger side of the car, helping Candy inside.

"Hello ladies, sorry it took me longer than I thought. Ms. Cain needed a ride home and I asked her over for dinner. Maybe I can convince her to stay to help even up the odds for the UNO tournament later, what do you all think?"

When Milly bobbed her head in instant agreement Davis closed Candy's door and jogged around the front of the SUV. He hopped inside and rubbed his hands together to ward off the chill from outside before putting the key in the ignition.

"Sounds like fun! Hi, Candy." Milly gave Candy a wide grin when she replied, instantly putting her at ease.

"Hi, Milly! I don't want to intrude on family night—"

"Please! You're not interrupting anything, is she Angel?"

Angelica took her cue from her aunt and agreed. "No, I guess it would be okay," she agreed, if a bit reluctantly.

"Your daddy needs all the help he can get," Milly laughed.

"Help for what?" he asked warily.

"Even up the odds in UNO, Daddy!" Angelica piped up, adding "Aunt Milly says you need all the help you can get!"

"Yeah well, if you and your aunt didn't cheat so badly, maybe I'd stand a fighting chance. But I'm not sure if Miss Cain wants to stay for cards, baby."

He shot Candy a questioning look.

"I think I'd better head home after all. It is getting late, and I don't want to intrude."

"You're staying for dinner and cards. Unless you can't handle

UNO, Ms. Cain?" Davis asked, and lifted one dark blond eyebrow.

"Are you . . . *challenging* me?" Candy asked, head canted to the side. When she heard the giggles from Angelica she upped her theatrics. "Oh no you *didn't*!" Candy snapped her fingers and clicked her tongue against the roof of her mouth. Angelica and Milly both released peals of laughter. "Didn't you know? I *never* walk away from a challenge. You're on!"

"*Never*, Ms. Cain?" he murmured the question loud enough for only Candy to hear.

"No . . . not anything, Davis," she replied softly.

Goosebumps tickled her arms as he slid his glance over her face, his eyes lingering on her lips.

"Consider that duly noted," he murmured and gave her one last hot look before he turned his attention to the road.

15

"Your home is beautiful," Candy said, allowing Davis to remove her coat.

"Thank you. Please have a seat, I'll hang this up for you." He took the coat and hung it up for her and Candy slowly trailed behind him.

When she'd walked across the gorgeous cherrywood floors in the large, immaculate kitchen, she'd instantly wanted to take off her shoes to avoid marking the shiny floors.

As they'd driven into the exclusive neighborhood, Candy had begun to feel uneasy, although she hated to admit it to herself.

Candy forced herself to shake off the feelings of *less than*. She recited reaffirming mantras in her head, sang in her head, lyrics from some of her favorite songs about being an independent woman . . . mentally doing *whatever* it took to remind herself she was no longer that embarrassed little girl from long ago.

She no longer needed to be afraid she'd break something valuable in one of the homes where her father worked and receive a scolding from the kitchen staff.

Angelica obviously didn't share Candy's fear of messing up the floors. After doing a cursory stomp-down of her snow boots once she hopped out of the SUV, she ran inside the house, and slung her backpack down to the floor.

"Come on, Aunt Milly, I want to show you the new game for my Game Cube Daddy bought me for Christmas!"

She'd happily raced up the spiral staircase, dragging her much slower moving, but laughing, aunt behind her to show off her latest game.

"That's fine, Angel-girl, but dinner will be ready soon—" Davis' voice trailed off when she and Milly disappeared from sight.

"Somehow I don't think she heard that," Candy laughed with him, over Angelica's excitement over her new game.

"No, I don't think she did."

Candy followed him, her feet sinking into the cushioned softness of the beautiful rug in the living area. Candy wanted to take off her shoes, as well as her tights, not for fear of dirtying up the rug, but just to feel its luxuriousness against her bare toes.

"Feel free to look around, if you want. I'm going to start re-heating the food," Davis said over his shoulder as he walked toward the open airy kitchen.

He'd taken off his shoes and, wearing nothing but socks, padded into the kitchen and removed the apron hanging from a hook. He donned it, allowing the ties to hang loose at his sides.

If it was possible for a man to look hot and domesticated at the same time, Davis Strong had that on lock down, Candy thought.

He prepared dinner with his shirtsleeves shoved up to his elbows to expose his lightly furred, muscular arms, as he set about pulling out cooking utensils.

When he reached above his head to remove the pots and pans hanging suspended above the butcher-block table, the ends of his dress shirt came out of his slacks and Candy was able to see a glimpse of his hard abs.

"Hmmm."

She thought he must have heard her appreciative murmur when he glanced at her, one dark blond eyebrow raised and a question in his eyes.

Candy mumbled some incoherent nothingness and he gave her a half-grin and turned back to his work.

There was nothing like watching a man who knew his way around the kitchen. Candy sat in one of the kitchen stools that ringed the island, perched her chin in her hands, propped her elbows on the counter and enjoyed the show.

Dinner had been delicious and Candy complimented Davis on the meal. She had been pleasantly surprised when a blush rose in his lean cheeks. They'd then gone to the family room and set up the UNO game.

When they first began to play, Angelica had treated Candy as she usually did whenever her father was around, with forced politeness, a step up from her occasional dismissiveness or complete rudeness. But soon she relaxed and even laughed at Candy's feeble jokes.

Candy noticed Milly would glance at Davis when she thought no one was looking, and she'd catch a certain look pass between them. Davis would quickly glance in Candy's direction when it happened, and she played off that she'd witnessed the exchange.

Candy was disappointed when the evening was over. She was surprised to see she wasn't the only one, when Angelica demanded one more tie-breaker game . . . for the third time.

"No Angel-girl . . . it's time to call it a night, I think." Davis stood and stretched his big body after sitting on the large throw pillows while they played. "Does anyone want anything else from the kitchen? I'm on my way in there."

When he cracked his back and stretched, the muscles in his back visibly bunched beneath his shirt. Candy bit her bottom lip with her top teeth to suppress a wistful sigh. When she dragged her eyes away, she caught Milly's amused eyes on hers and flushed.

Oh well, the man was fine, no use in pretending she wasn't sneaking a peak, as she'd been busted in the act anyway, Candy thought.

"I'm fine, Davis. In fact, I think it's time Angel and I got ready to go; it's getting late." Milly looked down at her watch.

"Why don't you and Angel stay tonight and wait until morning to leave? We can move the slumber party here, as easily as your house." Davis turned concerned eyes in his sister's direction.

"No way, Dad! You're not invited to the party," Angelica jumped up from her pillow and protested. "You promised I could have a sleepover with Aunt Milly! You promised!"

"Baby girl, I know I promised. But it's kind of late and too dark for you two to be out driving the streets alone—" Davis began only to have Milly glare at him and cut him off mid-sentence.

"Davis, I am more than capable of driving in the dark! I've been driving nearly as long as you have. I think I can handle a little ice on the streets, big brother," Milly scoffed.

"Yeah, Dad! Aunt Milly is almost as old as you are! She's been driving since forever!" Angel agreed, trying to be helpful, no doubt. Milly grimaced but laughed.

"Besides, you're taking Miss Candy home, or are you gonna let her stay over for a pajama party too?" she asked innocently. "Hey, that might be fun if we all had a sleepover together!"

Davis, Candy and Milly looked at one another, each with various expressions on their faces.

Candy envisioned what type of pajama party she and Davis

would have. The one instantly springing to her mind was worlds different than the one Angelica was thinking of.

Davis had a somewhat pained look on his face, searching for the right words in order to answer his daughter.

"I don't think we can do that, sweetheart. Miss Candy needs to get home. I'm sure she wouldn't want to stay for a pajama party with me . . . with us," he quickly corrected himself.

"Miss Candy, would you stay for a pajama party with my dad, if he asked you nicely? Wouldn't that be a lot of fun?"

"Yes, Miss Candy . . . would you stay for a pajama party if I asked nicely?" Davis said, gleefully turning the tables on her, if the evil glint in his eyes was any indication.

Candy gave Davis a wicked look before she turned and answered Angelica. "No, honey, as much as I'd love to, I'm afraid I can't. But I bet it would be a lot of fun! I've got to get home to take care of my cat. Russell gets pretty irked if he's not fed on time. He's got a schedule, and he's a total grump if I'm not home on time."

"Okay, Angel-girl, I think it's time for you and Aunt Milly to head on out, before it gets any later." Davis, thankfully, cut the conversation short.

"Your dad is right, Angel. Besides, we still have a movie waiting at home for us to watch!" Milly said as they began to walk toward the front door. Milly had parked her vehicle in the circular driveway instead of the garage.

"Goodbye Milly, it was nice seeing you again." Milly placed her coat on and picked up her cane. She then turned and surprised Candy by giving her a hug.

"It was nice seeing you too, Candy! I had a lot of fun. We'll have to do this again sometime."

"I'd like that."

Candy waited for Davis to help Angelica on with her coat before she spoke to her.

"I had fun with you too, Angelica. Thanks for allowing me

to spend time with your family." Angelica tried to hide her grin, but the adults all saw the way she smiled, pleased.

"Yep, that would be cool! But next time you can play on our team, all three of us together . . . huh, Aunt Milly?" she asked.

"Hey, that's three against one, no fair," Davis protested. "It's bad enough you and your aunt cheat, now you're going to take her from me? No way! I get to keep Ms. Candy all to myself, urchin . . . now let's go!" he helped her buttoning her coat.

Leaning down, he gave her a kiss on her cheek, and she in turn blew a raspberry against his cheek. Candy felt her heart clench at the simple, affectionate exchange.

"I'll be back after I walk them to the car," he promised, turning toward Candy.

"Goodbye, Milly, and I'll see you tomorrow, Angelica. An hour early." She gave a subtle reminder of their agreement.

Angelica glanced at her father, worrying her bottom lip with her teeth.

Candy faced Davis. "Angelica agreed to come in an hour early to help me and a few of the others set up for the party. I hope that's okay?" she said, more so to reassure Angelica that she'd keep her end of the bargain, as long as she kept hers.

"I don't see why not," he agreed easily.

"Thanks, Ms. Candy. See you tomorrow." Angelica placed her gloved hand in her aunt's and they walked out of the door.

"I'll be right back. Make yourself at home, I won't be long." Davis offered and quickly followed his sister and daughter.

16

When he closed the door, Candy slowly turned around and surveyed the formal living area.

It was immaculate. Although his entire home was beautifully decorated, this room had an untouchable aura of sophisticated elegance.

It was decorated in cool shades of black and cream, from the thick ivory rugs covering most of the hardwood floors, to the satin-covered occasional chairs and silk-lined drapes.

The art decorating the walls was sophisticated and abstract and Candy knew many of the prints would cost her a year's salary.

Definitely not the type of flea market finds adorning the walls of her home.

The fireplace was made of whitewashed brick, and was authentic, requiring logs and not gas or electricity. Although it wasn't lit, no fire burning brightly inside, she couldn't imagine that even if it were, it could extinguish the aura of cool elegance the room projected.

Not a knickknack was turned the wrong way inside the

glass-fronted hutch, no picture was situated wrong on the mantel of the fireplace. Everything was perfect.

Candy crossed the room. Curious, she looked at the few pictures set on top of the mantel. The majority of the pictures were of Angelica, but there was one small photo of a younger Davis, looking at a very pregnant woman whom she guessed to be Gail, Angelica's mother.

Candy picked the picture up to get a better look.

Gail had been an attractive woman. Her smooth oval face was the color of café au lait, her large eyes appeared dark brown and even in the picture she saw Angelica's resemblance to her mother.

She wore her hair straight and long with a slight curl at the ends, and wispy bangs fringing her wide forehead.

Her hands rested on her round stomach and although she had no smile on her face, she appeared to be happy. Or at least content. Davis stood next to her, and neither was he smiling.

As Candy carefully analyzed the photo, to her, they didn't appear to *fit* together. She got no sense of them as a couple.

When she heard Davis enter, Candy set the picture back on the mantel, feeling guilty for the psychoanalysis she'd been giving the couple in the picture.

"I had a wonderful time, Davis," she said, once he'd come further into the room.

"I'm glad you enjoyed it," he replied as he walked over to the fireplace. "Angelica and Milly had a good time as well. More so because you were here."

"I hope so. I enjoyed spending time with them, especially Angelica, outside of the center."

"Would you like me to start a fire?"

"Yes, that would be nice," she murmured.

On the floor next to the fireplace was a pretty white wrought iron basket filled with logs. Davis moved the gate in front of the fireplace and added two of them, lighting the fire.

"I know it's getting late, but would you like to share a glass of wine with me before I take you home? Or have you had enough for the evening, what with Angelica's cheating and all?" he joked.

Candy needed to get up early tomorrow, but it wasn't so late she couldn't enjoy a glass of wine in the romantic setting with Davis, alone.

"That sounds good."

"Great," he smiled lightly. "Hold on while I grab a few more pillows to sit on," he said.

He lifted the lid on an ornately carved, beautiful cedar chest, withdrew two large floor pillows from within and returned to her side.

After he placed them on the floor close to the fireplace, he held out a hand and helped Candy sit.

"I'll be right back."

He returned within moments with a bottle of wine in one hand and two fluted Waterford crystal goblets in the other.

"May I?" he asked, and when she nodded her head in assent, he filled the goblet halfway and handed it to her.

After filling his, he set the bottle on a small table next to the fireplace and sat down next to her.

"Ummm, this is good," she complimented his choice.

"You have beautiful hair. You should wear it down more often," Davis said, and surprised at the unexpected compliment, Candy automatically reached a hand up to finger her hair.

Instead of her customary French braid, today she'd worn her hair loose.

"Thank you. I normally wear it in a braid. It's so thick, it gets on my nerves normally if I leave it out," she said and wondered why she was babbling about her hair, when that was probably the thing he'd find least interesting in a topic of conversation.

"I like the French braid too; I like how you do the one braid down your head. I can never quite get it as neat when I do Angelica's hair," he grimaced and took another sip of his wine.

"You do Angelica's hair?"

He laughed. "You sound surprised. Who do you think combs her hair?"

The image of him combing Angelica's hair, parting and oiling her scalp, braiding it, flashed in her mind and she smiled, remembering her own father doing much the same for her.

She groaned inwardly, her admiration growing with the way he cared for Angelica.

As though she didn't have it bad enough for the guy.

He reached a hand out and fingered one of her kinky curls and her breath hitched in her throat.

"I love your hair. I like it when you braid it or twist it, but I love it out like this," he murmured.

"Maybe I should wear it down more often. You're the second person to compliment me today," she replied, shaking her head no when he offered her more wine.

"Oh? Who else?" he asked, casually, his hands leaving her hair.

Candy glanced up from taking the last sip of wine and noticed his casual tone was at odds with the look in his eyes.

"Nate did. But then again, Nate often gives me compliments. He's a nice boy."

"A nice boy who wants to fuck you. But I think you know that," he returned so smoothly, it took a fraction longer for the words to register. Candy almost spit up the wine she'd just swallowed. She carefully placed her glass on the lip of the fireplace, before turning back to him.

"Just what is that supposed to mean? And who told you you could be so damn crude?"

"What? That he wants to fuck you . . . and not just have you grade his papers? Or that you already know?"

"Both!"

"Come on, Candy. We're both adults, you know the deal as well as I do."

"I don't know what you're talking about. The next time you invite me to dinner, make sure it's not because your strange male ego was bruised because another man wanted me, and wasn't afraid to ask me out," Candy replied sharply and began to rise. "This has been great, but I think it's time for me to go."

The minute she realized what she said, she immediately wanted to bite her tongue out. She'd spoken as though there would be a second time, when this time had been a fluke.

"I didn't mean that the way it sounded," she tried to play it off, trying to save face. "I wasn't intimating there'd be a next time. Or that I *wanted* there to be one. I wasn't. I don't. I was just saying—"

The rest of her sentence was cut off when he placed a finger over her mouth, and gently pushed her back down on the pillow with his other hand.

"You're right; I shouldn't have been so damn crude. I'm sorry."

Candy allowed him to press her back down on the pillow.

"I want there to be many more times. Not just one."

"But the next time how would you feel about it being just you and me?" he asked. "And I can guarantee you I have no fear in asking you out."

When the small dimple flashed in the corner of his sensual mouth as he gave her one of his rare, but lethal, smiles Candy felt her irritability ease.

"Are you sure that's a good idea?" She murmured around the finger he still had against her mouth. He dipped his finger between the seam of her lips and fingered the inside lip, before allowing his finger to slowly trail away. The heat he'd generated from the simple touch remained.

"About as much as I am about this."

Davis cupped the back of her head with one of his hands, his fingers tunneling through the hair at the nape of her neck. He then pulled her completely off the plush pillow and his hand palmed her ass, bringing their bodies together, flush.

When his head descended toward hers, when Candy felt his cool breath fan against the corner of her mouth he was so close, her eyes shuttered closed.

She swallowed, hard, and waited with bated breath to feel his mouth on hers.

The moment she felt his firm, cool lips touch hers, his tongue licking the seam of her lips before he eased his mouth over hers, the ease of cream trickled, slowly gathering in her panties.

17

When he covered her plump, lush lips with his, Davis' heart thuded strongly inside his chest and his erection kicked into overdrive.

For most of the night he'd been in a state of semi-arousal, being so close to her. The only thing keeping him in check had been the presence of his sister and daughter. But now, with them all alone, and the feel of her soft lips beneath his, all bets were off.

He wondered if she knew how badly he ached for her. Her scent beckoned him, calling out, begging him to take what was his.

He'd behaved normally, done and said all the right things with his sister and daughter present, laughed at the appropriate moments, the entire time he'd been watching her, focusing on her. Accepting her nonverbal clues that she wanted him. Picking up on the subtle sidelong looks she'd given him when she thought he wasn't looking.

He knew he should take her home, knew it was getting late, knew the streets would be slicker the later it got and knew she needed to get up early the next day.

But none of that was going to stop him from sampling a bit of Candy.

Her accusations that he'd been interested in her solely because Nate showed interest was nowhere near the truth.

The fact that the gangly youth clearly had plans that didn't include just a ride home may have spurred his actions. But he'd wanted her for over nine months, and he was damned if he'd let the boy sample what was his.

He lightly brushed his lips across smooth full lips, back and forth, before he settled them firmly, slanting her head for a better angle.

He kissed her, his hands roaming over her curvy little body, her plump ass and thick thighs. Her small hands weren't idle. She matched him touch for touch, stroke for stroke.

Davis groaned out loud when her hands eased down past his chest, his stomach, until she settled them against his dick. His balls tingled when she feathered the tips of her fingers over his hardening erection.

He licked her mouth, raked his tongue across the fuller bottom lip before he dragged it deep into his mouth with his teeth. He then slowly allowed the plump lip to pop back out.

Soon the heated kisses weren't enough.

Davis felt his erection grow thick and heavy, his balls draw tight, with each stroke of her hand against the front of his pants. With every hot caress of his tongue against her mouth he continued to stroke his hands over her, the fever burning brighter.

He cupped her round, firm ass cheeks, massaged the thick globes and gave them a quick, hard squeeze, grinding her against his dick.

"Candy, I know I've said this before, but you taste so damn good, so sweet, so juicy," he said huskily, breaking away from her full, glistening, kiss-swollen lips to stare down at her flushed face.

His dick thumped when he saw the hot look of lust in her half-closed eyes.

He lifted her shirt out of the wrap, and his hands, which had been warmed by the fire, grew even hotter as they roved over her bare skin. Beneath his massaging fingers, her skin felt as soft as butter and just as smooth and creamy.

When he reached the front of her breasts, he gently cupped their small weight in his hand, after deftly unhooking the small front closure. When her small treasures bounced free, he lifted her T-shirt up and away as he allowed her pretty unbound breasts to fill his hands perfectly.

His thumbs gave rough, simultaneous caresses over her extended nipples, toying and lightly pinching the erect buds. Davis tore his gaze away from them, wandering if he'd hurt her when she cried out.

"Oh God . . . that feels good," she whimpered.

"So beautiful," he murmured, staring down at her passion-stamped face.

After one more stinging squeeze to her nipples, which to his delight made her moan again in enjoyment, he gently cupped each side of her face. He leaned down and rubbed his cheek against hers.

He'd wanted to feel her . . . taste her for so long. It was hard to believe it wasn't another one of his hot dreams.

"I love your skin, Candy. So smooth and beautiful."

"Thank you," she said huskily, licking her bottom lip. She glanced at him from the corners of her light brown, almond-shaped eyes, almost shyly.

He needed to get them both naked, soon.

Davis removed the bra from her shoulders and eased it down her arms, smoothly removing the small T-shirt she was wearing in one move. After a moment of fumbling, he unearthed the ends of her tied skirt and unknotted the fabric.

"I've always wondered how you did this. I've wanted to unwrap you for a long time, Candy," he admitted, his voice deep with need. He lowered her back down on her pillow and followed her, his body blanketing her.

She laughed huskily. "And you've unwrapped me so well."

Her exposed breasts, although no more than a handful, were pretty and plump. The chocolate creamy mounds, topped by darker brownish red, tight nipples, reminded Davis of some type of exotic, hot chocolate sundae, complete with dark, ruby red cherries on top.

At that moment all he wanted was to dip his spoon in the tantalizing dessert.

"Damn, you're hot," he murmured. Seconds later, he palmed one of her tits in his hand, leaned down and stroked his tongue over one of the small spiked nipples.

After a swirl of his tongue, he dragged his mouth across the valley between her breasts, and captured its twin, swirling and laving it as well. He alternated his attention, licking each one, giving them both equal attention, but it wasn't enough.

He couldn't get enough of her.

After months of fantasizing what it would be like to taste her, how her tight little nipples would feel scraping against the roof of his mouth, how her rounded curves would feel crushed beneath his body . . . he finally had her beneath him.

"God this feels good, please don't stop," she begged shamelessly.

Candy arched her back sharply the minute he pulled one of her hardened nipples into the hot cavern of his mouth and began to suck on her.

Each luscious glide of his tongue against her breasts, each pull of his mouth against her aching nipples, sent cream streaming from her pussy.

When he pulled away, Candy cried out in denial.

"Sssh, it's okay." He leaned down and gave her a hot kiss before he turned away.

When he picked up the bottle of wine from the table near the fireplace and gave her a heated look, Candy's heart stuttered, her body tingling in anticipation.

"Why don't we take this upstairs? This might get a little sticky." He took a small sip of the wine directly from the bottle and leaned back down and kissed her, transferring a bit of the sweet liquid into her open mouth.

"God, yes," she agreed after swallowing. She squealed when he lifted her in his arms.

He gave a guttural laugh in return, gave her one more smacking kiss on her lips, and carried both her and the wine bottle up the winding staircase.

In the darkness of the house, with no lights with the exception of the dim hall light on in the upper rooms to guide Davis, Candy felt secure in his embrace. He strode with purpose toward the partially opened door at the end of the hall and carried her inside.

They were silent during the short trip from the living area to his bedroom. The passion, the hush of expectancy of what was to come, was so intense it was a tangible, breathing entity.

No lights were on in the bedroom, yet the illumination from the moon streamed in from the open blinds, enabling her to see the room clearly. He carried her to the massive four-poster bed in the middle of the luxurious room, and gently laid her down.

The minute her body made contact with the bed, Candy glanced down. She'd expected to feel crisp, cotton sheets beneath her, and was surprised to feel the cool, slick caress of satin sheets against her skin instead.

She barely had enough time to enjoy the sensation as she rubbed her body against the sheets on the firm, yet soft mattress before he'd taken both of her wrists in one hand and raised them above her head. The action forced her small breasts to slap against each other.

He sat on the side of the bed and stared down at her nearly nude body.

"What?" Candy whispered, barely able to choke the question out.

He'd held on to the bottle of Merlot. With a wicked gleam in his eye, he held the bottle high above her body and tilted it, allowing several drops to fall and dribble down between the valley of her bared breasts.

"This is what I plan to do with the Merlot," he finally answered her question.

18
_____

"Oh God," she cried out sharply. His hot velvet tongue lapped a rough caress between her breasts.

His tongue lazily swirled a pattern around the underside of one of her breasts, lapping up the trail from the drizzle of wine. He popped one erect, taut nipple into his mouth and pulled so hard Candy felt a direct zing to the core of her femininity from his insistent tugging.

"Mmm, delicious," he murmured in satisfaction, releasing the bud and licking around one areola.

Candy squirmed beneath him as the moisture between her thighs increased from the contrast of his hot mouth and the cool satin of the sheets against her skin.

He released her breast and trailed his tongue down the midline of her body. He followed the sticky trail where the last of the wine had pooled in the deep recess of her belly button.

Although she'd had her belly pierced for several years, no one had ever given it the attention Davis currently was. He carefully licked the remnants of the wine from her body, swirling his tongue around the gemstone, until she wanted to scream, the pleasure was so intense.

Davis reluctantly shifted away from her belly with one last lingering kiss. He sat up and quickly stripped out of his shirt.

He undid his zipper and yanked off his pants, along with his boxers, shoving them both down his legs. Candy leaned on one elbow to watch. Her eyes widened when he stood before her, naked and deliciously aroused.

A sharp pang of desire furled low in her belly as she viewed his naked body. The moonlight filled the room, allowing Candy to see his body. Clearly.

And damn, what a body it was.

If she thought he had a hot body fully clothed, if she thought he was sinfully gorgeous before, it was nothing compared to what the man looked like stripped down, standing before her, hot and hard. His body looked as though it belonged in a centerfold for *Playgirl* magazine. His impossibly long, beautifully hard cock curved so enticingly against the dark sprinkle of hair on his stomach. Candy squirmed, clamping her legs together in eager anticipation.

He didn't have one bit of extraneous flesh on his hard body, not one ounce of flab marred his lean waist.

Candy bit the inside of her cheek to prevent an irresistible desire she had to thank God out loud for the fine specimen of manhood walking toward her.

Once he was within touching distance, she brought herself to her knees, and allowed her hands to rest on his chest.

Her fingers followed the fine dusting of hair that matted the broad expanse of his densely muscled chest; they dipped and feathered beneath his hard pecs.

She placed a finger in her mouth and licked it before she returned it to his chest, swirling and circling his small, erect nipples.

He uttered a harsh groan and she glanced up. Candy smiled at him before turning her attention back to his beautiful male body.

Her gaze and fingers followed the V of hair as it ran down the length of his upper body, past his muscle-ridged abdomen, before her gaze halted. She stared in helpless fascination at the long, hard length of his smooth, lightly veined cock.

Candy reached out and curled her hand around the steely shaft.

"Oooh," she groaned, whimpering in hot anticipation when her hand wasn't able to close around his thickness.

She brushed a thumb over the small eye at the head of his penis, catching a bit of his sticky pre-cum dew and when he groaned, low in his throat, she gave an answering purr of delight.

Her palm caressed his plump bulbous end, transferring more of his essences over the broad head, before she stroked her hand over him. She fondled him from his tightly drawn balls back to the tip of his erection, once, twice . . . and watched in fascination as it grew longer, harder.

The soft smooth feel of his skin was in direct contrast to the hard length of dick she was holding in her hand. It turned Candy on that she was holding so much raw masculine strength in her hand.

"It's beautiful," she whispered. Davis released a sound that was halfway between a groan and laugh. One of her hands remained on his cock, the other grasped his lightly furred, drawn-up balls.

She let go of his balls and grasped his dick with both hands, caressing him, rotating her hands in opposite directions, while stroking the length of his erection.

"Baby, what are you doing? I want to—"

His words were cut short. He shouted in pleasure when Candy stopped her movements, grasped the base of his penis firmly with both hands and eased her mouth over the bulbous head.

She flicked her tongue in a series of quick licks over the entire circumference, before she swallowed as much as she could of his length inside her mouth. Slowly, she released him, allowing his cock to ease out of her mouth.

She didn't give him a chance to react. She quickly engulfed him again, deep-throating him until she felt the end of his cock brush the back of her throat.

"Shit, Candy!" Davis groaned, as he thrust his hips, forcing more of his dick to glide further into her mouth.

As big as he was, and as far as she had him into her throat, she couldn't fit half of his hard length inside. Her pussy quivered in expectation of housing all of his magnificent length.

Candy eased him out of her mouth and licked the combined juices of her saliva and his pre-cum off, swirling and laving him clean.

His hands went to the sides of her head to pull her away.

"Baby, I have a lot planned for you, for us. As good as this feels, I have to stop you. I don't want to come like this, not the first time with you."

With reluctance, Candy allowed him to withdraw from her and push her back down on the bed.

"Now where was I? And why are you still wearing these?" he asked, his fingers toying with the scrap of panties she still wore.

He eased his big body between her legs and spread her thighs wide, waiting for her answer.

"Because it's cold outside and I don't want frostbite on my kitty," Candy replied saucily.

Davis grinned and kissed her mound through the silk of her panties. He moved the elastic aside, and using his thumb and forefinger, separated the lips of her pussy. He leaned in closer, and inhaled, deeply.

"Damn, your pussy even smells good," he said, his hot tongue slicing between the seam of her creamy opening. She hissed, squirming around his tongue, moaning in delight.

He carefully lapped along both sides of her crease, taking his time, swirling his tongue around, above and below her clit, over and over . . . Candy wanted to cry when he avoided actual contact with her clit that had peeked out the minute, *the minute*, his tongue had come out to play.

He glanced up at her, licking his lips. "Your kitty?" he asked and it took her a minute to recall their conversation.

"Yes, that part of my anatomy you're making purr, right about now," she groaned, barely recovering from his caress.

She knew the sound she made from her throat was that a satisfied kitten would make, but damn if that wasn't how she felt. Or would feel, if he continued his oral lovemaking.

"Do you always say the first thing that comes to your mind, Candy? Do you have reservations? Walls or barriers?"

He'd eased his hands out of her panties, and now his fingers were brushing back and forth against her mound, through her soaking panties. No physical contact was made, yet his touch through the silk was just as erotic, electric.

Again, he fingered aside the elastic of her panties and separated her folds, rubbing his finger over and around her clit.

She cried out when he inserted one thick finger and then a second inside, stretching her wide as he worked her. "Oh God!"

"Well, Candy? Do you?"

Candy couldn't think straight. His talented fingers were manipulating her sex, and when he added another finger to the mix, stretching the opening of her vagina even further, she bit back a groan.

"Do I what?" she asked, panting.

"Have any reservations?"

"When it comes to life, and love . . . no. I don't. You only get one chance at life, as far as I know—"

Davis chose that moment to apply direct pressure to her pelvic bone as his fingers continued to play with her, and incredibly, she felt an orgasm hovering.

The orgasm broke free when he lifted her ass cheeks, snatched her panties down to her knees and covered her entire pussy with his mouth and suckled.

The unexpected feel of his velvet tongue as it stroked her aching sex, with hot delicious glides, ministering to her clit, forced the scream, along with the orgasm, to erupt. Licking and stroking her from her streaming entry to the top of her hood, he didn't miss a bit of flesh in between.

He gently grabbed the nubbin of her clitoris and worked it, using tongue, teeth and lips, giving it all the hot attention she craved, and more. Candy's body went up in flames as she accepted his tongue loving.

She tossed her head back and forth on the satin pillow, lost in sensual agony, coming long and hard as he continued to glide his tongue inside the lips of her vagina.

Just as she thought the orgasm had reached its peak, when she thought he'd wrung out the last bit of sensation from her weakened body, he spread her lips wide and added another finger to her sopping entrance.

Licking, sucking and pumping his fingers in her sheath all at the same time forced another orgasm to erupt and she screamed, bucking against him, her eyes tightly closed.

She screamed and came, yelled and cried until she was hoarse.

By the time her release was complete, by the time she'd returned to a semblance of normalcy, her heart was beating so fast, she was afraid she'd have a heart attack it raced so out of control.

She took deep, panting breaths, trying to calm her heart when Davis leaned down to softly caress her forehead before kissing her, sweetly, on the mouth. She could taste her own essence on his lips.

It took a while before she opened her eyes. Davis was reaching around her, opening the drawer of the side table next to her. When he withdrew a foil package she closed her eyes again.

He wasn't through with her yet.

"We're far from through," he confirmed her thoughts. She felt the curl of excitement in her belly when he ripped open the foil package and sheathed his long, thick organ, his hot, lust-filled eyes never leaving hers.

19

Davis was so excited it was a wonder he was able to roll the condom down over his dick, his hands shook so, as he readied himself for her.

She lay down on the bed, eyes half-closed, panties around her knees, with the stamp of sexual satisfaction on her beautiful face, all because of him.

He felt like beating his chest and going completely caveman, claiming his woman. He'd never experienced the high, the near nirvana eating her out had given him, with any other woman.

Her unique smell, her tight, soaking wet pussy, the little moans she uttered as he'd licked her, drank her, *ate her,* had his dick swelling to near record proportions.

Damn.

With a harsh groan he grabbed her panties and, after lifting her legs, eased them completely off her body. He was careful not to yank them because if he did, as badly as he wanted to do her, spread her legs and fuck the shit out of her . . . he would have ripped them from her body.

His dick was hard and ready to plunge into her tight, sweet snatch. He was afraid he'd hurt her.

It had been a while since he'd last made love ... had sex ... he automatically corrected himself, mentally ... with a woman. Actually, not too long after meeting Candy for the first time, almost nine months ago, had been the last time.

He'd tried bedding a hot, beautiful blonde after going out to the bar with Rodney one evening after work, a few months after Candy had come strolling into his world.

But damn if it wasn't Candy's face, Candy's smile ... Candy's body he'd imagined in place of the woman he lay with.

And after an embarrassing performance, although he'd left the woman satisfied and he'd achieved a semblance of orgasm, he hadn't had sex with anyone else.

What the hell was the point?

Once had been enough to tell him that unless he exorcised Candy from his mind, until he could somehow rid himself of the fantasies he'd constructed around her, it was useless for him to try and make love with anyone else.

His hands shook as he placed them on each of her thighs and settled into the V of her spread legs, her tight curly hairs wet and glistening from her own juices.

"Are you ready for me, baby?" he asked.

She nodded her head in agreement and licked her lower, plump lip and inhaled deeply, as though to prepare herself.

With a tight smile of anticipation, he lifted her thighs and placed them over his arms. Within moments he was slowly feeding her his dick, inch by inch, until she grabbed on to his forearms, sinking her short nails deep into his flesh.

"Oh damn ... wait ... ummm," she hissed, "Davis, you're so big and it's been a while for me. Give me a minute, please." The hot words made his dick grow even bigger as he halted.

"Baby, don't worry, we'll go nice and slow. We'll take this easy. At your pace," he promised and leaned down to grab at her bottom lip, sucking it into his mouth before he reluctantly released it.

"Mmmm, okay, thank you," Candy panted against his lips.

After several tense moments, she nodded her head for him to continue, and he slipped more of himself inside her juicy, tight channel, carefully feeding her the rest of his shaft.

Seated to the hilt, his balls tapping against the soft seam of her perineum, in that space between her anus and the lips of her pussy, they both released groans of pleasure.

Yet, he waited.

He didn't want to hurt her, so after he adjusted her snug sweet snatch on his dick, he waited.

When she whispered, "Okay . . . I'm okay," he moved his hand under her bottom and brought her flush against his body and flipped them, without losing the connection of the intertwined bodies.

"You ride me, Candy. I don't want to hurt you, and your pleasure is my main goal, my only goal."

He'd said things to women in the past, words designed to get them in bed. He'd said pretty words to make a woman think she was the most important woman in the world, but he meant what he said to Candy.

He didn't want to think deeply into why that was as she slowly began to ride him.

Her plump butt was nestled firmly against the top of his thighs, both knees were lying close to his body, her hands were braced near his hips and her hot slick vagina had eaten all his dick . . . and then she moved.

She slowly glided up and down his cock, riding him nice and slow in a way that had him clenching his jaw as his hands grasped her grinding hips.

Every bounce and glide along his shaft made her small breasts slap together enticingly. Davis sat up and grabbed one of the small treasures and latched on, nursing her as she rode him.

As he laved her tight, beaded little nipples, his fingers gripped her round ass, massaging the hot globes, squeezing them together as she rode him, as he ground his dick into her.

He pulled her as tight to his body as he could, but it still wasn't close enough. He dug into her deeper, working her sweetness in tight strokes. She continued to bounce her plump ass, jostling and riding him as she moaned and cried, her sounds of pleasure spurring him on.

He could tell she was close to coming when he felt her walls tightening on him, clutching and gripping him in smooth rhythm with his strokes until she cried out harshly.

He placed a hand between them, found her hot, swollen nubbin and continued to work her along his cock. He rubbed her stiff, blood-filled clit, hard, until her orgasm broke.

She screamed her release, crying and bucking against him, clutching at him frantically as she came, but shit, it *still* wasn't enough, not for him.

Davis felt crazed with the feel of her tight pussy walls milking his dick as she completed her orgasm. As soon as she finished coming, he lifted her off his penis, despite her cry, and lay down on the bed.

He placed her on top of his body, and eased his body down until her legs straddled either side of his face with his hands supporting her, around the waist.

He placed her drenched pussy directly over his face, his mouth, and started eating her out as though it was his last meal. He rubbed his face against her pussy, completely devouring her.

Within minutes her wrenching cries erupted, her body shook uncontrollably yet he continued to consume her, until she screamed loud and long, her cries ending in a sob.

When she released again, Davis couldn't hold back. With her body sagging from the back-to-back orgasms he'd given her, he lowered her quivering form down his, and carefully flipped his body so that he lay above her.

He spread her thighs into a wide V, settled between them,

sank into her as far as he could and started fucking her, driving into her as far as he could reach.

She groaned and cried out as he lifted her leg and leveled his dick inside her streaming heat.

At the angle he had positioned her he knew she would easily get off again, as he pumped inside her drenched sheath. He smoothly adjusted her body lower on the bed so her head wouldn't bang against the headboard as he jammed her body.

Caught up in the sheer pleasure of stroking into her, of having his fantasy of being with her fulfilled, he grabbed both of her wrists in his one hand and forced them high above her head. With the other hand he began to roughly massage her small, perfect breasts, delivering tight corkscrew thrusts, burying his face in the crook of her neck, as she groaned.

"Do you want to come again, Candy?" he whispered against the side of her neck, frenzied in his need.

"Yes . . . lord yes!" she cried out.

"Then come for me, baby, come *with* me, this time," he encouraged her and grabbed one of her small tits that he'd been playing with and nearly engulfed the entire small globe inside his mouth.

He released his hold on her bound wrists and eased his mouth away from her breast, and concentrated on rocking his dick in and out of her juicy pussy.

Before bliss took over and he had one final moment of coherency, he glanced down at her. The look on her beautiful, passion-filled face forced the orgasm to explode from his body.

He held her down as he gave one, two, three . . . hard, grinding thrusts, sending them both over the edge.

Their cries, one deep, the other high, blended, melded, into one wailing note of passion, as on one accord they released.

20

Their heartbeats and deep, harsh breaths were the only sounds in the darkened bedroom.

Davis had placed her in front of him after their shared, mind-blowing orgasm, crossing both of his big arms over her breasts, nestling her bottom tightly against his semi-erect penis.

Candy was dizzy and her breath was still coming out in harsh gasps. Her heart settled into a relaxed pattern, and she inhaled deep, calming breaths of air into her lungs.

She couldn't believe what she'd just experienced with Davis.

She'd had orgasms before, had enjoyed a healthy sex life, but she'd never experienced the connection with anyone that she had with him. And the explosiveness of their first coming together . . .

She feathered her fingers back and forth along his lightly furred arms.

Candy felt him kiss the top of her head before he laid his cheek against her hair.

"I'm sorry, Candy. I didn't mean to go . . . crazy like I did. I hope I didn't hurt you," he murmured, and she could hear the tension in his voice and was puzzled.

"What? I loved it, it was the most incredible experience I've ever had, Davis. God, if that's going crazy, lock me up on the ward and throw away the key, because that's the kind of crazy a woman can't get enough of." She groaned softly when he adjusted her body more comfortably against his groin.

He played with the gemstone in her belly ring. Candy lightly squirmed against him, still zinging from her orgasm, every nerve ending in her body alive and on fire.

She groaned and laughed at herself. The memory of how he almost made her come from playing with her belly ring earlier caused a surprising response, her nipples instantly beading.

"Oh my God, this is crazy," she laughed. "I can't believe you can still drag a response from me."

"Did you like what we did? I wasn't too much for you . . . too wild?"

"Are you kidding me, Davis? The yells, screaming, near speaking in tongues didn't give you a clue how good it felt?" she asked, incredulous. She felt the tension ease from his big body with her response.

He pulled her closer to his warmth. They were silent, each in their own thoughts, until Candy spoke.

"Davis, you made a comment about me saying what was on my mind . . . you asked me if I had any walls or barriers," she reminded him of his earlier question. "Why did you ask me that?"

She felt some of the tension return to his body and waited. She'd been so caught up in the moment, so hot that she hadn't been able to concentrate on what he was saying when he'd made the offhand comment.

Now with her sexual tension eased and completely sated, she was able to fully concentrate. Upon reflection, his words hit a discordant nerve.

"It seems as though you don't allow anything to stop you

from doing or saying whatever it is you want," he started and stopped as though trying to search for the right words. "You're so free with everything."

Candy relaxed.

She didn't detect any type of judgment in his tone, so she didn't think he meant it as a slam, probably just curious as to what made her tick.

"Davis, I grew up homeless, or as close to being homeless as you can."

From his sharp intake of breath, it was obvious it wasn't what he expected to hear her say. She plunged ahead, ready to share a piece of her history, her life, with him. She felt no shame about the way she grew up. Not anymore, she didn't. It was a part of who she was, what forged her into the woman she was, today.

"We never stayed in one house, one city more than a year until I turned fifteen and we moved here, to Stanton. I was able to graduate from high school. When I got a scholarship to the University, I didn't take it until Dad promised he'd stick around." She uttered a humorless laugh. "I should have known better. After my freshman year, he told me he needed to go."

"Needed?"

"My father was, *is,* the type of person who believes in experiencing life to the fullest. It was only for me, I realized later, that we stayed in Stanton as long as we did. He never liked conventionality. It *was* one of the things that drew my mother to him, she once said."

"Was? You say that as though it isn't true anymore," he murmured, stroking a hand over her belly as they lay close, her back snug against the hardness of his chest.

"Yes. *Was,* is right. My parents stayed together just long enough for me to enter grade school, before she left."

"So your father raised you?" he asked.

"Yes, he raised me and my older brother, Corey."

"I thought for some reason it was just you and your dad. Kind of like me and Angelica."

"No, I have an older brother. He's a lot different than Dad and me. More like Mom. Or what I remember of her."

"In what way?"

"Corey was quiet, not as expressive in his feelings. Although he made it clear when he turned sixteen, he no longer wanted to move around, was embarrassed by the way we lived, was the way that he put it."

"What did he do? Leave?"

"Yes. He graduated from an alternative school—the type we normally went to because we were transient a lot of times—and got a scholarship to a university on the East Coast. Dad and I didn't hear from him, just like Mom, for years afterward."

The pain of desertion by her brother stung as deeply as it had when her mother decided she, too, no longer wanted to be a part of their family. Candy blinked several times to keep the unexpected tears from surfacing.

"So in the end, my brother chose the more conservative route, I guess you could say," she smiled without humor into the dark of the room. "Last thing I knew of his life, he wore Brooks Brothers suits, drove a gas-guzzling SUV—sorry," she said, remembering Davis too drove an SUV, "and held a high-powered job as an investment broker in D.C., close to where our mother lives. At least as far as I know, as I haven't had a real conversation with my brother in a number of years."

"And your mother?"

She released a grunt that even to her own ears sounded as painful as it felt.

"My mother? I haven't heard from her in years. At any rate, unlike my brother . . . and mother, I chose the more liberal way of life. I'm not for trying to fit into someone's ideal of who I should be, what I should look like, where I should live, or how I should dress. I am completely comfortable in my own skin," she finished and if she sounded as though she were trying to convince him, he remained silent about it.

Davis smoothed a hand over her hair and the constricted feeling began to ease from her chest with his soothing touch.

Candy no longer wanted to think about her past, her family, her mother . . . or anything. All she wanted was to feel.

She turned to face him and reached up and kissed him lightly on his sensual mouth.

Surprised, he captured her lips with his, sucking gently on her fuller lower rim. Candy hummed around his kisses, having already noticed he enjoyed pulling her lips into his mouth.

As he sucked on her lips, she groaned as his teeth bit gently into the lower one. The slightly painful sting was instantly soothed when his tongue lapped a hot caress across both lips.

"Sorry," he murmured, once he released them. "I didn't mean to hurt you. Sometimes I can't always hold it back."

"Hold what back?"

"My desire . . . need . . . to get a little rough," he admitted and buried his face in the crook of her neck, nuzzling aside her soft kinky curls and biting a trail down her neck.

"Ummm," Candy murmured and arched her back, "I don't mind, Davis. You weren't rough at all with me. God, I loved it. All of it," she said and reached both hands up and pulled his face to hers and initiated a kiss he quickly took over. When he released her, she was completely breathless.

"Good, I never would want to hurt you. Tell me if anything I do is too much for you," he said and Candy laughed, thinking he was teasing her.

He pulled away from her, looking deep into her eyes, and although it was dark, she could see the earnestness in his expression. "I'm serious, Candy. Tell me, promise?"

"Of course, but, Davis, I can't see you ever hurting me on purpose."

"No, I wouldn't," he murmured and nestled her against his

chest as they lay in companionable silence. "My first wife, Gail, was never very receptive, once we were married, to me being 'aggressive' in our lovemaking."

This was the first time he'd mentioned his wife's name, willingly, and that he did so now caused her heart to speed up in excitement. That he was opening up to her on something so personal was a milestone in their relationship.

"When we first dated, before she left for college, she seemed to enjoy the way we made love," he started.

"You were high school sweethearts?" she murmured.

"Not sweethearts. Her grandfather had worked for the company before he passed on; she and I ran into one another once in a while, at company-sponsored events," he replied.

His hand continued to stroke over her hair, his voice sounding distracted, his mind obviously in the past. Candy remained silent. She didn't want him to stop opening up to her, sharing a part of his past with her.

"I was a few years older than her, but she'd always flirted with me. But like I said I was older, and didn't view her in the same way." He paused and captured the finger that was tracing small circles on his chest and placed a small kiss on the tip, before he picked the conversation back up.

"I came home after I'd graduated from college, with my degree in architecture. She'd just completed her freshman year at the university she attended, up north. We attended the same party one night. I had been drinking, having a good time, she and I started dancing... kissing, kind of doing the grab-ass thing," he gave a short humorless laugh. "One thing led to another, and before I knew it, we were in bed together."

21

"One thing led to another?" Candy asked, one eyebrow raised that Davis could see, even in the dark.

"That's about it . . . one thing led to another. Not hard to do when there's alcohol involved; inhibitions fly out the window. That was the beginning of a sexual relationship that lasted the summer. It wasn't supposed to go beyond that . . . just a summer fling."

"But obviously it became something more," Candy murmured.

"Yes. When it was time for her to go back to school at the end of the summer, it was obvious that she was pregnant. At least a couple of months, and as we'd been sexually active, exclusively, I thought the baby was mine. Fool that I was, I didn't even question it. But she wasn't. I wouldn't learn that until Angelica was born."

"I'm sorry. That must have been hard."

"It was. For a long time I was in denial, that Gail would lie to me, when she knew . . . shit. I don't feel like going into all of that, right now."

"Davis, I believe that it's hard for Angelica to hear things about her mother and not be able to talk to you about it. The cruelties of others, saying you're not her biological father, pales in comparison, I think, to being teased about what type of person her mother was, when she feels as though she can't defend her, because she doesn't know anything about her," Candy said cautiously.

"Yeah, you're right, it's common knowledge that Angelica isn't my biological daughter. But I love her as though it was my blood in her veins. I love her more than anyone on this earth."

"Davis, you don't have to convince me. I know that," Candy murmured.

"I have her best interests at heart. I don't know how to tell her about her mother. It's not as though any of that knowledge affects how I feel about her, but hell, if I tell her, I don't know how that'll affect my child. I can deal with other people's doubts, but I don't know if I could handle it if Angelica ever doubted for a moment my love for her. I don't want to risk that. Not now. Maybe when she's older, I'll tell her about her mother's and my relationship . . . but not now," he finished, adamantly, and Candy decided to leave the subject alone for the moment.

There wasn't anything she could do to force him to talk to Angelica about her mother. The reality of it was that Davis had a skewed view regarding his relationship with his deceased wife.

Added to that, feeling guilty about not wanting Angelica when he'd first learned she wasn't his child, biologically.

"Isn't there something more pleasurable we should be doing, than dredging up the past?" he asked and leaned down to capture her lips with his. Now it was his turn to leave the pain of the past alone and turn to her as she had done to him when speaking of her family.

With a small lift of her lips, she gave him a half smile, and ran a hand down his cheek. "If I can't think of anything, I'm sure you can," she said.

Davis reached a thick arm around her body and pulled open the drawer to the bedside table and withdrew another foil package.

"Candy, that was incredible. God, I don't know what to say," Davis said as the last tremors of his intense orgasm left his body.

He carefully pulled out of her and after discarding the condom, placed her in front of his body, tightly spooning behind her, his mind a chaotic whirl.

He had an inkling that the sex would be incredible between them, there was no way it would be anything but, yet what we they'd shared, the connection, had come as a total surprise, something he hadn't expected.

Although he hadn't planned the night, had no intention of asking her to dinner, much less bedding her, he knew it was inevitable. It was only a matter of time, whether he chose to acknowledge it or not; his subconscious *knew* it.

She'd gotten under his skin from the first moment he'd laid eyes on her, and as much as he might have wanted to deny it, he'd more than wanted her. He craved her.

Badly.

And now, like any addict on the street, one taste . . . make that several *tastings*, counting their last marathon of sexual exploration . . . wasn't near enough to satisfy him.

And no amount of fantasy or erotic dreams could replace the real thing.

Now that he'd experienced the real thing, he knew that he was in trouble.

Damn. He sighed, gathering her closer to his body, listening to her ragged breathing even out as she came down from their last orgasmic high.

After he'd pushed into her tight, warm pussy ... Davis glanced down. One of his legs was casually thrown over both of hers, pinning her to the mattress.

His dick, soft now as it lay against her plush ass, began to stir to life the minute he thought of what it felt like to push into that pretty kitty of hers ... shit.

Candy had been right when she referred to her sweet pussy as a kitty; he loved to hear it and her purr when he made love to her.

And although they'd had sex more times than Davis had in nine months, he still wanted more. He needed more of her.

The soft penis of moments ago began to take on a life of its own, and Davis felt the instant response from Candy when, with a groan, she pushed her round ass cheeks against his dick and softly ground against it.

He kissed the side of her neck as they quietly, with no words except the occasional soft moan or low grunt, took pleasure with each other.

He placed one of his hands on the top of her hip, forcing her legs tightly together as his dick knifed back and forth along the crease of her ass and swollen vaginal lips. He felt her tremble as his shaft angled against her clitoris.

"Do you want to come again, Candy?" he asked in a voice grown hoarse.

When she nodded her head, not saying a word, his other hand gently manipulated her swollen sex as he ground against her, fucking her, no entry needed as her pussy wept and saturated his dick, easing the glide. Within moments they both went over the edge, again, together.

They were silent, as he held her tight against his chest, drowsy and sleepy. There'd been no penetration, yet the feeling, the orgasm had been just as intense for Davis as it had the other times they'd made love that night, and it scared the shit out of him.

He thought maybe one time with her, one time and he'd be able to exorcise her from his mind and go on. But that was before tonight, before he'd made love to her, before they'd shared their history with one another . . . before he'd gotten to know even more about her.

And everything he learned further let him know that he needed to be careful around her. Because if he wasn't, there was a distinct chance she'd do more than work her way into his dreams, she'd work her way into his heart.

And that was an added complication he didn't need.

He'd ridden Candy strong and long throughout the night, unrelenting in his desire to fuck her good and hard, needing to quench his increasing thirst for her . . . and get her out of his mind, once and for all. To erase her from his thoughts.

But each time he'd surged into her heat, it had been pure nirvana and he knew he had to have one more taste of her. One more taste of Candy and he'd be satisfied. But each time only served to make him want more. And he hadn't been gentle with her.

Hell.

He never wanted to hurt Candy like he did Gail the one time he'd engaged in sex that had been too much, too intense, she'd said.

He still remembered the way Gail had looked at him like he was a monster, when he'd suggested tying her up while they made love. She'd allowed him to, but it hadn't been a pleasurable experience for either one of them. Davis hadn't ridden her hard, nowhere near the way he'd made love with Candy, but he'd felt as though he hurt her.

And Gail never let him forget it.

Afterward she made him promise to never do that, never suggest it again, and he'd gladly agreed.

The memory made his gut clench.

He gathered Candy close and allowed himself to drift off to sleep.

In that state in between sleep and consciousness he promised, "I'm sorry, Gail, I didn't mean to hurt you." He kissed the back of Candy's hair and promptly fell into a deep sleep.

Candy too was in the state in between sleep and wakefulness. So much so that she wasn't sure if she what she heard was real or not.

If Davis had, in his sleep, called out the name of his wife after making love all night long with her.

22

"Oh no! Not again," Candy moaned out loud.

Blindly she tapped her hand around the bed, near the vicinity of her head, until her hands came into contact with the pillow. She shoved it on top of her head.

She'd done it again.

Had another crazy erotic, wake-up-with-her-panties-wet, fingers-smelling—

In the middle of her mental rant, as she began to chastise herself for having another Davis-inspired erotic dream, she stopped. Clear as day, she heard the distinct sound of a man's voice singing in the . . . *please Lord, let me be dreaming* . . . shower.

She quickly shoved the pillow off her head and opened her eyes, only to tightly close them again. It was too bright in the room, with the blinds open and the glare of the sun shining off the snow. It took a moment for her eyes to adjust.

As well as her foggy brain.

Panicked, she glanced around at her surroundings and down at her naked body. Quickly, she threw her legs over the side of the mattress, trying to gather her wits.

Okay, so it was true.

It hadn't been another erotic dream. It had been all too real what she'd done last night. *All night.*

Her dream lover couldn't take the credit for the deliciously sore feeling she felt between her thighs, the minute she swung her legs over the side of the bed, or the sticky evidence of her own cream between her legs.

The images of Davis holding her down as he did her, sliding into her so far she thought he touched her womb, burned bright in her mind.

His perfect penis, so thick and long . . . the way he'd given careful attention to her tattoo that lay low on her back, in the curve of her waist . . .

The way he'd dictated when she'd come, making her beg for it at times, before making love to her, doing her so hard, so deliciously attentive to her body that she sometimes felt faint . . . goosebumps peppered her flesh.

And the last time. She remembered how sweet it had been, how he'd loved her from the back, without penetration, the feeling indescribable, before they'd both eased into sleep.

She *thought* she'd be in seventh heaven. She *thought* she would be over the moon. They'd made love and it had been everything she imagined, hotter than any of her fantasies had ever been. It had been one of the most erotic nights of her life.

So why in hell did she feel a strange nervousness settle in her belly? Why was she reluctant to see him?

Some of the things they had done until the wee hours of the night were enough to make anyone blush, Candy thought.

But she knew the problem, the reason for her hesitancy in seeing him.

Although she'd been almost asleep when he'd finally allowed her to rest, the last words he said rang loudly in her mind.

I'm sorry, Gail. I didn't mean to hurt you . . .

The singing in the shower came to an abrupt stop, and Candy looked around, frantically trying to find her clothes to cover her body.

Although why was completely beyond her. She'd allowed him to lick, caress, massage, nibble and explore every inch of her body, so it wasn't as though she had anything to hide—he'd explored every nook and cranny of her body as he made love to her.

She jumped up from the bed, ignoring the ache between her legs, and hobbled—sheet haphazardly wrapped around her body—over to the side of the bed. She found her panties and searched frantically for the rest of her clothes.

She stopped the search when she remembered Davis had stripped her down in the living room.

Oh, hell.

She was in the process of doing a quick re-wrap with the sheet—marveling at her own talent with fabric, even in a rush—when Davis stepped out of the shower, looking fresh as a daisy, and stopped.

His wet, dark hair was spiked, after he removed the towel which he was vigorously rubbing over his head. Water clung to the soft mat of hair on his sculptured chest, down the center line of his chest and abs, glistening in the hair above the plush towel he'd casually wrapped around his lean hips.

Although he'd covered himself, she caught a glimpse of his long cock peeking out, and could imagine the way his balls, drawn tight against his groin after showering, would look . . .

Candy forced her lusting eyes away.

She had some things to sort out; questions about last night. The last words he uttered were fresh in her mind, before she engaged in any more . . . escapades . . . with Davis.

"Good morning. I didn't mean to wake you." His eyes searched hers, his voice low-pitched.

"I think I'd better get ready to go, I have a lot to do today," she blurted, unsure what to say. The main thing on her mind was to get home and away from Davis Strong. She needed to think. She couldn't do that with him standing before her, nearly naked, staring at her as though he was ready to pick up where they left off in the wee hours of the night.

"You can take a shower. I would have woken you up and asked you to share one with me, but you looked so peaceful laying there, I didn't have the heart to wake you up. You looked tired," he murmured, carefully scrutinizing her face.

"I'm fine. I think I'll just get dressed, and if you could take me home—"

"Is everything okay?" he asked, confusion on his face. He stepped nearer to her when she stood. Candy felt like a deer caught in the headlights, unmoving, in the middle of the floor.

"I'm fine, last night was great. Like you said, I'm just a little tired—"

"God, I'm sorry. I didn't mean to be so demanding. It was all my—"

"No, it wasn't your fault," she finished for him this time, seeing the direction he was going.

Candy didn't need to hear him apologize for giving her the best night of her life. She didn't want to see the way his nostrils flared or his eyes trailed to her mouth when she licked her suddenly dry lips, either.

She particularly didn't want to see the guilty-looking expression flash across his handsome face.

The guilt probably came from thoughts of last night, the way he'd loved her, the incredible way they'd loved one another, as he was thinking of his wife, Gail.

Feeling as though he'd somehow betrayed her memory, or worse, wishing she had been the woman in his bed, instead of Candy.

She straightened her shoulders and gave him a determined, carefree smile.

"It was amazing, Davis. And I would love to take you up on the offer of breakfast, but I think I'd better go. I have a lot to do this morning and afternoon, to get everything ready for tonight."

"But you still have to eat, Candy, it won't take me long—"

"Look, I would like for you to take me home," she interrupted him, again. This time a set look crossed his face and he gave a short nod.

"Fine. Let me grab something to put on, and as soon as you're ready—" he paused, and his gaze roamed quickly over her sheet-wrapped body "—I'll take you home."

"I'll be ready as soon as I find my clothes," Candy replied and turned to leave the room in search of her abandoned clothes.

She swallowed, hard, when she glanced over her shoulder and noticed the way he tented the towel draped over his lean hips.

Candy hurried out of the room, in search of her clothes, compelled to be far, far away from his hot gaze roaming over her sheet-covered backside.

23

" Karina, Liza, I can't thank you ladies enough for helping out with the dance! I wouldn't know what to do without you, sometimes. You're both a godsend," Candy said to two of her volunteers, Karina Woodson and Liza Toulson.

She stood from her crouched position with an armful of items. She carefully moved aside the dish in which a colorful assortment of condoms were placed and set her bundle down.

She made a mental note to remind herself to remove the bowl before any of her girls came into her office. She'd picked the prophylactics up at the drugstore after she'd agreed to give a safe sex class at the women's shelter she volunteered at once a week.

She definitely didn't want any parents getting the wrong idea and thinking she was teaching their girls about safe sex. But if she had her way, she would. Many of her teens were having sex, and unfortunately it occurred without the majority of their parents' knowledge.

Some protected themselves, while others played Russian roulette, not understanding the ramifications of unsafe sex.

After she moved the bowl aside she smoothed down the hem of her short wrap skirt and glanced over at her two favorite volunteers.

Liza had begun to volunteer six months ago, and Karina had been volunteering at the center before Candy came on board as the director. Karina had spent many Saturday afternoons helping out wherever she was needed, usually with the younger girls.

Because Liza was a licensed social worker, Candy considered herself a blessed woman to have her help with the counseling sessions with the older teens.

Both ladies were dedicated to the success of the young girls who attended Girls Unlimited, as both had been members of the center as young girls themselves.

In the beginning, Liza had been hesitant, hadn't known how the girls would react to her. She'd not been to the old neighborhood since she left after graduating from high school, purposely putting the pain of her youth far behind her. Unlike Karina, she'd wanted no ties with a past that for her had been filled with poverty and a mother who neglected her.

Candy allowed her glance to slide over Liza. She was crouched down next to Karina as they scoured the many boxes on the floor of her office in search of decorations for the dance.

Liza was always turned out to the T. Even in the jeans she was currently wearing, which she'd coupled with a designer sweater, she exuded sophistication. Her tall, model-like slim body seemed perfectly suited for anything she wore.

Her perfectly coiffed, relaxed bob had subtle light brown highlights and feathered up at the ends, with fringed bangs framing her high forehead. Her beautiful deep-brown complexion was flawless, makeup always impeccable. And although she had a slightly reserved personality, she was very approachable and the girls she helped to mentor had come to respect her.

Candy turned to look at Karina and felt a smile automatically stretch her lips.

As for Karina, she'd been a volunteer on a regular basis, since her undergraduate days at the state university. She too grew up on the north side of town, alongside Liza. But unlike Liza, she'd grown up in a loving home, with her grandmother and mother, and had known nothing but affection.

Karina volunteered often on the weekends as well as the occasional evening, when she could spare the time between building her new web design business and her new marriage.

Karina was a self-proclaimed nerd, loved her computer and would talk your ear off about the latest HTML or ColdFusion product that hit the market. She'd started giving a small class on Saturdays, teaching the girls how to use the computer, and it had been a great success.

The girls loved her, but then again, most people loved Karina. She was similar in height and body type to Candy, hips and thighs, not overweight, but she definitely was curvy. But unlike Candy, Karina had boobs. Even before she was pregnant, she was an impressive C cup, unlike Candy, who was lucky to fill an A.

She wore her hair natural, as did Candy, but instead of wearing her kinky mane loose, she wore it locked. She sported cowrie shells and hair jewelry on several of the long, light brown locs, which framed a pretty, café-au-lait-toned face.

Her wire-framed glasses were perpetually dropped down low on her round nose, causing her to constantly push them up the short bridge.

Although Candy tended to be a bit of a loner and had few girlfriends, she enjoyed being in both of the women's company. She'd once accompanied them on a rare shopping expedition to the mall, and although she hadn't actually bought anything, she'd enjoyed being with the ladies.

Candy never had any close friends growing up, because of

the way she constantly moved from city to city and job to job with her father. She learned quickly that to form friendships ended up being more painful in the end, when, inevitably, she'd have to say goodbye.

Yet, over the course of the last months of her association with Karina and Liza, she'd gradually, without even being aware of it, become friends with them.

Karina had the type of personality that drew people like magnets, male or female. She had an open and friendly disposition that was so infectious, it was no surprise to Candy she had become one of the few friends she had within her inner circle.

She'd only recently gotten married, six months ago, and was still in the honeymoon stage. Although Candy was happy for her when she first told of her upcoming nuptials, she had to admit too, she was selfishly afraid she'd lose Karina as a volunteer once she'd gotten married.

In Candy's experience there weren't that many men she personally knew who were willing to give up their wives on a Saturday to volunteer, let alone have them devote the amount of time that Karina did, but that was before she'd met Karina's husband, Cooper.

Since their marriage, Cooper was at the center, volunteering alongside his wife, and it was clear he was not only besotted with his wife, but had grown just as committed to the center as she had.

"Girl, please! It's no problem. You know how much we love it here. I think I benefit more than the girls do," Karina chuckled, head deep inside one of the boxes on the floor of Candy's office.

"No, I think the girls are lucky to have you and Liza here," Candy countered, with affection.

She walked over to where both women were hunched down on the floor, sifting through and lifting out various decorations for inspection.

"Let me help you with this," she said and took an armful of

the supplies Karina ferreted from the box in the storage closet. She set them on a chair before offering her hand to help Karina stand.

"These should work out fine, don't you think?" Karina asked, looking down at the small pile of decorations as she rubbed her round belly, absentmindedly.

Karina was nearly six months pregnant with twins; her belly was nice and round, but she didn't let it stop her from remaining active. She'd disclosed to Candy that early in her pregnancy the doctors were worried when they found out she was pregnant with twins. One of the babies didn't look to be developing at the same rate, but as the months passed, things seemed to be going well with the pregnancy. Nonetheless, Candy was still concerned for her.

"Everything going well with the babies?" Candy asked.

"Everything is great!" she replied.

Karina gratefully eased her body down in the oversized chair in front of Candy's desk and took a deep breath.

"Are you okay?" Liza asked, concern in her voice, as she too sat down in one of the chairs facing the desk.

"Oh, I'm fine! Just a cramp, I think. Hmm. Wait a minute, I think it's heartburn." She placed a splayed out hand on her chest as she furrowed her brow. "Girl, it's probably from eating, *inhaling*, too much junk," she groaned. "It's not the babies' fault their mama is addicted to those doggone Little Debbie Oatmeal Cream pies," she groaned and they all laughed.

"I was hoping for the more traditional pickle cravings I keep hearing about. Something a lot less fattening than what I'm devouring, at any rate. No such luck for me," Karina good-naturedly grumbled. "In fact, I think it's getting worse if my growing girth is any indication. And, nut that my husband is, he keeps feeding my addiction!"

"What's he doing?" Candy asked and laughed inwardly, preparing herself. She and Liza exchanged a look.

There was no telling where this was going. Karina was hilarious at times, with the stories she told about her smitten man.

According to Liza, Karina had been a studious bookworm before she met her husband Cooper. She'd not dated much, devoted much of her time to building her Web business, and tended to be shy around men.

That all changed when she'd met Cooper. The man had introduced sweet, mild Karina to a few sexual adventures Liza swore up and down were illegal in certain states and which Karina would gleefully tell Liza all about.

From that day on, Candy looked at the mild Karina in a totally different light. Looks were definitely deceiving.

"Girl, last night I was seriously jonesing for some Little Deb's and Cooper drove across town to Wal-Mart to buy a box when the gas station a few miles away from our house didn't stock them! If that's not feeding this addiction of mine, I don't know what is!"

Although she complained, the look of bliss etched on her face clearly said how much she loved the attention. Candy felt a pang of jealousy, her thoughts sliding toward Davis and their current situation. To have a man so totally devoted to a woman was a rare thing.

Candy blew out a breath of disgust at herself, forcing her mind to leave the puzzle of Davis alone for a hot minute.

She wasn't up to analyzing, again, the events of the previous evening.

Candy plastered a smile on her face and replied, "That is too sweet. You and Cooper are blessed."

"Yeah, we are," Karina grinned, and pushed her small wire-rimmed glasses further up her short nose. "We got to hear both of the babies' heartbeats at my last ob appointment! Cooper was beyond himself. The man all but thumped his chest and went all he-man on me, when the doctor identified Gabriel's beat," she laughed.

"Oh, Karina, I'm so happy for you! I can imagine just how that would make a man go 'he-man'," Candy laughed along with her.

Because of the early fear that both twins weren't doing well, they'd agreed to have an amniocentesis, to determine if both babies were healthy, and with the positive results came the news that one of the twins was a female, and the other a male.

"It felt good to know both twins are doing well. And now we know their sex. Coop and I are happy we have a boy and girl. Gabriel may be smaller than his sister, but that sure doesn't stop him from playing kick ball with her. I swear those two have formed their own football team and my belly is their arena!"

The three women talked about babies and husbands for a bit. Although Candy had experience in neither area, she participated in the conversation, laughing at some of the things Karina told them of the measures Cooper had begun to go through in his quest to baby-proof the house.

When Candy heard the strains of music, as it filtered into her office, she glanced up at the clock in the corner of the room and noted the time.

"I think some of our kids will be here shortly. I asked the volunteers to be here an hour before the dance starts. I think the DJ is setting up now. Someone must have let him into the gym."

Candy walked back to her desk and began to fill one of the small boxes with the decorations they'd chosen. Liza stood and walked to the desk to help.

"Girl, sit down, we have this. It takes you too darn long to waddle these days," Liza told her friend as Karina was pushing herself up by the arms of the chair. Karina stuck her tongue out at her but sat back down with a grateful sigh.

"So how is everything going with you . . . with Angelica?" Karina asked and, surprised, Candy turned back to face her.

"Everything is fine. Why do you ask?" No sooner had she spoken when she instantly knew the answer. Pauline Rogers.

"Oh, Sister Pauline mentioned you were doing some special type of mentoring with her, that's all," Karina replied with the answer Candy already knew.

She continued to place the decor items in the box and wondered how much to disclose to the women. She didn't know how much Sister Pauline had already told them. Although Pauline tended to give her opinions a bit freely, Candy trusted her.

"Hmm. *Well*, it's going fine. I think. We're beginning to form an understanding at least. I think she's beginning to trust me. At least she's beginning to open up a little more than she ever has."

"That's good. She's a confused little girl, I think."

Candy turned questioning eyes in Karina's direction.

"What do you mean?"

"Well," Karina began and stopped for a minute, head cocked to the side, as though considering her words carefully. "I think she has had a bit of a hard time, not having a mother around. Luckily, she has her aunt Milly, but I think when Milly left town for a while, poor Angel was even more alone. And it definitely didn't help when she started hanging around some of the girls she's been with lately, at the center." Karina mentioned the same girls Candy, as well as Davis, had identified as part of the problem.

Candy stopped filling her box and thoughtfully looked at Karina. "I'm not sure how much you're aware of what's going on with Angelica—" she asked, including both women in the question.

"I know that she's getting in trouble at school. Seems to be a bit more defiant lately, much more than she used to be," Karina said with a shake of her head. "It's too bad. She's basically a sweet little girl. She's just having a hard time, lately, I think."

"I only know what Karina has told me. I don't get to see her that much, I'm usually with the older girls," Liza replied.

"If you don't mind me asking, could you tell me what your thoughts are on Angel? I'm trying to help, in whatever way I can, with what's going on with her."

She decided to bring Karina and Liza a bit more into her confidence, and shared some of what was going on with Angelica at school. She also shared what role she herself had agreed to play in helping to resolve some of the child's issues. When she finished speaking she turned to Karina.

"I've known her since she was six years old and first came to the center. She's always been a precocious little thing. Girl, that child has more attitude than someone four times her age!" Karina said after Candy finished.

Candy agreed with her. Angelica often displayed a sweet disposition, but when she was in one of her moods, she would quickly turn to smack talking, head rolling, hands on her little hips and everything, as she gave her opinion on whatever was on her mind.

Candy noticed that this happened whenever Angelica was angry or when she was upset, but didn't want anyone to know it. It was her way of showing her displeasure.

"You know who she reminds me of, when she was a child?"

"Who?"

She and Liza exchanged a look.

"Believe it or not, Liza."

At first Candy was surprised, but then she recalled when Liza disclosed what it had been like for her, growing up. She had spoken to the girls during a group gab session over six months ago, when she first started volunteering, and shared how as a young girl she'd been a lot different than the put-together woman she was today.

The woman had it together. It didn't matter that her upbringing had been so rocky, Candy thought with a small bit of envy.

"As together as you are now, I have to admit it's still hard to believe," Candy replied.

"Yes, I know!" Liza smiled slightly. "But Karina and I both grew up in the same neighborhood, both came to the Club," she said, referring to Girls Unlimited. "I think the difference was, although we both grew up without a pot to tinkle in, was that Kari always had her Big Momma and mother," Liza replied, referring to Karina's grandmother.

Karina picked up the rest by saying, "And Liza usually had to fend for herself." Karina shook her head sadly.

"Yeah, girl. As a kid my motto was strike out first, before being struck. But as a social worker I learned later that was the way it was for a lot of children who were abused, either physically, or emotionally, as I was."

"Fortunately, for Angelica, I don't think this is going on in her home. It appears as though her family home life is positive, nurturing," Liza both asked and stated to Candy.

"Yes, I would have to agree. Davis is a good dad. I hope I'm able to help them come to some resolution. Maybe I'll be able to help unearth the reasons for Angelica's behavior."

"I'm sure you will. If there's anything you ever need, if I can help in a professional way—" Liza began.

"I know I can come to you, Liza. I appreciate it." Candy smiled and glanced up at the knock on her door. "It's open."

"Ms. Candy, I hate to bother you, but the volunteers is here and you'd best to come on and get 'em started on what you want them to do," Pauline Rogers said, barging into the room.

"Okay, Sister Pauline, thank you. Did you happen to see if Angelica Strong and her father were here?" Candy asked, as all three women left her office.

She turned around and turned the light off in her office, closing and locking the door behind her, and missed the significant look that Sister Pauline gave the two women.

"Little Angelica is here, but her daddy dropped her off, she said." Pauline answered her as she turned back around and followed the women down the hallway.

"Her aunt Milly is here with her, though, so that should be some help for us," Pauline said, slyly glancing at Candy from the corner of her eyes. "Unless you was wantin' to know if her daddy was coming here for reasons other than volunteering."

Candy ignored the question and the sly look the old woman gave and opened the door to the gym. She further ignored the accompanying guffaw from Pauline and the look of amusement she caught from both Karina and Liza as they followed her inside.

24

"Come on, Miss Candy, come out and dance with us! I know you know how to do *this* dance! Whenever my mama and her sisters go out clubbin', this is their favorite!"

"No way! You all are *not* going to laugh at me," Candy protested.

Shantella, one of her older girls, tugged on Candy's arm trying to force her out on the dance floor.

She literally dug in her heels as the other girls teased her. They were trying their best to convince her to come out on the dance floor and do the cha-cha slide with them.

She ignored the part of Sherry's comment, that she should know how to do the particular dance, because Sherry's mother knew how. The implication was she was the same age as Shantella's mother. To girls Sherry's age, all women over twenty-five were ancient and belonged in the same genre, anyway.

Which, as Candy thought about it, was probably close to the truth. She knew Chanel, Shantella's mother, was in her early thirties, having had Shantella her senior year in high school.

"Okay okay, I'll dance!" she grudgingly agreed, and allowed the girls to pull her onto the dance floor.

"Aw, snap! Miss Candy's gonna get her dance on!" one of the other girls laughingly said as she helped to push Candy on the floor.

Candy jumped into the circle of dancers and after a few missteps, caught the rhythm and shuffled, jumped, and cha cha'd with the rest of the dancers.

Soon, the floor was filled with dancers of all ages, from the younger kids who were surprisingly good at following the simple dance routine, to several of the volunteers, who happily joined in, comfortable with the more familiar dance and music.

By the time the D.J. finished remixing the extended version of the remix, Candy was completely out of breath, and when the music changed to a faster, more furious beat she held up both hands in defeat.

"Sorry girls, I'm out of my element here! I'll catch the next 'old chicks' song!"

Despite her heartbeat pounding against her chest from the impromptu exercise, Candy laughed and readjusted the band she wore around her hair. She wiped the dew of perspiration that had misted her forehead with the tips of her fingers.

"Aww, come on Ms. Candy, can't you hang?" One of the girls asked as they crowded around Candy, all flushed and laughing.

"Yeah, Ms. Candy . . . can't you hang?"

The oh-so-familiar goosebumps feathered down the length of her arms when she heard the whispered comment, against the back of her ear, from the deep, *I've-got-what-you-need* voice she knew too well.

Although it was dark in the gym and no one was paying her any attention anyway, she felt as though a high beam was aimed directly on her *and* her ridiculous-acting nipples.

Candy twisted her body around and came face-to-face with the owner of the sexy, deep, voice.

As she'd spun around she'd nearly lost her balance until his big hands reached out and spanned her waist, catching her before she could fall. One of Candy's hands splayed across his muscled chest, the other grabbed on to a bicep to catch her balance.

"Davis, I didn't think you were going to be here."

"And why would you think that?" he had to lean closer so she could hear him speak. The smell of his breath was warm and minty, and Candy's reaction was predictable and immediate.

She pushed away from his hard body and adjusted the fabric covering her breasts.

"I assumed you wouldn't be coming when Angelica came alone, with Milly."

Davis had pulled her back closer into his arms and maneuvered between the dancing couples, finding them a spot in relative isolation from the wild dancing teenagers.

"I had some things to attend to, so I could be here. I told Milly to tell you I'd be here, didn't she?" he asked.

Although the song was a fast-paced rap tune, Davis pulled her close as they danced. The feel of his hard body moving back and forth against hers had Candy wanting to go into straight cat mode and slide her body up against his, despite her conflicting feelings about him.

There was no denying the man had a body that was lethal, more sex appeal than should be legal, and the way he was moving against her made her want to do things to him, right there in the middle of the gym floor, that she knew would get her arrested.

Aware of the sweat on her body after dancing with her girls, she tried to move away, but Davis wouldn't allow her to.

"This is a fast song, Davis! Besides, I'm nasty and sweaty. You don't want to dance close to me, now."

"And since when did a little sweat hurt a man? Last night

the way our slick bodies ground against each other as we exchanged all that good and nasty sweat wasn't a problem . . . what's changed?" Davis asked, lowering his face close to hers, murmuring the words directly for her ears alone.

Their surroundings seemed to fade into the background as their eyes never left contact with the other.

"Okay, kids, let's switch the pace!" The D.J. said as the final beats ended for the remixed version of the *remix version* of *some* song, Candy had not a clue. "Let's mix it up so our volunteers can catch their breaths!" he finished. "There's nobody who does it better than Mr. Luther Vandross, as I'm sure our volunteers would agree."

"This is better. Come on, dance with me, Candy."

Candy slowly, at first with hesitancy, raised her arms and rested her hands on his chest, and allowed him to pull her tight as they danced.

The new song began to pour from the speakers booming from the center stage where the D.J. had set up his equipment.

The song was considerably slower and much more sexy. Although it was one of Candy's personal favorites, she eased out of Davis' hold, more than ready to leave the dance floor, and even more ready to clear her mind and get away from him.

"Where are you going?"

"I've been dancing for the last twenty minutes straight! Besides, I need to check on the kids," Candy answered, her voice breathy, although their dancing had nothing to do with her breathless state.

"The kids are fine, there are plenty of volunteers. Besides, I don't think one more dance will hurt, do you?"

Before she could answer, Sister Pauline was right behind her, pushing her back into Davis' arms.

"Go on and dance, Ms. Candy, I'm on patrol, don't worry 'bout a thing. I don't like how close some of these boys is dancing with our girls, I think I need to circulate on the dance floor.

I got my baton right here," she said pointing to the small club she had holstered to her side, better than any cop. "And my whistle," she said and pointed to the whistle dangling from the familiar string hanging around her neck. "Just in case I need to separate 'em."

With a gleeful look in her eyes she turned and surveyed the kids as they began to dance. "You have fun, I got this, baby." Sister Pauline murmured, and with an absent-sounding good-bye she left Candy and Davis.

"See, even Sister Pauline thinks you should keep on dancing with me. Come on, we'll move to a corner away from the others," he said and led her to an isolated area of the gym.

As she allowed him to pull her back into his arms, she gave up fighting it. She wanted to be in his arms, wanted to feel his arms wrapped around hers. She lay her head against his chest, and felt the steady, strong beat of his heart against her ear.

Davis pulled Candy against him and began to sway to the soft music.

Before he'd found himself in the parking lot of the center, Davis hadn't been sure he was coming, although he'd told Angelica and Milly he'd return later. After he'd dropped Candy off at home, he'd driven to his sister's house. Surprised, she'd welcomed him inside, and he'd disclosed to Milly, or better yet Milly had manage to pry out of him, the conflicting emotions he had surrounding the woman he now held, nestled, in his arms.

"What brings you here? This is supposed to be a girl's week-end," Milly said and briefly hugged Davis. She moved to the side and allowed him to enter.

"I know," Davis replied shrugging off his coat. "I won't stay long, just thought I'd drop by and see Angel before I head in to the office."

"Angel is still asleep. We stayed up pretty late watching a SpongeBob marathon," Milly groaned.

"Hell, better you than me. I can't tell you the times I've been forced to watch that particular marathon," Davis grunted, completely unsympathetic to his sister's pain.

"Aw, come on Davis, loosen up. You know you like the square one just as much as Angel does!" Milly accused.

"I guess he's not that bad," he laughed. "Actually, it's okay that Angel's not up yet. It will give us a chance to talk. We haven't talked about how the return to the office is going for you," Davis said.

The smell of bacon pleasantly assaulted his nose as he followed Milly into the kitchen.

"Oh, it's going fine, I guess."

She handed him a glass of orange juice before walking over to the stove and turning the sizzling bacon in the skillet. Davis sat at the island in one of the high-backed bar stools and thanked her before taking a sip. After taking a cautious drink, he put the glass down.

He thought he'd hidden his grimace, but when she turned accusing eyes in his direction he knew he'd been busted.

"Sorry, Mil, you know I don't like it from a carton. At least get the kind in a glass container. This stuff tastes like cardboard."

Davis knew he had it coming when Milly turned away from the stove after turning off the flame beneath the sizzling bacon and faced him, one hand on her ample hip.

"You know Davis, at first you had tendencies. But now I think you're a step away from some kind of compulsive disorder. You know what's next, right?" she asked, biting the inside of her cheek to prevent the laugh from escaping.

"No . . . what?" Davis knew her answer.

"Full-out dementia, big brother. Drink the damn juice," she laughed and turned back to the oven.

"So, how's it going Mil?"

He carefully observed Milly as she bustled around the kitchen, removing plates from the hutch and setting out silverware, and gave a mental sigh of relief when he noted that her limp was barely discernible. When she turned to face him again, plate in hand, he made sure his expression was light.

"It feels good to be back. I think I'll have to relearn the office. In the short time I've been gone, there've been some changes," she said and turned back and filled his plate.

"Take your time, there's no rush. Rodney has an assistant who seems to be working out—"

"Yes, I know. Letty," she interrupted, her smile tight. "I met her when I visited yesterday." She placed his food in front of him.

"Didn't know you'd come by the office, yesterday. I was there most of the day," he said and took a bite of the bacon, his eyes trained on Milly.

"I think you were with a client. I wasn't there long. I met Letty, she seems nice."

"She is. But I think Rodney would prefer working with you. He said no one could ever replace you."

When Milly stumbled and nearly upset the plate of food she was carrying, Davis leapt to his feet and steadied her and the food.

"I'm okay, Davis! Just a little stumble," she said, averting her face.

Davis took the plate from her hands and settled his hands on her shoulders, forcing her to face him. "Are you okay? Look, Milly, we know each other too well to try and bullshit each other. Lately, every time I mention Rodney you either get angry or butterfingery."

"Butterfingery Davis?" she chortled.

"You know what I mean. What's going on with you two?" he asked after leading her to sit in one of the matching high-backed stools.

"I wish I knew. I'm just about as clueless as you are. I'm not sure what to make of him. He's so damn irritating, I swear! I'm back for less than a few weeks, and already the man is trying to dictate to me what I can or can't do."

"I think I'm missing something! When did this all start?"

Milly shook her head. "It's confusing, Davis. I wouldn't even know where to start. I don't even have it worked out in my own mind what's going on with us. If anything. I'm not ready to talk about that, right now. When I need to talk, I know where you are," she smiled, slightly. "I think you have much more pressing things going on with you than anything I have going on with Rodney, at any rate. So spill, before Angelica makes it down here."

They both heard the unmistakable sounds of Angelica pounding her way down the stairs, and knew she'd be in the kitchen in a matter of moments.

"What the hell is going on with you and Candy, and did you two finally do the horizontal shuffle, or *what*?"

Davis nearly choked on the toast sliding down his throat as he turned to face his sister.

"How the hell did you know?"

The look on her face told him that she hadn't . . . but now she did. Chin perched in her hands, elbows on the counter, Milly listened in open-mouthed surprise when he quickly filled her in, in succinct detail, on what happened between Candy and himself.

25

The singer crooned over the loudspeakers and Davis rested his chin lightly against the top of Candy's head, moving it softly back and forth against her soft curls.

Angelica had saved him from giving his sister a detailed account of exactly how well he and Candy had done the "horizontal shuffle," as she put it, even if he'd been inclined to give details.

Which he wasn't.

But he'd never been able to hide anything from Milly for long. He had no idea she'd even known he'd been attracted to Candy, much less that she would guess they'd made love last night.

Pressed as close as he was to Candy, he could feel every soft curve on her small body molded to his larger one, perfectly. As though they were two halves of the same whole.

He pressed his nose close to her hair, and inhaled deeply the intoxicating scent she seemed to naturally exude.

Chocolate and sweet peppermint.

Sweet and addictive, just like her name. Just like Candy.

From the first time he'd met her, her unique scent had reached out and enveloped him in its heady embrace.

The scent was all over her, and not simply her hair. He'd discovered for himself last night how much a part of her it was, how intoxicating it was to all of his senses. As he'd licked every part of her body, her scent had transferred to him, and his to hers in a tango of bodies and hot desire.

The thought of the things she'd allowed him to do, how he'd handled her in the way he'd dreamed of . . . he felt his body's instant response; the front of his button-fly jeans grew taut and his cock swelled.

It had been the hottest night of his life.

The longer they danced together, their bodies moving as one, the harder he got with every sensual glide, every soft stroke of her belly against his jean-covered shaft.

Davis had both of his arms wrapped around her waist and he allowed one of his hands to lightly grip her sweet bottom, giving her a hot massage in response to her touch, before he moved it back to her waist.

The gym was dark and they were dancing in one of the least populated areas, and no one could see them as his hands caressed her body.

Her small hands weren't idle either. Soon, he stifled a groan as they feathered caresses over his chest, swirling patterns against his nipples, mimicking what she'd done last night to him.

He didn't think she was aware of what she was doing, the effect she was having on him. It was becoming increasingly difficult to maintain his composure with her hot hands playing with him, yet he pulled her closer, until there was not a single hair's breadth separating them.

Her hot movements against him were tantalizing and electric. Davis was forced to close his eyes as he expelled a long breath and felt the cum swell in his balls.

"As much as I'm enjoying this, I think we'd better stop. I don't think I can keep going like this. This is agonizing having you so close, feeling your body slide against mine . . . with all these eyes on me, it's torture, Candy" Davis whispered hoarsely into her ear.

He leaned back to look at her face and within moments, the sensual cast on her face was gone.

She pulled away from him as the last strains of the song faded. When the song ended, someone turned on a set of the lights near the stage, and Davis could clearly see Candy's face, illuminated against the dim lighting.

The faraway look of pleasure had been erased when his words penetrated her brain.

Candy had been completely engrossed in the song. The feel of Davis' body pressed so intimately against hers, the hard, thick ridge of his shaft pressed insistently against her stomach had left her aching, instantly wet.

Despite her surroundings, despite the questions she had about him, his wife . . . none of it mattered in that moment. She wanted him so badly she'd do anything to be alone with him so they could carry out what they'd started on the dance floor. But she wasn't about to allow her lust to have her make a complete fool of herself.

Candy glanced up into his harshly sensual face.

"Well, it's a good thing the song is over. Now we can stop this . . . torture . . . without causing speculation," she answered, tightly. "I had better get back to my duties. Thanks for the dance."

With that she moved away from him and with a purposeful saunter in her walk, one she hoped to hell showed confidence and verve, instead of wobbling uncertainty, she walked away.

Candy was stopped by one of the volunteers as she walked away from him, and as she spoke to the parent, she could feel his eyes boring a hole in the back of her head. Unable to resist the lure, she turned her head enough to cast a final glance in his direction.

He stood in the exact spot they danced in; his penetrating gaze intent, unwavering before he turned away from her.

Had he not been the one to turn away, Candy wondered how long she would have stood like that, watching him watching her. She was oblivious to the parent who blithely went on talking and didn't pay the woman much attention; Candy's attention was solely focused on one man.

With a disgusted shake of her head she plastered a smile on her face as she listened to her volunteer's ideas on an upcoming fundraiser for the center.

26

Candy eased down in her chair, placed her head in both hands and rested her aching head on her desk. It had been a long day, and the party had just ended at—she forced herself to raise her body enough to look at the watch on her wrist—midnight.

She'd seen the last of the volunteers out of the door, after most of the kids had left the gym. The few stragglers left were mostly children of the few remaining volunteers, who were helping to put the gym back to rights.

With a groan she laid her head back on the desk. After her one dance with Davis, Candy had managed to avoid him, for the most part, for the rest of the evening.

She'd caught the questioning look on his face, and knew he wondered what was wrong with her, why she was avoiding him.

"He is so clueless, has absolutely no idea what happened between us from last night to this morning," she mumbled out loud. As she spoke, her breath fanned the fine hairs that sprinkled her arm as she rested her head against it.

"Especially after all that hot sex we had," she continued her one-sided dialogue, as usual, to no one in particular in her empty office. "I knew it was too good to be true, that he wanted me for me, and not just a warm body, a substitute for his wife. Damn."

Her wallow in self-pity was cut short when a loud knock on the door forced her to sit up in her chair. "Come in," she called out, tired and not feeling up to speaking to anyone.

She reluctantly stood from her chair, ready to grab her purse and head out for the night. It was probably one of the two off-duty police officers they'd hired for security for the evening.

She felt a tingling start in her toes and run through her body as she gathered her things. The sensation usually meant Davis Strong was within her general vicinity.

She knew, before he opened the door and walked inside, who it was. Once again her body seemed to know whenever Davis was within a ten-foot radius of her.

"Everyone is gone. I assured the officers that I could see you safely out of the center and into your car," Davis said as soon as he opened her door.

Without preamble, he walked inside her office and carefully closed the door behind him, locking it. He caught the surprise in her eyes as soon as she saw him.

"Now ... are you done hiding from me, for the night?" he asked.

As he waited for her reply, his glance slid over her, top to bottom. She had been in the process of standing when he entered, with both hands braced on the desk. With his entrance, she slowly sat back down in her chair, behind her desk, her eyes warily assessing him.

She didn't say a word, yet somehow the whole scene was strangely familiar to Davis as her beautiful, light brown eyes continued to assess him.

He walked further into the room and stopped, several feet

away from her desk, his legs spread apart, arms crossed over his chest and waited for her reply.

"Are you sure you want to know the answer to that, Davis?" she finally answered, leaning back in her seat, her eyes locked with his. Searching for some answer; he had not a clue as to what.

"Just as much as I'd like to know why you went all cold on me this morning. Why the woman I slept with—"

"We hardly slept," she interrupted, her smooth brown cheeks flushing.

As he'd been speaking, he'd walked the small distance he was from her, and stood less than a foot away from her.

"Why the woman I *made love* to, until the early hours of the morning—" he noticed that his clarification only served to heighten the blush she already had going "—was a vastly different woman from the one I faced when I got out of the shower, this morning," he finished.

"I guess I decided I wasn't up for a game of substitute. I've never been one to sit on the bench and be happy when I'm called in for a pinch hit," she retorted, sharply.

"Did I miss something here? When did this become a conversation about baseball?" he asked.

He adjusted his pants when his dick thumped against his zipper after her small breast pushed against her dress when she inhaled deeply. The imprint of her pointy nipples was visible through the soft fabric of the wrap.

It dawned on him why the scene was all so familiar. With small exception, it was eerily familiar to one of the erotic dreams he'd had of Candy, weeks ago.

In the dream, she sat behind her desk, wearing one of her typical fabric wraps, much like she now sat. Just as she had in the dream, her skirt was short, brushing the tops of her thighs.

In his erotic dream, she'd had one leg thrown over the arm of the chair, swinging back and forth. She'd given him peek-a-boo glances of her sweet, naked pussy, as she'd taunted him, wearing no panties beneath her clothes.

Unlike in the dream, however, she was wearing tights and knee-high boots, and both feet were firmly planted on the floor.

He had no idea if she was wearing panties now, but he was damn sure determined to find out.

"Not talking about baseball, Davis. That was a metaphor for the fact that I don't think you're ready for me."

"You don't think so?" he murmured.

Davis didn't give her time to react before he reached over and plucked her up from her chair and plopped her round little ass on top of the desk, ignoring her indignant yelp of protest.

He positioned himself between her thighs, widening them as she leaned back on her elbows and warily observed him. She watched him from beneath lowered lids as he raised her legs, one at a time, and slowly unzipped the knee-high boots she wore and eased them off of her feet.

The thud of the boots hitting the floor was muffled by the sound of her gasp when his long fingers firmly massaged the bottom of one of her covered toes.

"Hmmm," she groaned and half closed her eyes in response, with her foot braced against his chest, the other dangling over the edge of the desk.

Davis had learned last night how responsive she was to his touch on her feet. After several more light massages, which elicited heartfelt groans of pleasure from her, with reluctance, he allowed her foot to drop.

With his eyes trained on hers, he lifted her bottom from the desk. Slowly, he pulled her tights off of her body, past her rounded hips, thighs and knees and off her feet.

"I wondered," he murmured and she felt him brush his fingers back and forth against the curly thatch of hair covering her mound.

"About what?"

"If you were wearing any panties. Just like in my dreams, you aren't," he replied, the satisfaction evident in his voice as he bent his head to take a deep breath.

"And you smell just as good as you did last night . . . just like you always do in my dreams." The look in his lust-filled eyes made her breath catch.

"I'm in your dreams?" she asked, heart thudding in her chest as he continued to toy with her.

"You are," he affirmed. "On a regular basis," he murmured, his voice distracted, his mind obviously elsewhere. "But having the real you beneath me is so much better," he finished huskily.

When his big fingers separated her folds Candy could have sworn her heart stopped beating, before it began to thud loudly, and very audibly.

She swallowed and held her breath in anticipation, wondering what he would do next.

She was rewarded when his talented tongue swiped a hot caress against her folds. She arched her back sharply off the desk. She knew they were all alone, no one was in the center but the two of them, yet she shut her eyes tightly and held on to the sides of her desk, trying to stave off the scream of delight from behind clenched teeth.

He separated her pussy lips and carefully nibbled her creaming folds, licking up her juices as he laved her channel until Candy didn't think she could accept another heated stroke.

When one delicious lick hit a particularly hot spot her upper body jerked, forcing her into a near-sitting position on the desk.

She opened her eyes and gazed down at the sexy image of him between her spread legs, one of her thighs draped over his muscled forearm, the other dangling to the side as he catered to her.

"But no way in hell did my dreams ever prepare me for the real you. Now lay down . . . I'm not done with you yet," he replied, glancing at her with her cream on his face, referring to her question of appearing in his dreams.

She allowed him to gently push her back down so that she lay prone on the desk, once again, as he continued to minister to her silken core.

When he captured her hood and furrowed out her tight, feminine bud and drew it into his mouth, this time the scream of delight she held in check was forced out as he paid homage to her blood-filled, stiff clit.

He licked, stroked, and swirled her clitoris, using teeth, tongue and lips all designed to give her the ultimate pleasure.

Working it and her until she felt ready to die—the pleasure was so intense.

Her moans of delight increased when he separated her lips and eased one, and then a second finger inside the slick, tight opening and pumped them in and out, mimicking the action of his shaft the night before.

As he continued to torment and delight her at the same time, Candy could no longer hold back the orgasm she felt churning.

She clamped her legs against his face, capturing his head between her thighs more securely. Her body jerked as she ground into his face, bucking and crying out as she came long and strong, the orgasm she felt hovering now ripping through her entire body, leaving her weak and limp from the explosive release.

Her body relaxed against the hard desk, completely wrung out from his hot loving. Her legs dangled, limply, over the edge of the desk, as he continued to lave her, until her body had halfway calmed and some of the tremors had left.

The only sound in the room was her dying cries of release. Candy slowly opened her eyes and stared down at Davis.

He stood from his crouched position between her thighs and in the semi-darkness of her office she was able to see the evidence of his oral loving on his face as he unfastened his jeans.

Davis didn't give her time to recuperate before he pulled her further down the desk, until her ass cheeks were on the very edge. He kept his eyes on hers, and the tingling sensations returned. Candy stared helplessly at his perfect cock, as it jutted free from beneath the confines of his fly.

She swallowed the constriction in a throat grown dry and watched him grab his penis by the base and deliver a short smooth stroke, from the base, to the bulbous, pre-cum-dripping end.

He continued to hold her helpless gaze as he reached over with his free hand, and obtained one of the condoms in the small bowl. He ripped the package open with his teeth, sheathed himself in one fluid motion, lifted her legs and spread them wide and stepped in between them.

"Tell me . . . what do you want from me, Candy?" he asked, his dick in his hand, hovering at the mouth of her dripping entry. His other hand rested on her rounded hip, with its fingers digging lightly into the smooth flesh.

She had no idea what he wanted her to say. She couldn't even think straight for staring at his thick, cum-filled dick straining to get at her.

Candy's gaze reluctantly left the tempting visual to stare helplessly into his hot, lust-filled grey eyes, which had darkened with his arousal.

She wanted to scream at him and beg to be filled with all ten inches plus of that beautiful straining beast and not ask her a darn thing that might actually require thinking beyond the here and now.

"Davis, I want you. You know that."

"But what do you want from me?" he insisted and Candy felt her nose scrunch in confusion and her brow lower as she wondered what magic word he wanted her to say.

"I want you to love me ... fuck me, Davis. I want you to fuck me," she stated boldly, quickly correcting her statement. Candy simply wanted him to ride her, hard, and give her what she needed, what they both needed.

He eased a bit of the bulbous tip into her opening and her juicy pussy eagerly latched on greedily, wantonly striving to be reacquainted with his thick, hard-pounding, dick.

She groaned and licked her lips. What did he want from her?

27

Davis stared down at the hot visual she presented and knew that if he wasn't careful, he'd embarrass the hell out of himself and spill his seed before he had a chance to get in her good.

Shit.

She'd smelled and tasted so fucking good as he ate and licked her out that he'd damn near come from the experience. He'd been forced to clamp the end of his penis with his fingers to prevent himself from coming, just as he had last night when he'd first sampled from her juicy, streaming sex.

There wasn't one damn thing about her he didn't find attractive, appealing . . . addictive.

"What happened to the woman I made love to last night? And why don't you think I'm ready for you?" he both asked and demanded as he pulled her to the edge of the desk, until her rounded bottom was halfway off. In one move, he stroked into her, deep, as far as he could.

"Listen—" she started to speak. Her words came to a grinding and immediate halt as she screamed when he impaled her on his rock-hard dick.

"Oh God, Davis," she whimpered, the unexpectedness of

his plunge forcing her to clutch the sides of the desk. Davis felt her pussy walls quivering, desperately clenching his cock, almost sending him over the edge, without him having to lay one stroke in her.

"Damn! Don't move, please. Just . . . don't . . . move. I need you to be still for a minute," he said harshly and pulled her squirming body closer to his, flush with his groin, forcing her body to still.

He gripped her hips tightly with one hand, and the other, he shoved up her shirt, fumbled until he unhooked the front closure of her bra and squeezed one breast as it spilled into his warm palm.

"Davis, please. I need to move, I need you to move," she whimpered and Davis's heart beat loudly as he stared into her upturned, beautiful face. There was a fine sheen of sweat covering her brow and her breaths were coming in short, hot gasps.

"I'll move, eventually. Right now, I need for you to be still," he demanded, readjusting her, fitting her comfortably on his shaft.

He then pushed her further back on her desk, spread her legs in a wide V, and shoved her knees up, until her feet were planted firmly on the desk.

He closed his eyes.

He didn't want to come before he'd stroked her, and incredibly, he felt the cum as it swelled his balls. He knew that if he stared down at her lying splayed out in front of him, legs wide open, skirt hiked up her legs, pussy hairs glistening . . . it would be over before either of them wanted.

And so he moved . . .

. . . and when he moved, his dick kissing the back of her womb, Candy reveled in the delicious feeling of being stuffed.

His strokes began slow and methodical, as he stretched her, preparing her for his full girth. As he stroked into her heat, jostling her body as his thrusts grew stronger, Candy desperately clutched at her desk, scattering papers and documents everywhere in her need to grab hold of something . . . anything . . . to steady herself for the ride.

His hold on her hips was steady, the expression on his handsome face intense, as he rocked into her. Candy gritted her teeth to keep from crying out from the exquisite feel of his penis as it slid in and out of her, tight against the lips of her sex. At the angle he had her, the top of his penis, close to his groin, was able to tap a steady rhythm against her clit.

When he increased the tempo and depth of stroke, Candy cried out, "Yes, Davis . . . yes! Please, keep it right there, ummm," she screamed when he moved one hand from her hip and pressed down against her pelvic bone, the pressure forcing her G-spot into direct contact with his cock.

"Yessssss!" she cried. Her head moved back and forth on the desk, in a mindless state of sensual heat as he continued to drive into her.

"I love how you feel wrapped around me, so wet, so hot . . . ummm," he groaned, "and tight. Damn, you're tight! This pussy was meant for me, only me! I can't get enough of it, I can't get close enough, baby, damn!" he ground out. "I need to come!"

"Yes, Davis, please," she panted.

His hot words, the way he was working her over, digging into her, loving her so perfectly, Candy felt the tingling sensation of an orgasm unfurl in her belly.

Davis reached a hand between them, spread the throbbing lips of her vagina and using her own lubricant, spread it over and along the seam of her vagina, hood, and clitoris in small tight massages.

The intimate massage, coupled with his hot strokes, sent her over the edge.

The moment he felt her walls begin to milk him, relentless as she climaxed, Davis dropped his hands from playing with her pussy and lifted her cheeks completely off the desk and pumped into her, hips moving like a piston.

As his gaze settled on hers, the mindless way she was moving her head back and forth, seemingly in agony forced his orgasm to release and he grunted harshly when he felt the cum eject from his balls and fill the condom.

As he emptied his seed into the condom, he felt resentful, for the first time, of the need to use the protection. He wanted to feel skin on skin, no barriers, and God help him if he didn't want the satisfaction of emptying his cum deep inside her warm wet snatch.

After they came, for long moments, they were both quiet, both of their breaths ragged as they inhaled deep breaths of air. Davis felt masculine satisfaction when she hissed, with the accompanying satisfying wet, suction sound when he reluctantly pulled out of her.

"I'm ready for you, make no mistake, Candy," he picked up the thread of their conversation, as though they'd just ended it.

Candy leaned up on both elbows, and eased her shaky legs down, allowing them to dangle over the edge of the desk.

"Are you sure you're ready for me?" he asked as he tucked his penis back inside his boxers and buttoned his jeans. "If you are, come home with me, tonight. And we can finish what we started here." The look he leveled her way was so hot, she wasn't sure if she could handle much more.

"That is, if you're not afraid. Are you Candy? Afraid?" he asked.

She may feel trepidation, but Candy had never backed down from a challenge, especially one that was guaranteed to bring the type of satisfaction she knew she'd get at the end of this one.

"Davis, my daddy taught me one thing. Fear is a totally useless emotion. I'm ready."

28

―――――――

"Just a minute, I'm coming, Davis!" Milly mumbled as she grabbed her cane and quickly walked to her front door.

She glanced at her watch as she did so.

Didn't that man have a life? It was almost midnight, Angelica was in bed and she was in her ugliest pajamas, face scrubbed clean of makeup, watching the late, late, late show.

She laughed at herself.

Who was she making fun of? She was alone, watching the late, late, late show and if her niece wasn't upstairs, she'd still be at home, alone, watching the late, late, late show.

"I thought you would be with Candy, what are you doing here at this time of—" she began as she opened the door, the end of her sentence dangling into nothingness as she peered up into the eyes of a man that was not Davis.

Definitely not her brother.

There wasn't anything brotherly about the way she felt about *this* man. She shivered and forced herself not to step back from his overwhelming presence.

"Woman, what the hell is wrong with you, opening the door without asking who it is? People get killed that way!"

"The only lunatics running around this time of night are the domesticated garden variety types. I think I'm pretty safe," she said, unable to resist pulling the tail of the tiger.

The owner of that tail stalked further into the room and closed the door behind him, locking it in place. He turned back to face her, and Milly shivered from the look crossing his handsome chocolate brown face.

"Safe huh?" he asked and grinned. It wasn't a very nice grin Milly thought, with nervousness settling in her belly. It was the type of grin a predator, much like the tiger she likened him to, gave his next meal.

The thought of this big fine man devouring her did more than send nervous jitters racing along her spine. Instead of it frightening her, it caused that part of her that had been dormant so long to flare to life.

He began to walk toward her, stalking her as she backed up. She stopped when her bottom hit the back of the sofa and swallowed hard as she gazed up into his deep brown eyes.

He brought a hand up and she refused to flinch. Lightly he ran rough, caressing fingers down her skin and she halfway closed her eyes before she could stop herself.

"Is there a good reason you're here at—" she glanced at the clock mounted on her wall and finished, "one o'clock in the morning?" and raised her eyebrow at him.

"Angel sleeping?" he asked.

"Yes."

"Good. This is why I'm here at one o'clock in the morning." With no further words his large hands grasped her by the tops of her shoulders and hauled her close, bringing their lips and bodies together. The look in his dark eyes made her heart pound in her chest before she allowed her eyes to slowly drift close as his dark head descended toward hers.

With a groan she willingly went into her lover's arms.

* * *

"I think the water is warm enough."

Candy stuck a hand in the running water, testing it to make sure it was the right temperature. "Just right," she said, glancing at Davis as he stood against the wall of his bathroom, arms folded across his chest, his light eyes steady on hers.

"It'll be just right, when you join me," he said, matter-of-factly, as he casually began to disrobe, his hot gaze steady on her.

Candy shivered from the look in his eyes, despite the warmth that emitted from the hot water steaming the bathroom. The water, along with the candles he'd lit, bathed the room in a warm, sensual, amber glow.

Candy moistened her lips with her tongue and allowed her gaze to roam over Davis as he undressed. He boldly stood naked before her after removing his jeans and shirt.

His thick penis was semi-erect as it jutted free from the dark thatch of smooth hair covering his groin. His balls hung low enough so she could see them dangle behind his cock, looking like two juicy plums, ripe and ready.

The ride home had been hushed, mostly filled with an occasional murmured comment, or an occasional glance, one to another. But the sexual tension she felt in the dark, intimate confines of his SUV had filled her with hot anticipation for what he was thinking, what he had in store for her.

What he wanted to do to her.

They'd only made one stop, at her house, for a change of clothes, and had then driven back to his home.

He'd offered her something to drink and eat, but she'd said no. She'd turned from admiring a painting to find his gaze almost moodily watching her and she'd shivered. He had taken her in his arms and walked up his staircase with her into his bedroom. She'd been surprised when he walked through the room and entered the large, adjoining bathroom before he'd set her on his feet.

She'd turned questioning eyes on him and he'd told her he wanted her to prepare a bath for him. Nervous and unsure of what he wanted, she'd done his bidding. He'd walked out of the room, quickly returning with several candles and lighting them, placing them alongside the Jacuzzi-style tub.

Now as he stood naked in front of her, his hand stretched out, palm up, for her to accept his. She nodded her head in agreement, and stood. She walked up to him and halted, less than a foot from his body.

"Okay," she answered in a hoarse voice. She cleared her throat. "Let me undress."

"No, let me undress you."

She bit down on her full bottom lip, and worried it between her teeth and hesitated.

Davis reached a hand out to stroke down her soft cheek. "Please," he added when she looked as though she wanted to bolt.

When she nodded her head in agreement, and allowed him to pull her shirt up and out of her wrap, Davis' excitement grew.

"Lift your arms," he instructed, his voice low, throaty. His excitement escalated as she readily obeyed him, raising her arms to allow him to pull it over her head.

After he hooked his fingers inside her bra, his thumbs caressing the soft cushiony underside of her sexy breasts, he cupped one warm mound in his hand, and thumbed the tightly drawn, beaded nipple.

"Hmmm," she murmured.

Davis leaned down and captured the dark wine-colored nubbin in his mouth for a quick, slick caress before reluctantly releasing it.

As he undressed her, it was one of the most erotic things

he'd ever done with a woman, the feeling of taking care of her, of her willingly standing before him, allowing him to take her clothes off, to prepare her.

He had become quite adept at untying her wraps, and within seconds he had removed the short skirt from her body, leaving her semi-nude.

After they'd made love in her office, she hadn't bothered to put her tights she'd been wearing back on, and now she stood wearing nothing but a hesitant smile and a tiny scrap of panties that barely covered her mound, and a lacy half-bra dangling off her shoulders.

After he removed the bra and tossed it to the side, Davis' gaze settled on the thatch of hair at the apex of her round thighs, barely contained by the silky lace.

She presented an intoxicating vision of lush womanhood, with her rounded curves and smooth, creamy brown skin.

His eyes moved over her body, past the small indentation of her belly, with the gem sparkling from the center, to her breasts with their beaded stiff nipples, standing at attention, beckoning his mouth to lay claim to them, again.

His arousal grew just from looking at her, as the soft amber glow from the burning candles silhouetted her sweet body enticingly.

With a hesitant, almost shy look in her doe-shaped eyes, she watched him as he assessed her. When he reached out and pulled her against him, she came, willingly, into his arms.

"You're so beautiful, Candy," he said and lifted her high.

He carried her the short distance to the tub, and carefully stepped inside and sat down, settling her against his body.

Once he'd settled her in front of his body, Davis picked up the face towel that lay over the small shelf near the tub and lathered it. The soap looked almost too pretty to use, a mottled brown color, with flecks of what looked like almonds embedded inside. Angelica had given it to him, telling him she'd learned to make it in a class Candy had given the girls at the center.

"This smells good enough to eat," he murmured, taking a whiff of the unique soap and Candy laughed, lightly.

"That's one of my bars, isn't it?"

"Yes, Angel brought it home."

"I make soaps and taught the girls how. Although I use oatmeal and almonds in the ingredients, I don't think it would be all that appetizing," she laughed lightly.

"Hmmm, it smells good. Everything about you is different, unique. Even your soap is different," he said as he began to lather the towel.

"Does that bother you?" she asked, squirming a bit as he lathered her breasts.

His towel-covered hands squeezed and massaged her, paying careful attention to her areolae and nipples. When he finished, her nipples were stiff, sensitive and erect from his nearly painful ministrations.

"Does what bother me? That you're different?"

"Yes. You've mentioned it a couple of times," she replied.

He dipped the towel in the tub and rinsed off the soap before he squeezed the warm water over her breasts and tummy, washing away the light coating of bubbles.

Davis opened his mouth to give an automatic rejection of her question, before he closed it and thought about her it.

"At first, Candy, it did bother me, that you seemed so oblivious to conventionality. You didn't seem to care one way or the other about what anyone, me included, thought of you," he said, carefully weighing his words.

"Hmmm," was her one-word response and he could tell by the slight stiffening of her back that he had offended her. But he had to be honest.

Their relationship over the last few weeks had evolved to the point that for him to be anything less than honest and forth-coming would seem unnatural.

He sighed, deeply, and re-lathered the towel before running the sudsy cloth down her belly, over the swell of one hip, beneath the water, before landing at the apex of her thighs.

"I don't feel that way anymore, Candy. I think for a long time, I wanted to ignore this . . . attraction . . . between us. It was easy for me to maintain my guard around you, if I pretended I disliked your personality, your natural carefree way. But I have always known there was more depth to you. You're a free spirit, make no mistake," he laughed, "but you're an intelligent professional woman, who not only enjoys what she does, but you're damn good at it. Everyone can see how you've changed the center's direction. Added programs, tirelessly working with the board," he complimented her, "and the girls all love you, including Angelica. And that says more than anything, how much the girls you mentor love and appreciate you," he finished.

As he spoke, he'd kept a light pressure on her mons, lathering, separating the lips of her vagina, and thoroughly cleansing her. Candy was torn between being highly aroused, to blushing pride at the wealth of compliments he'd showered upon her, all so matter-of-factly.

She knew her approach to working with the young girls at the center had been different than the previous director's. She knew many—like Davis—viewed her as younger than her actual years and without enough experience to run the center.

To hear him tell her how much he admired her, complimenting her as well as sharing his reasons for hiding his feelings for her, allowed the burden of doubts she secretly carried to ease away.

Candy relaxed, against his chest while the fragrant bubbles caressed her breasts. She groaned in delight when she felt his hand sink into her scalp and his strong fingers began to massage.

He deftly loosened the thick, long braid, and within moments he had her hair loose. Her kinky curls felt free, cushioned against his chest and falling down to her shoulders.

"That feels good," she murmured.

She moved her head to the side and when his strong fingers massaged a spot near the base of her scalp Candy groaned in pleasure.

"You like that?" he murmured hotly, against the side of her neck, his hands reaching around her in order to cup her breasts.

"Yes, I do. A lot," she breathed the words.

"Maybe you'll enjoy this even more, Candy."

He lifted her legs at the bend of her knees and placed each one on either side of his legs. They were spread in a deep V and the angle left her wide open and vulnerable.

He then lifted her by the waist and eased her down over his erection. She cried out at the sudden invasion. "Davis!" she shrieked as he adjusted her on his shaft.

He knew she could take all of him in this way, yet he paused, slowly easing her down until she was seated firmly on him, embedded as deep as he could go, nestling her ass against his stomach.

He groaned, harshly, as he felt his naked dick throb a happy welcome inside her slick walls.

Damn, she felt good. Hot and wet.

He wasn't wearing a condom and knew he shouldn't make love to her no matter how good her pussy felt wrapped around him.

"Oh God, this feels good, Davis, but we shouldn't—" she paused, and expelled a short, hot breath, before finishing her sentence. "—damn . . . we shouldn't be doing it like this," she continued on a hissing pant of pleasure. "I'm on the pill, but still . . ."

His lips curled into a tight grin of satisfaction when she keened after he delivered one short thrust into her creaming snatch.

"I know, baby. Don't worry, I'll take care of you. I won't come inside of you. I'll be responsible, no matter what happens. Just . . . damn . . . Candy, don't make me pull out now. Trust me, I'll take care of you," he repeated the words, harshly.

"Okay . . . I trust you," she cried out, and with those words Davis felt his heart squeeze and pound in an erratic pattern. He gripped her hip tightly with one hand, and the other reached around her small waist. He used his fingers to spread her slick lips, found the apex of her sex, and began to manipulate her clit as he dragged his cock in and out of her tight pussy.

29

Candy felt stuffed as she sat astride him, her legs thrown over his, hands braced alongside the rim of the tub as well. When she felt him move away she glanced over her shoulder and saw that he had eased his upper body back against the tub.

She began to ride his cock and he allowed her to set the pace, his hooded eyes concentrated on her ass. She rose up and down his length and he kept her body steady as he pumped inside her.

He moved one hand from its steadying position on her waist and buried his fingers in her dark, tight curls, manipulating her clit as she bounced on his dick, increasing her pleasure.

Candy turned back around, facing forward and closed her eyes. She inhaled a long shaky breath.

His hard, massively engorged penis eased between the cream-slick, plump lips of her vagina in smooth, easy glides.

She felt nothing but pure pleasure when he hit her clit, G-spot and every nerve ending *just* right pumping into her, jostling her body.

She opened her eyes and glanced down and the sexy picture of his hand buried in her dark, tight curls. The image provided a sensual visual that heralded the beginnings of an orgasm.

"This is real, so good, Candy. This is what lovemaking—" he paused and grunted, delivering several tight strokes to her streaming sex—"is supposed to feel like."

The tub was perfectly sized so they were able to comfortably share the space as he fucked her.

"Yessss," she hissed in agreement.

Forming a coherent thought and having the ability to actually speak amazed her as the sensuality, the sheer passion of the moment, overwhelmed her senses.

She clenched the edge of the tub tightly, her breath coming out in gasps. She rolled her bottom against him, writhing on his cock, and ground her body against his. Thrusting, bucking, they both strived for the ultimate release.

It didn't take long.

"This is mine," he grunted and thrust heavily into her desperately clenching sex. "Say it. Say it's mine . . . you're mine," he demanded and Candy groaned, nodding her head in assent.

"Hell no, Candy. That's not good enough. I want to hear you say it. Tell me it, and you, belong to me."

"God, yes, Davis, Yes! Ummm, baby I'm yours, I'm all yours!" she moaned and cried.

"Good," he replied, his voice harsh.

He pushed away from his reclining position against the back of the tub to sit upright and pumped tight strokes into her drenched cunt.

"By the time I'm through with you, your pretty pussy is going to be molded for me, and me only. You're mine. Now come for me, baby. Come for me!" he demanded.

Candy screamed and came, grinding her body on his, moving and bouncing her ass against him as the orgasm overtook her, leaving her spent and depleted when it was over.

Davis lifted her body off his still-erect cock, and Candy thought he was done with her.

He wasn't.

He eased his erect penis out of her milking walls. He re-arranged her body and spread her ass cheeks before he poised the broad head of his penis against her tightly puckered anus.

Candy's breath hitched in her throat. Damn . . . did he want to . . .

"May I?" he asked in an almost formal tone, so much so that Candy felt a desire to laugh.

"Do you trust me . . . do you want this?" he asked huskily.

"Yes," she answered both questions in a low voice.

Her sex tightened in anticipation as he shifted her body. He adjusted her backside to his liking and rubbed his cock against her opening, moving her into a semi-kneeling position in front of him.

All desires to chuckle came to an immediate halt when he slipped one hand around her hipbone, and stroked the small bud hidden inside her tight, moist vaginal lips, and the other lifted her ass out of the water.

He placed two fingers deeply inside her vagina and scooped out her cream, lubricating his hand with her juices.

He uttered a sound of satisfaction deep in his throat and quickly spread the cream over her anus, preparing her for his invasion.

His thick penis probed at her opening, not moving forward, just playing with her, while at the same time his fingers spread the lips of her vagina, continuing to stroke her clit in short, tight circles.

Davis raised himself to his knees, aligned his dick with her opening, and pushed her against the side of the tub. Her small breasts lay sweetly on top of the rim of the tub, her ass tilted up and inviting. He groaned from the visual alone.

He leaned in closer to her, moved her damp hair aside and laid a small kiss on the side of her neck. She looked so damn beautiful, so hot and willing, ready for anything.

He tested her entry, wanting her creamy and ready for him. He knew that she'd just orgasmed and her sphincter would be relaxed. It would be easier for her to accept him, but he didn't want to hurt her.

He gently pushed one lubed finger inside the puckered rosette and when she only moaned softly, and arched her back against the pressure, he pressed one more inside. He stopped when she cried out.

"Wait—" she whimpered, head hung low as she accepted him.

"Are you okay?" he whispered against her ear. He hadn't come yet, his dick was on fire, yet he would wait until she was ready.

"Yes—okay, I'm okay," she panted, her tone low.

With her assent, he pressed a third finger inside.

Again, she groaned harshly, but from the tone, he knew it wasn't from pain.

Davis proceeded to rotate his fingers inside of her ass, easing the tightness of her opening, his dick rock hard and throbbing as he thought of how tight she'd feel wrapped around it.

Once she was sufficiently loosened, he eased his fingers out, and laid a kiss against the back of her neck.

"Baby, you're tight, this may be a little uncomfortable at first, but stay with me, okay?" he whispered gutturally and clenched his teeth tight, when she whimpered.

He fed her his dick carefully, slipping the bulbous head inside, but not going any further when he felt her tight ring squeeze hard against his invasion.

He hoped the pain-pleasure would only last a short time, before it was all pleasure. But she needed to be completely relaxed for that to happen.

"But, it's going to be good, Candy, so damn good," he promised before he eased more of himself inside, one hand kept steady, manipulating her sex, the other braced against her hip bone.

Although he felt the tight inner muscles of her ass relax around him with each incremental inch he gave of his dick, she was so damn tight, gripping him so mercilessly, he knew he wouldn't last long.

He kept their bodies close and slowly ground into her. His dick swelling to massive proportions, he felt her stretch and accommodate his length and girth.

She moaned and keened, crying out desperately and Davis slowly, carefully worked her ass.

He was relentless. He held nothing back as he fucked her. She screamed while he rode her, body shaking, arms quivering yet accepting his tight hard thrusts. But he didn't stop.

He held onto her tightly and felt every shiver, every moan, her body naturally resisting his invasion as she bucked back against him . . . and when her pussy creamed all over his hand, and she cried out sharply in ecstasy, he knew she was no longer feeling any pain, it was all pleasure.

"Just feel, Candy and let it go," he whispered and groaned huskily as he pumped into her, joining her in her moans of pleasure as he rode her ass.

Candy felt helplessly and sensually trapped beneath Davis' big body. And she didn't give a hot damn, it felt so incredibly good, what he was doing to her.

She'd tried sex this way only once and the experience had been anything but enjoyable, and she'd never been the type of woman to suffer in silence.

She'd promptly bucked the man off of her and despite his angry response she'd *refused* to allow his non-caring, rutting ass on her ever again.

Once had damn well been enough.

What Davis was making her feel was nothing like that one-time, horrid experience. He took care to make sure she was ready for him.

Although it had hurt like hell as he stretched her, the pain had eased and she'd felt herself cream as he rotated his fingers inside her, easing the initial burning.

But when he'd began to feed her his rock hard dick . . . damn.

The burning returned ten-fold and she'd tried her damnedest to get away from him. The pain forced her eyes to tear momentarily as she gripped the rim of the tub, her body on fire and shaking.

But quickly the burning receded and was replaced with hot, scorching pleasure. Her cry of pain turned into a purr of satisfaction as he *worked* her, fucking her so good she nearly fainted. The pleasure was so indescribable, so intense.

And damn if it wasn't the best "working" she'd ever had.

He moved inside of her, gently, not pumping into her hard, only gliding his greased cock in and out smoothly with one hand buried inside her pussy.

Candy felt as though he touched all of the nerve endings in her body simultaneously, making them strum all at once. He played with both ends of her, stroking inside her ass with his cock as his fingers toyed with her pussy.

"Come for me, baby," he whispered the demand against her ear, leaning closer. He bit the lower lobe of her ear, before suckling the small injury, and she shivered.

He'd told her she was his, demanded that she acknowledge his possession earlier, and without a doubt, Candy knew she did indeed belong to him. She gladly accepted his demand that she come.

Davis continued to stroke, pumping into her with short plunges, his grunts animal-like, before he released a primal shout, yet he didn't come.

"Davis," she cried out, her hands reaching blindly behind her to clutch at him, arching her body away from his. She felt the orgasm creep up on her, engulfing her. Her body shook with the power of her climax.

Candy came for so long, she felt as though she blacked out, momentarily, and when she came back to awareness, it was to feel Davis steadily pumping inside of her, until he too, came.

When Candy felt Davis release, his cum jetting from his body, she experienced a second orgasm along with him.

When she felt the heat of his seed erupt inside of her ass, her cries joined his in the purity of the moment of mutual release. Her vision blurred and she felt completely numb, the moment of pleasure was so intense.

The hiss of the dying candle, along with her long sigh of pleasure as he eased himself out of her, were the only sounds in the bathroom for long moments, until Davis spoke.

"You're mine," he said with such finality in his tone that, completely spent, Candy could only nod her head weakly, in affirmation.

30

He carefully removed her from his body and, after he stepped from the tub, he pulled her into his arms. Davis grabbed the fluffy white towel she'd laid out for him and after giving himself a cursory wipe down, folded her in the towel as he strode from the bathroom and walked into the bedroom.

Weak, Candy slumped down, limp as a dishrag against him as he carried her to her bed. After turning down the bedding, Davis laid her down.

He covered their bodies with the sheet after he lay down behind her. There was contented silence between them for long moments, until Candy cleared her throat.

"Davis, I know you said your wife wasn't forthcoming about Angelica's paternity," Candy began, and he interrupted her.

"You mean she lied? Yes, what of it?"

Although she was uncomfortable with out and out asking him about his relationship, she knew that for Angelica's sake, Davis needed to confront his feelings about what had happened, once and for all, if not for his own healing, then for his daughter's.

She forged ahead, despite the forbidding tone of his voice.

"Obviously, Gail knew she was pregnant before she came back home," she hazarded a guess and when she felt him murmur an assent, nodding his head, with a short motion, she continued.

"After you found out Angelica wasn't yours, what happened?"

"She knew all along that Angelica wasn't mine," he began and Candy nodded her head to encourage him to continue.

"After Angelica was born, she told me she hadn't been sure when she told me she was pregnant if the baby was mine, or a college boyfriend's. I believed her, and although it was hard as hell in the beginning, I forgave her and we started to raise Angelica together, as though she were mine. I didn't want to turn my back on them. They didn't have anyone else besides her grandmother, who was elderly."

"Her grandmother raised Gail, didn't she?"

"Yes. I didn't learn until later that she'd gone to her grandmother and told her she was pregnant . . . two weeks before she returned home from summer break," he said and allowed his words to penetrate. When they did, Candy felt the color leave her face.

"She knew," Candy whispered into the dead silence.

He gave a short, humorless laugh. "She knew. I overheard her having an argument with her grandmother, when Angel was two years old. In short, the man who'd fathered Angelica was nowhere to be found and wanted nothing to do with Gail, or the baby. It had all been a lie. She planned it as soon as he told her he hadn't wanted to be with her."

"Oh God, that's awful. Why did you stay? Most men would have packed up and left," she shook her head in amazement. "What you did was beyond honorable. That you stayed with her, after hearing a second lie which was so much worse than the first."

"It wasn't for any noble reasons, I assure you. Although I'd grown attached to Angelica, she was my child at that point, DNA didn't have a damn thing to do with it. I wanted nothing to do with her mother. In my eyes, she was nothing more than a manipulative bitch, always playing a role with me, so genteel and conservative, butter wouldn't melt in her mouth she was so pure . . . and I fell for her act, hook, line and sinker and felt all types of fools for having done so."

Candy was silent and allowed him to speak, the anger so palpable she felt it reverberate from his body to hers. She wasn't surprised when he rose from his position behind her and sat on the edge of the bed.

"She begged me to stay, if not for her, then for Angelica. She said she was sick. I didn't believe her, I cursed her out and called her all kinds of liars, and told her I didn't want her or her kid and left. Well, this time she wasn't lying. A few weeks later, her friend Anita Watson—"

"Angelica's school principal?" Candy asked.

"Yes. They'd been friends, if you can call it that, for years. At any rate she called and told me, weeks after I'd left, that Gail was in the hospital, that she had a malignant tumor and the doctors didn't know how long she had."

"Davis. Oh baby, I'm so sorry," Candy felt saddened over the cruel twist of fate. "What did you do?"

He inhaled deeply. Candy didn't think he was going to answer. Eventually he turned to face her, and in his face she saw anger, disappointment and overwhelming sadness, all swirling together in a kaleidoscope of jumbled emotions.

He swallowed, and hung his head. "I walked into the hospital room and felt trapped."

"Trapped?"

"I had no plans to return to her or Angelica. Angelica wasn't mine, I had no ties with her . . . I was a free man."

"So why did you feel trapped?"

Candy's heart, if possible, expanded even more, as his words sunk in. Whether he knew it or not, even before he'd come back, before he decided to reunite with Gail, he'd already accepted Angelica as his child, already loved her as his own.

"Hell, I guess why any man would feel trapped. I knew I couldn't walk away from her, or Angelica. They needed me. That's all there was to it. I couldn't desert them. I'd feel like the biggest son-of-a-bitch on the planet earth, if I did."

There was a pregnant pause as Candy digested all that he had shared with her.

"Davis, have you ever thought that it would be a good idea to share this with Angel?" she asked, glancing over her shoulder at him.

Candy watched as his once-content, sated expression changed, as his face tightened. The familiar guarded look returned and she wanted to scream out of sheer frustration.

"Look, I told you before, Candy, I don't want to talk about that, not only to Angel, but consider the damn subject closed for you as well." His anger and frustration were palpable.

He pulled away from Candy and sat up in bed. He threw his long legs over the side of the bed and reached down, grabbing the T-shirt he'd hastily discarded in order to disrobe.

After he pulled the shirt over his head, without a word he stood and walked bare-assed over to the pile of clothes lying in the middle of the floor. He unearthed his shorts and yanked them up his long legs before he turned back to face Candy.

The set look on his handsome face was so unapproachable Candy felt tears sting the back of her eyes.

As close as they'd gotten over the last month, as much progress as she'd thought they'd made with Angelica as well as each other, he still refused to allow her in, that last inch.

He was damn near obstinate in his tenacious hold on the past. It became clear to Candy, in that moment, as he stared at her, his expression tight and closed off, that Davis would never let go of the guilt he still carried like a heavy blanket.

He couldn't deal with the guilt associated with Gail, the events surrounding Angel's conception, or own up to the feelings of betrayal his dead wife's duplicitous behavior had on his affection for Angel.

Candy understood that to do so would open up a flood of emotions, feelings and consequences that Davis wasn't nearly ready to embrace.

But she felt she had to help him try.

She wanted so badly to help him understand all Angelica needed was for him to open up with her about her mother.

He didn't have to disclose the more intimate things, but Angelica deserved to have Davis talk about her mother, to tell her things no one else would or could tell her, good things and not-good things Angelica was hearing through nasty gossip.

"I mean, on the one hand you pretend as though everything was good between you and her mother; you set her up as a woman who was nearly perfect. Yet on the other, you refuse to talk about her. And she hears awful things from her friends, things that have been blown up out of all proportion about her mother, and when she asks you about it, you refuse to talk to her about it, Davis! It's one of the main reasons she's having problems lately, Davis."

"So now you're like the rest of them?" he questioned, his face stormy.

"What rest? What are you talking about?"

"Like that damn Anita Watson, or hell, even Gail's own grandmother for that matter." He angrily turned away and stalked over to the large bay window and stared out into the darkened night.

Candy threw her legs over the side of the bed and walked to the bathroom and found her discarded T-shirt. She shoved her arms through the sleeves, and without bothering to try and find her panties, she wrapped her fabric around her body, quickly clothing herself.

She felt vulnerable and exposed at the moment with him dressed and angry at her—and at himself.

"Hell, her own grandmother was quick to be negative, was the first one to say I had no business raising Angel when Gail died, but she damn sure didn't want to have anything to do with raising her, so I raised her as my own, *on my own*. I may have had a real hard time coming to terms with what happened between her mother and I, but I never deserted her."

Candy walked up behind him and placed a hand on his back, and was so startled when he spun around, his face red with anger. She took an involuntary step back.

"Davis, I know you're angry, I know that you're frustrated with a lot of things going on with Angel. I'm on your side; please don't make this into something it's not. Sometimes a child needs to know where she comes from, in order to understand where she's going. That's all I'm saying, baby. It's not your job to screen what she should or shouldn't know about her mother. It was her mother. It's her right to know."

She tried to lay a soothing hand on his chest but he pushed her away and Candy refrained, barely, from flinching.

"You have to trust she'll be okay, Davis. The knowledge of who her mother was, that she wasn't this perfect woman you've created in your mind, this vision of what the perfect mother is, won't make her think less of her. She'll be fine. She'll be more than fine. She won't feel there's this constant image of perfection she has to live up to. Some unattainable perfect person who she'll constantly let down."

Candy released a deep breath and tried to stem the flow of tears running unchecked down her face as she spoke. "Angel deserves not to have to constantly try and live up to perfection," she insisted. "No one is perfect."

"So I should raise her like your father did, Candy? Tell her that her mother didn't give a damn about anyone but herself? Should I tell her everything she did, she did with calculation, that she manipulated everyone and anyone?" he asked, shrugging her hand away from his arm.

His voice was filled with such cold disdain that Candy felt the effect as though he'd opened up a window and allowed the cool air from outside the frosted window to come inside.

She crossed her arms over her breasts in defense.

"You're a fine one to talk about the mores of parents. You, whose parents didn't even bother with the normalcy of marriage," he laughed harshly. "How loving and caring mothers are, how misunderstood. Yours was such a shining example. She didn't stick around to give you any guidance at all. But unlike Gail, she didn't have the convenience of death as a reason not to. And look how great you turned out without the guidance of a mother. Half the time you're thumbing your nose up at convention, the other half you're trying to prove you're just as good as everyone else. That you're no longer the little homeless girl everyone made fun of, and no one wanted around. Well I'm sorry but I don't want that for Angel."

The retaliation was swift and brutal, and the minute the words flew out of his mouth, the minute he'd ended his tirade, they both stared at each other in shock. Both were stunned at his words.

"Go straight to hell, Davis," she forced the words out without allowing a quiver to enter her voice. His words caught her unawares and struck hard like a tight-fisted punch.

Candy took an involuntary step back, her hand went to her chest, settling over her heart as though she'd felt the blow directly there. But she was proud of the steady way she held his eyes, the total lack of emotion she allowed to enter her voice.

"Damn, baby, I didn't mean that the way it sounded . . . I had no right—" he began, advancing toward her, a hand held out in conciliation.

Candy continued to walk backward; the only emotion that showed was her nostrils flaring, jaw clenched tight as the impact of his words hit her.

"No, you meant what the hell you said. People only say in anger what was brewing in their hearts all along. Just like children, who haven't learned to control their words, in anger we say what we mean," she replied, her voice low, controlled, as she was teleported back in time to the little girl, the little homeless girl who was taunted and laughed at by others.

Just as he began to walk toward her, hand out in conciliatory apology, Candy heard a sound outside the partially closed bedroom door.

She and Davis both turned at the sound and heard the distinct sound of crying and raced toward the door. Davis reached it first, and flung the door open wide and there, standing in the shadowed hallway, was Angelica, tears streaming down her stricken face.

31

_____

"How much did you hear, Angelica?" Davis asked and reached out to take his daughter in his arms.

She wrenched her body away, backing away from him. "I heard enough, Daddy," she whispered and Davis' heart broke, with the very quiet and almost adult sadness in his Angelica's voice. "Aunt Milly dropped me off a few minutes ago to grab my teddy, and I heard you and Miss Candy arguing, and wanted to know what you'd said to make her mad," she said and looked away.

That she naturally took Candy's side and assumed Davis was the reason for the argument didn't escape his attention. At any other time he would have been glad, as it showed how much she cared for Candy.

However, at the present, his entire concentration was focused on wondering how much she'd overheard, praying she'd come in on the latter part of their conversation, and was upset they'd been arguing and not because she'd actually overheard what had been said.

"If you didn't want me, if you only stuck around because

you felt guilty about Mama being sick, then why didn't you just give me away?" she cried.

All hopes that she hadn't heard the details were dashed. Although he didn't turn around, didn't need to, Davis felt it the moment Candy was standing behind him, in the open doorway.

"Sweetheart, please . . ." he reached out again and this time she turned furious tear-stained eyes in his direction.

"Oh yeah, that's right. Nobody wanted me. You were stuck with me."

Her small chest heaved as the tears streamed down her small face. She wiped her face with the back of her sleeve and tried to stop the flow of tears as she glared at Davis.

Davis withdrew his hand, but hunkered down to eye level with her and placed both of his hands on her narrow shoulders, forcing her to turn around and face him.

"Look, sweetheart, I'm sorry. It's not true that no one wanted you. You overheard a conversation I wish to God you hadn't, and Daddy was feeling upset and said things that weren't true."

When she refused to look at him, tears running unchecked down her face, he felt close to tears himself and turned to look at Candy who stood in the doorway, helplessly observing their exchange.

"I need to talk to my daughter. I'll be back," Davis said and Candy nodded her head in agreement, not able to look at him. She wanted, desperately needed, to get away from him as quickly as she could before she completely broke down.

"That's fine. Don't worry about me, go take care of Angel," she said and quickly turned away.

She saw him hesitate, and silently prayed he would just go and take care of his daughter so she could get away.

"Will you stay? After I take care of her, you and I need to talk as well," Davis said, quietly.

Candy turned around and faced him, her bag slung over her shoulder and a determined smile plastered on her face.

"I think I'd better go, Davis. I think it's best for everyone right now," she replied, trying damn hard to keep it together.

"Look, you have to wait for me, you don't even have your car here. Let me take care of Angel, and then you and I can talk. Please."

"Go take care of your daughter," was her only response and with a slight hesitancy he nodded his head and stood, placing Angel's small hand in his and walked away.

Once he and Angelica reached her room, Candy withdrew her cell phone from her purse and called Karina.

Candy was relieved when she said she could pick her up within ten minutes.

She flipped the receiver down on the phone and quietly walked down the hallway toward the winding staircase. As she walked past Angelica's room, she could hear the low rumble of Davis' voice, and was just able to see, through the crack, the way he held Angelica's hand tightly with his own.

32

Why Candy thought the blues would take *her* blues away, she had no idea.

The stirring, soulful melody and heart-wrenching lyrics of love gone wrong poured out of her small stereo speakers and invaded her chaotic mind, as she sat in her favorite rocker in her living room.

She absentmindedly scratched behind her cat's ears while he purred loudly, eyes half-closed and content, sitting in her lap.

At least one of them was happy, Candy thought staring sightlessly out of her small living room's window at the fading light of the day.

With her hands sunk deeply in Rus' thick fur, her head pillowed by the slightly worn cushion on the old rocker, she inhaled, deeply, and blew out a short breath.

She was still able to smell *him* on the overlarge T-shirt she wore.

Candy closed her eyes and listened to the lyrics of the song.

Karina had called her earlier, but like all of the messages she'd gotten over the last week, Candy had ignored it, and allowed the calls to go directly to voice mail.

"You know, ignoring the machine won't work, any more so than you taking time off at the center, or hanging out, all by yourself in your house. And neither is ignoring Davis going to do you a bit of good. When are you going to talk to that man?" This had been the latest message on her machine and Candy had ignored it, as she had the others.

It had been nearly two weeks since she'd seen or spoken to Davis Strong. And in the two weeks, he had spent the first week calling her, coming by the center, trying to speak to her, but she'd always managed to avoid him, or be surrounded by others so she'd been able to slip away and not have to talk to him.

After a few days of avoiding him in person and his calls, he'd taken to sending her e-mails. She'd promptly deleted them, not having any real desire to even *read* what he had to say. There wasn't anything she wanted to hear from him. Not now. Maybe not ever.

With a sigh, she leaned further back into the rocker. When Russell made mewing sounds, she allowed him to jump from her lap and leaned back into the rocker.

When Karina had picked her up from Davis' home she hadn't asked what happened and Candy hadn't felt like sharing at the time.

She was not only hurt but mad as hell. She'd come to care more about Davis and Angelica than she should have. And she felt ten times the fool, for doing so. He had no right to say the things he had, to attack her like that, no matter how stressed he was over his situation with his daughter.

She understood that he was stressed. She understood that he was uncertain about how to broach the subject of Gail to Angelica, how much to disclose, how much was too much . . . too little. But she wasn't the bad guy. She only had their best interests at heart.

For him to claim she needed to work through her own abandonment issues before she could give him or Angelica any advice stung, deeply.

It stung even more when she went home and cried herself to sleep. Not because of the words he'd slung angrily, in the heat of the moment.

No, she understood that. It pissed her off no end, but she understood it was anger and frustration, mostly self-directed, that spurred his tirade.

The reason she'd cried herself to sleep was because some of his comments had hit home.

Damn.

When he'd said she was a fraud, she'd angrily told him off, yelled at him, telling him he didn't know what he was talking about. The issue was him and his daughter and the fact he was too damn scared to tell her the truth about her mother and get over it. He was the one lying and avoiding the past, pretending it was something it wasn't, for no good reason. He was the one with the issues. Not her.

Damn, damn, damn, she thought.

Davis forced her to acknowledge her own unavoidable demons, and in doing so, she came face to face with a few revelations that had been stewing in her subconscious for years.

They weren't issues she was unaware of. Simply, she'd placed them in individual compartments in her brain, and mentally bookmarked the *delve into later . . . much later* file. But she'd never quite gotten around into delving into that particular file.

It was too painful.

She sighed. "But sometimes life has an annoying habit of forcing a woman to clean her mental office," she spoke out loud as she continued to stroke Russell's thick pelt.

She'd always been comfortable with who she was. Well, as much as any woman could be, she thought. But Davis's hurtful words had forced her to acknowledge painful truths. She did thumb her nose at conventionality for a reason.

As much like her father as she was, or *told* herself she was . . . there was a part of her that always wanted to fit in.

When her mother, and later her brother, left them, Candy had been heartbroken, and no matter how many times her father expressed his love, told her she wasn't the reason they left, she'd secretly harbored a desire to go with them.

And that had made her feel the guiltiest of all.

As a new song began to play, by one of her favorite acoustic guitar artists, she allowed herself to be swept up in the smooth rhythms, letting the disturbing thoughts ease from her mind. Or go back to their *delve into much later* file, she thought.

She welcomed the satin tones and haunting lyrics as they washed over her, enveloping her in their heady embrace.

She parted her lips as the feathery strokes played against her bottom lip, tugging and pulling. She felt the velvety strokes against her straining nipples, the simultaneous touches leaving her breathless . . .

She quickly opened her eyes, realizing what she was doing, or about to do.

Lord, have mercy.

Not only had the last two weeks been difficult as she thought of her past, while trying to avoid speaking to Davis until she sorted out her tangle of emotions, they'd also been nearly impossible in trying to keep thoughts of him, of them making love, out of her mind.

And she wasn't helping matters by sleeping in his T-shirt just so that she could envelop herself in his scent. A T-shirt she'd worn every night since they'd separated.

All alone she sat smelling his shirt just to catch a whiff of his scent like some Victorian maiden whack job. With disgust, she tore the shirt from her body. Wearing nothing but her wrap and a sports bra, she flung the shirt to the floor.

She raised herself up from the chair and followed the loudly mewing Russell into the kitchen to feed him. While in the kitchen she decided to brew herself a fresh batch of chamomile and rosemary blend herbal tea.

Lord only knew she needed something to calm her chaotic mind, if simply listening to music had the stimulating effect of arousing her, her thoughts obviously on Davis.

She'd thought of Angelica, as well, over the last two weeks. Candy hadn't expected to see her the previous week, knowing the schools were out for spring break, but she'd thought she'd be in the following week and when she hadn't, Candy had been tempted to call their home, to find out if she was okay.

Maybe that had something to do with why she hadn't seen or heard from Davis over the last week.

Whatever the reason he'd stopped his calls and e-mails the last few days, Candy reminded herself it was what she wanted . . . what she *needed* for the time being.

"I don't need someone in my life who is trying to validate who he is, and in the process forcing me to self-examine." Candy spoke out loud, to the room at large.

She filled the yowling tabby's bowl and placed it back down on his place mat and rubbed the top of his head. "Don't you agree, Rus?" she asked, but of course, as usual, Rus only had eyes for his food.

"Again . . . the male chromosome has no respect for species, men are all the same. One thing on their mind, and again, it doesn't seem to be me."

Candy felt as though she'd said the same thing, on more than one occasion, to an unresponsive audience. She watched as the big tomcat began to devour his food in record time.

Afterward he strolled away from his dish, plopped his butt down on the floor, raised his leg and licked his balls clean.

"Dang, Rus . . . that is *so* nasty."

He paused mid-lick and his golden, slanted eyes assessed

her. Candy could have *sworn* he gave her a wink, along with a superior look that mocked her, telling her in cat language that because he could . . . he did.

With a loud mew, he returned to his task and Candy had an irrational desire to throw something at the smirking cat.

Yes, males were all the same, didn't matter the species.

Give them what they wanted and they licked their balls and forgot all about you, she thought.

Despite her dour mood, she laughed out loud at her ridiculous thoughts as she poured her tea and carried it out of the kitchen to return to her living room.

After she placed the mug of steaming tea down, Candy picked up the discarded T-shirt she'd thrown to the floor and held it between her hands, absently, her mind a million miles away as she caressed the soft, worn cotton.

Davis had completed several drive-bys, circling her block four or five times, before he came to a halt and parked his SUV down the street from her small house.

If he wasn't careful, her neighborhood watch would be all over him, considering the lateness of the hour.

He could have sworn he saw a woman who looked a hell of a lot like Sister Pauline, standing on her neatly manicured lawn, staring him down. Her hands rested on her ample hips while the light streaming from inside her house from the door she'd left open showed the suspicious scowl on her face as she stared at him as he made the fifth drive-by.

Deciding he didn't want to get arrested for suspicious behavior, he started the engine back up, drove down the street, pulled into Candy's driveway and cut the engine.

As he glanced out of his rearview mirror, he noted the woman with the resemblance to Sister Pauline continued to stay rooted in her spot, not moving a muscle.

With a resigned sigh, he opened the door and climbed out of

the car. He knew if he didn't the woman would give him only so long, before she called the cops.

"Hey you . . . aren't you Davis Strong?" she called out. Surprised when he heard her voice, he turned toward her, and realized that she didn't resemble Pauline Rogers, she *was* Pauline Rogers.

"Sister Pauline?" He began to walk toward the old woman.

She was wearing a thickly matted, faux-fur coat, buttoned completely to the top, and although she wore a big white fluffy knit cap on her head, complete with white puff ball, Davis could see the tips of her of her curly, gray wig peek out from beneath. He felt the beginning of a smile tug at his lips.

"Mmm, hmmm . . . it's me. I'm over here taking care of my sister while she's recuperating from that ugly hip replacement surgery. Although God in heaven, and his heavenly host only know why Nadine is even bothering with all that at our age! I'm younger than her by eighteen months so I don't *exactly* know what she's going through, but still," she said.

She patted her wig in place through the hat on her head and made the familiar popping sound with her tongue against the roof of her mouth.

Davis wanted to laugh, but checked himself. He'd learned from Candy that Sister Pauline, although a professed saved, sanctified, God-fearing, church-going woman . . . had no problem losing her religion, so to speak, if someone tested her, as Candy put it.

Davis had no desire to test her.

"The doctor said Nadine's last replacement would last another five, ten years before she'd have to replace it; hell, this new one will last longer than she will!" the old woman cackled, a wicked, humorous glint in her dark eyes.

"Well, I'm sure she's glad you're here to take care of her. Nothing like a sister's love and devotion at a time like this."

The old woman "hummed" and squinted her eyes at him, looking over the tops of her fogging half-lenses.

"It's too cold to be running around outside. The weatherman can say it's going to be an early spring all he wants . . . but it ain't warm yet."

The way her eyes bored into him, Davis felt like an errant boy in front of his mother and resisted the urge to straighten and button his leather jacket.

"What are you doing around here anyway? Here to visit Ms. Candy?" she asked and rolled her tongue with her signature pop against the roof of her mouth.

It had been two weeks since he'd spoken to Candy. The first week he'd done everything in his power to talk to her, apologize . . . beg for forgiveness. She'd been right about so much.

The night she'd left, he and Angelica had stayed up until well past one in the morning talking. After he realized Candy had left, twenty minutes into talking to Angelica, he'd been worried and had one hand on the phone when he discovered the note she left, telling him she'd called a friend to take her home.

Unbidden, wild jealousy ran rampant when his first thought was that the friend was Nate, her intern from the center. He'd called her cell phone and she'd answered, assuring him she was safe and at home.

He'd demanded, like an idiot, to know if she'd called Nate to bring her home and she'd quietly hung up the phone on him. That was the last time they'd spoken.

He'd then gone back to Angelica and they had spoken about things that in the beginning he felt uncomfortable sharing with her. Although he tempered his words, he was honest with her. Direct.

But after the initial sadness he caught in her eyes, the tears that tugged at his heart, she sat back against the headboard of her canopy bed and smiled around the tears, when he told her about her mother.

Sharing stories of what she was like growing up, how funny she was, her dry humor and quick wit that he knew Angelica had inherited from her.

In the end it had been emotional for both of them. But it was needed, way overdue.

The following week, Davis had left work early and picked Angel up from the center early. Every time he'd come, Candy had found an excuse not to be there. He'd done his best to try and catch her alone, but either she was with a child, or Sister Pauline would run interference and, frustrated, he'd started to e-mail her.

She hadn't answered those any more than she had his phone calls.

At spring break he decided to take Angelica on a small vacation, deciding they both could do with getting away from Stanton. He'd returned on the weekend, and like an addict, he'd driven by the center on the pretense of discussing the spring plans for construction for the center only to find out Candy had taken the last few days off.

Frustrated, he was determined enough was enough. She would see him, they would talk, and she'd quit acting like a kid and admit she loved him. And forgive him for acting like an ass.

Because he sure in the hell loved her.

He hadn't realize how much until he felt as though someone kicked him in the gut after he'd hurled the hurtful words her way.

The proud way she'd stared him down didn't hide the pain in her eyes.

He could see past that. She'd gotten so far under his skin that he *knew her.*

And he realized he felt like this only because he loved her. The kind of deep, soul-wrenching type of love that came only once in a lifetime. It had been building for almost a year. Slowly creeping up on him, sneaky. Irritating as all hell, it was. It confused him, had him twisted all up, dreaming of her at night, hot scorching dreams where he would wake up damn near in pain his dick was so hard, cum all over the damn sheets as he'd made love to the woman in his dreams, the woman *of* his dreams.

Because even though he hadn't claimed her, she'd been his from the first moment they'd met.

It had taken his mind longer to catch up with what his heart already knew.

Shit.

And now he needed to "re-claim" his woman. And he wasn't about to take no for an answer.

He turned his attention to Sister Pauline and felt the burden lift with his resolve.

"No, Sister Pauline, It's deeper than that. I'm here to get my woman back."

She stared at him, squinting her eyes behind her fogged-up glasses for long moments. Then the old woman's mouth twitched before she let out a loud guffaw and popped Davis so hard on the back he nearly fell face forward in the melting snow.

"Well hell it's about time! What in the name of heaven took you so darn long, boy? Go on in there and get your woman and quit playin' around!"

33

"Hold on, I'm coming," Candy yelled.

She dropped the shirt she'd clutched in her hand like it burned her when she heard the banging at her front door.

She quickly picked the T-shirt back up and walked toward the door, glancing at the old grandfather clock in the corner.

At nearly midnight, she wondered who was coming to visit her so late and cautiously raised herself on tiptoe to glance through the peephole.

Before she saw his large frame filling her lit porch, Candy already knew who was at her door banging like he'd lost his mind.

Davis.

She looked down at the T-shirt clutched in her hands and was torn. She either put the shirt back on, or answered the door wearing nothing but her bra and brazen it out.

With a mental shrug Candy decided she might as well put his shirt back on and hope Davis wouldn't notice it was his.

"Hold on, please. I need to take off the chain," she spoke loudly over his banging and yanked the T-shirt down over her hips.

She drew back the chain and carefully opened the heavy door. Candy inhaled a deep surprised breath when she saw he stepped further into the light, and she could see his face.

His normally closed expression was an open book and a wealth of emotions flashed across his face, ranging from desire, anger, frustration . . . to love.

It was all there and Candy forced herself not to respond, not to reach out and grab him by the lapels of his leather jacket and haul him close to her.

She carefully kept her features neutral, not wanting one bit of her feelings, none of her emotions, to show.

"I love you, Candy," he said staring down at her with such an incredibly intense look in his light gray eyes that she nearly staggered back from the effect.

"I said I love you, Candy," he repeated and cleared his voice before he drew in a deep breath. "Will you marry me?"

Davis stared down at her and waited, with an expectant look on his handsome face.

"Well, aren't you going to say something?"

When she made no response, a small tic appeared in the corner of his sexy, chiseled lips before the hesitant smile that had began to flower gradually began to wither away and all but disappear.

"Did you want to come inside, Davis?" she asked calmly and when he nodded his head shortly she stood back and allowed him to enter.

She closed the door and locked it, before she turned to face him. He'd only taken a few steps into her living room before she spoke.

"What did you want me to say, Davis? Did you want me to jump up and down and shout to the heavens in gratitude that my man loves me?" she asked, her voice only squeaking just the smallest bit.

"That my man reached down *deep*," she said, warming up to her topic. She not only emphasized the word "deep," but dragged it out as far as she possibly could.

Davis crossed his arms over his leather-clad chest and raised a brow at her theatrics. He opened his mouth to speak but Candy beat him to it.

"And discovered that he loved me? That he couldn't live without me? Me with all my strange unconventional ways," she began and watched warily as he took his leather jacket off and carefully laid it over the back of her small forest-green sofa before turning back to her.

"Go on," he said when she paused when he took steps closer to her.

"A woman who not long ago he didn't think was suitable to give advice to his daughter, much less a group of impressionable young women? Yes, I know I have some things to work out, but who doesn't? But you know what?"

Davis cocked his head, encouraging her to continue. "Tell me what, Candy?" he asked.

She glanced up, caught off-guard, wondering how he'd gotten so close so quickly. He now was standing less than a foot from her.

Candy felt her renegade nipples response to his sudden nearness, but she refused to allow that to stop her until she'd had her say.

"I neither want, nor do I need your or anyone else's stamp of approval over my life. I am an educated, intelligent woman who has a lot to offer not only to the young women I mentor— which I do a damn fine job of, by the way—but also to the right man. A man who doesn't judge, a man who will love me for me, tattoos, piercings, and all. A man who loves me with all his heart. For that man, I will give my all. I won't hold anything back from him, the good, the bad, whatever . . . all of it. He'll be worth it. Because he'll know that I'm worth it, and I won't have to prove a damn thing to him," she finished, unable to hold back the tears that trickled down her face.

"I don't fucking deserve you, but God, I love you, Candy," he said and that was all.

Tears had escaped her eyes as she'd spilled her heart to him and his hungry gaze had roamed over her beautiful face, over every beloved feature before traveling over her body.

He felt the unexpected sting of tears in his own eyes by the time she'd finished speaking and clenched his teeth tightly.

The corners of his lips lifted slightly when he noticed she was wearing his shirt over one of her funky little fabric wraps and thick grey granny socks on her feet. Her hair was gathered into a sloppy topknot on top of her head and she was the most beautiful woman he'd ever seen in his life.

He didn't say anything else, simply reached out to her over the small distance separating them and pulled her into his arms.

"Shut up, Candy. I was an ass, no two ways about it, but you love me and you know you do," he said and lowered his head and kissed her.

She struggled for a respectable amount of time before her lips softened and she returned his kiss. He slipped his tongue into the seam of her lips and groaned when she allowed him entry.

He knew she loved him, it was there in her face, despite the carefully neutral expression she'd tried to erect and maintain. She had every right to be angry with him, had every right to tell him to go to hell after what he'd said to her.

But he knew she wouldn't. Because she loved him almost as much as he loved her, no matter what.

Her body's response to his was instant. He could feel her tight little nipples stab him as she pressed herself against his chest, groaning as she wound her arms around his neck.

After several long minutes, he dragged his mouth away from

the nirvana of her lips long enough to ask, "You do believe me, don't you, Candy?" he asked, his breathing heavy.

Her tongue snuck out and nervously licked the full bottom rim of her lip and he placed a finger beneath her chin and raised it.

"I'm serious, Candy. I need to know. Do you believe me?" he asked and felt more nervous than he ever had in his life, as he waited for her answer.

"Yes, I believe you," she finally answered and a part of the pressing weight on his heart lifted with her answer. "But we need to talk—" she started to speak, but Davis placed a finger over her mouth, hushing her.

"I know. Baby, I know we do. But all of that's going to have to wait. I have to feel you, Candy. I need to feel you wrapped around me before I lose my damn mind. Two weeks without you has me climbing the walls, and if I don't get to that pretty kitty of yours soon . . ." he laughed shakily, a husky catch in his throat. When she nodded her head in agreement, he lifted her in his arms.

"Where's your bedroom?"

She pointed the way down a hallway in her small house and Davis walked with his beloved bundle down the short hallway that led to her bedroom.

He didn't bother turning on the light, simply walked to the bed and lay her down, immediately crushing her small body with his.

Between muffled kisses, groans and soft sighs, they managed to undress one another other and soon she lay naked and compliant beneath his body.

"I don't know how long this is going to last, Candy. God, I've missed you so much!" he said and slipped a hand between their bodies, separating her vaginal lips and testing her readiness for him.

He groaned harshly when she was creamy and ready for him.

"That's okay, Davis. Please, just love me," she begged.

Davis tried to be gentle as he moved her thighs further apart, afraid he'd hurt her, he was so damn randy for her. He guided the head of his penis into her streaming entry and carefully pushed into her moist heat.

Once fully embedded inside, Davis paused, not moving as he enjoyed the feeling of being one with her.

He felt complete, whole. He'd never felt like this while making love with another woman, the way he did with Candy. Making love with her went beyond the physical act, and became a total expression of love, of finding the other, perfect half to him.

He adjusted her sweetness on his cock, and carefully lay on her, blanketing her with his body. He held her hips steady as he slowly, with excruciating slowness, ground into her, nestling deep inside her warmth.

As impatient as he was to make love to her and how badly he needed to come, he still rocked her nice and slow, easing in and out of her creaming heat with care. This time as they made love he wanted to *feel* her.

He wanted to relish her, saturate and drown himself in her essence. In the short time they'd been intimate, Davis had become addicted to her sweetness, and now that he had her beneath him again, he intended to take his time, and reacquaint himself with her.

When Candy wrapped her legs around his lean hips and tried to hasten his pace, the heels of her feet pushing against his taut butt cheeks, he gave a rough masculine laugh, and she groaned.

"Oh God, I missed you, missed this" she whispered as she accepted, gladly, his short easy glides.

He was feeding her *just* enough of himself to feel good, but not enough to completely satisfy her.

When he picked up the pace of his strokes and roughly

pulled one of her breasts into the warm, wet cavern of his mouth and sucked, Candy felt her body hum, tingling as the orgasm began to churn through her.

"I'm coming, baby . . . Davis, I'm coming . . ." she screamed.

As the orgasm overwhelmed her, he began to rock into her hard, both hands grasping her hips in a grip so harsh she knew she'd have marks in the morning.

But now she didn't care, all she cared about was the pounding thrusts and the tight suction he maintained on her titties as he plummeted into her pussy.

She reached between their close bodies and cupped his tightly drawn balls and he reared his big body away, and yelled.

"I love you, Candy," he yelled as he came, his hot seed bursting, jetting into her like a geyser, splashing the walls of her uterus, her womb.

"Oh God, I love you too, Davis!"

With a few more deep strokes together they went up in flames, reaching their peak in unison.

34

"Enough that you'd consider marrying me?" Davis picked up the conversation where they'd left off, before they'd slaked their first-round lust for each other's bodies.

He had her small body positioned in front of his and they lay facing one another on her soft bed, amid all one hundred and one of her pillows. He hadn't noticed how many she had when they'd laid down, because his entire focus had been on getting them both naked.

"Did you hear me, baby?" He felt his heart thud in his throat the sound was so loud, while he waited for her answer.

When she remained silent dread settled in his gut and he pulled her tight against his body, his hands wrapped securely around her small waist.

"You may as well say yes, Candy. I won't accept anything else," he warned, darkly.

"Oh? Is that a fact?" she responded. Davis detected a hint of lightness in her voice and he felt a bit of the constriction around his heart ease.

"Yeah, that's a fact."

"We have a few things to discuss, before we go there, don't you think?"

"Yes, we do," he agreed, solemnly.

He raised her chin with two fingers and stared down into her beautiful light brown eyes, eyes which had haunted his dreams for almost a year.

"Candy, I owe you a lot."

"You owe me?" she echoed, and he heard the surprise in her voice.

"I do. You've helped me connect with my daughter, which forced me let go of the guilt of the past. Without you, I don't know if I would have been able to do so," he admitted.

"You would have eventually, Davis. But I'm glad I was able to help. And neither do you owe me anything. I care about you and Angelica. If I was able to help in any small way, that's payment enough."

His heart did a flip when she smiled up at him, and in the dark, her smile illuminated the entire room. She traced the cleft in his chin with featherlight touches with the tips of her fingers. Davis captured her hand and lay a small kiss in the center of her palm before releasing it.

"At any rate you helped me realize my daughter needed more than what I was giving her. No amount of love and overindulging could make up for gifting her with the truth."

"How did it go?"

Davis sighed and pulled her closer. He lay back against one of the large pillows with her. She rested her head on his chest, her hands playing with the scattering of hair around his pectoral muscles.

"Angel was so hungry for information about her mother, any information, that she didn't seem to be as badly affected by learning about how we became a family as I thought she would. In fact, it pained me that I'd been the source of causing my baby so much angst."

"How were you the cause?"

"Had I not been so bent on pretending nothing had been out of the ordinary, that we had been a happy family before her mother passed, things would have been different. For both of us," he said.

He filled Candy in on the conversation with Angelica. How in the beginning of their talk he'd been uncomfortable, not sure how much to disclose, but in the end he told her as much of the truth as he could.

"I kept back that I felt betrayed by her mother. Neither did I tell her Gail knew she was pregnant by another man. Maybe in time, when she's older, we can go there, but for now that wasn't necessary to tell her, I didn't think."

"No, I agree, that's too much for a nine-year-old. To understand the complexities of adult behavior can confuse the most sophisticated of us," Candy murmured in agreement.

"Definitely. I was a convenience for Gail; there was no need to tell Angelica that. It was more important she learn what her mother was like, her personality, her likes and dislikes. Something I'd never shared with her, because I avoided discussion about Gail," he said and shook his head at his own male, ego-driven folly. "It was important she understood her mother loved her deeply, without reservation, and wanted the best for her. That was the most important information I could impart."

"Yes, she did want the best for her, Davis. And I believe that although what she did to you was wrong and completely unethical, I do understand. She knew you would be an amazing father for her child."

The sincerity of her words struck him in the middle of his heart. When he laughed self-consciously, Candy leaned up and away from his chest before she grasped the both sides of his face between her warm hands.

"Davis, it's true. You are such a caring father, such a loving man, a woman would be foolish as hell not to want you to be the father of her children. I know I would love to have you as the father of any child I'd be blessed to conceive."

When the words left her mouth, Davis saw the way her eyes widened, her own words penetrating her brain, and a wide smile split his face.

"You invaded my dreams almost a year ago, Candy. No matter how many times I told myself I was too old for you, you were too different, you wouldn't want me . . . none of that mattered because I started falling in love with you from the moment I laid eyes on you," he said.

He pulled her close and gave her a lingering kiss before he released her.

"Hold on, I need to get something," he said, giving her a sweet kiss, licking the tear away from her cheek before he bounded from the bed.

Candy propped her chin in the palm of her hand and rested her elbow on the bed. She grinned and enjoyed the show as the moon streaked light across his taut, chiseled buttocks and ran down the length of his thick, muscled legs as he bent over and picked up his jeans.

She watched in curiosity and then dawning realization when he withdrew a small gold box, topped with a small foil bow.

Her heart began to pound heavily as he walked back toward the bed, took the proverbial knee and opened the box. The princess-cut emerald nestled inside winked beautifully at her as he took her hand in between his.

"I love everything about you, Candy. Your intelligence, your uniqueness, your scent, your beauty, your zest for life, your beautiful caring nature, your dedication to Girls Unlimited, how you love your girls and they love you. How you love me and my daughter," he finished his litany huskily and paused to clear his throat.

This time Candy allowed the emotion to run through her and felt tears sting the corners of her eyes. He withdrew the ring and tossed the box over his shoulder and she gave a small laugh around a hiccup.

"You said you loved me, Candy," he reminded her, with a hint of smugness to his voice. "And I think I've gotten to know you well enough over these last months to know when you love, you do it completely, no holds barred, full steam ahead . . . am I right?"

"Yes," she agreed and bit the inside of her cheek to prevent herself from smiling.

"Well, I'm here on the clichéd bended knee to ask that you love me enough to allow me and Angelica to become a permanent part of your life. The last few weeks have been unlike any in my life, as we've gotten to know one another, and not just physically. It goes beyond the physical in a way no one would understand unless they've experienced true love."

Joy welled inside Candy as his loving words cascaded down on her like welcomed rain after a drought.

"Baby, you complete me, and I'm asking you to allow me to show you I'm willing and ready to do whatever it takes to make you happy. I want you in my life, fully, wholly. Trust me, Candy. I won't ever knowingly hurt you. Your well-being and happiness will always be placed above all others, yours and Angelica's. Do you have enough faith to believe I will always take care of you? That I love you, mind, body and soul?" he asked, his eyes earnest, the emotion on his face raw, real.

Candy, who prided herself on her communication skills, was unable to utter a word, her mind in a whirl as she considered his request.

She allowed her eyes to roam his face, looking for what, she didn't know, something to help her make the most important decision of her life.

The only thing she saw, the only thing that mattered, was

the light of honesty and love she saw reflected in his eyes and her decision was made.

She loved this man with all her heart, had loved him from the moment she laid eyes on him.

The last months had only sealed her fate, a fate that had been decided long ago, before they'd even met. She needed to be with him. There were no two ways about it. She loved him, loved Angelica and there was no way she was going to let either one of them go.

With a nod of her head she gave her answer and he let out a loud "whoop!"

With shaking hands he eased the ring on her finger. Tears of joy ran down both of their faces, as they grabbed on to one another and clung as though for dear life before Davis smothered her faces with kisses.

"Yes, baby. Yes, I'll marry you." She promised and saw a wealth of emotion pass over Davis's handsome features; relief and joy only some of them.

"You'll never regret it, Candy. I'll make sure of that. You can trust me. I have you now, and I'm never going to let you go," he told her gruffly. "Now why don't we seal this bargain with a kiss?"

He captured her mouth with his in a toe-curling kiss, and with a sigh of happiness she allowed him to tumble them back on the bed.

Her last coherent thought, before he covered her body with his and eased inside her welcoming sheath was that the kiss was only metaphorical. Candy's fate had been sealed the moment she'd met Davis, the moment they'd laid eyes on one another. They belonged together.

Turn the page for a preview of
Kate Pearce's new novel,
SIMPLY SEXUAL!

Coming soon!

1

Sara pressed her fingers to her mouth to stop from gasping as she watched the man and woman writhe together on the tangled bedsheets. Daisy's plump thighs were locked around the hips of the man who pushed relentlessly inside her. The violent rhythm of his thrusts made the iron bedstead creak as Daisy moaned and cried out his name.

Sara knew she should move away from the half-opened door. But she couldn't take her gaze away from the frenzied activity on the bed. Her skin prickled, and her heart thumped hard against her breasts.

When Daisy screeched and convulsed as if she were suffering a fit, a small sound escaped Sara's lips. To her horror, the man on top of Daisy reared back as though he'd heard something. He turned his head, and his eyes locked with hers. Sara spun away, gathered her shawl around her shoulders, and stumbled back along the corridor. She had her hand on the landing door when footsteps behind her made her pause.

"Did you enjoy that?"

Lord Valentin Sokorvsky's amused voice halted Sara's hurried retreat. Reluctantly she turned to face him. He strolled toward her, tucking his white shirt into his unfastened breeches. His discarded coat, waistcoat, and cravat hung over his arm. A thin glow of perspiration covered his tanned skin, a testament to his recent exertions.

Sara drew herself up to her full height. "The question of enjoyment did not arise, my lord. I merely confirmed my suspicions that you are not a fit mate for my youngest sister."

Lord Valentin was close enough now for Sara to stare into his violet eyes. He was the most beautiful man she had ever seen. His body was as graceful as a Greek sculpture, and he moved like a trained dancer. Although she mistrusted him, she yearned to reach out and stroke his lush lower lip just to see if he was real. His hair was a rich chestnut brown, held back from his face with a black silk ribbon. An unfashionable style, but it suited him.

He arched one eyebrow. Every movement he made was so polished, she suspected he practiced each one in the mirror until he perfected it. His open-necked shirt revealed half a bronzed coin strung on a strand of leather and hinted at the thickness of the hair on his chest.

"Men have . . . needs, Miss Harrison. I'm sure your sister is aware of that."

As he moved closer, Sara tried to take shallow breaths. His citrus scent was underscored by another more powerful and elusive smell that she realized must be sex. She'd never imagined lovemaking had a particular scent. She'd always thought procreation would be a quiet orderly affair in the privacy of a marriage bed, not the primitive, noisy, exuberant mating she'd just witnessed.

"My sister is a lady, Lord Sokorvsky. What would she know of men's desires?"

"Enough to know that a man looks for heirs and obedience from his wife and pleasure from his mistress."

She felt a rush of anger on her sister's behalf. "Perhaps she deserves more. Personally, I cannot think of anything worse than being trapped in a marriage like that."

His extraordinary eyes sparked with interest as he appeared to notice her nightclothes and bare feet for the first time. Sara edged back toward the door. He angled his body to block her exit.

"Is that why you frequent the servants' wing in the dead of night? Have you decided to risk all for the love of a common man?"

Sara blushed and clutched her shawl tightly to her breasts. "I came to see if what my maid told me was true."

"Ah." He glanced back down the corridor. "Daisy is your maid?" He swept her an elegant bow. "Consider me well and truly compromised. What do you intend to do? Insist I marry her? Go and tell tales to your father?"

She glared at him. How could she tell her father that the man he regarded as a protégé was a licentious rake? And then there was the matter of Lord Sokorvsky's immense wealth. Her father's seafaring enterprises had not fared well in recent years.

She licked her lips. His interested gaze followed the movement of her tongue. "My father thinks very highly of you. He was delighted when you offered to marry one of his daughters."

He leaned his shoulder against the wall and considered her, his expression serious. "I owe your father my life. I would marry all three of you if such a thing were allowed in this country."

"Fortunately for you, it is not," Sara snapped. His face resumed the lazy, taunting expression she had come to dread. "As to my purpose, I thought to appeal to your better nature. I wanted to ask you not to dishonor my sister by taking a mistress after you wed and to remain true to your vows."

He stared at her for a long moment and then began to laugh. "You expect me to remain faithful to your sister forever?" His eyes darkened to reveal a hint of steel. "In return for what?"

"I won't tell my father about your dishonorable behavior tonight. He would be so disappointed in you."

His smile disappeared. He stepped so close his booted feet nudged Sara's bare toes. "That's blackmail. And there's no way in hell you would ever know whether I kept my word or not."

Sara managed a small triumphant smile. "You do not keep your promises, then? You are a man without honor?"

He put his fingers under her chin and jerked her head up to meet his gaze. She found it difficult to breathe as she gazed into his amazing eyes. Why hadn't she realized that beneath his exquisite exterior lay a deadly iron will?

"I can assure you, I keep my promises."

Sara found her voice. "Charlotte is only seventeen. She knows little of the world. I am only trying to protect her."

He released her chin and slid his fingers down the side of her throat to her shoulder. To her relief, his air of contained violence dissipated.

"Why didn't your parents put you forward to marry me? You are the oldest, are you not?"

She glanced pointedly at his hand, which still rested on her shoulder. "I'm twenty-six. I had my chance to catch a husband. I had a Season in London and failed to capitalize on it."

He curled a lock of her black hair around his finger. She shivered. His rapt expression intensified.

"Charlotte is the most beautiful and biddable of my sisters. She deserves a chance to become a rich man's wife."

His soft laugh startled her, and his warm breath fanned her neck. "Like me, you mean?"

Sara stared boldly into his eyes. "Yes, although . . ." She

frowned, distracted by his nearness. "Emily might be a better match for you. She is more impressed by wealth and status than Charlotte."

"You possess something neither of your sisters has."

Sara bit her lip. "You don't need to remind me. Apparently I am impulsive and too direct for most men's taste."

He tugged lightly on the curl of her hair. "Not all men. I have been known to admire a woman with drive and determination."

She lifted her gaze and met his eyes. Something urgent sparked between them. She fought a desire to lean closer and rub her cheek against his muscular chest. "I think I will make a far better spinster aunt than a wife. At least I will be able to be myself."

His lazy smile was as intimate as a caress. "But what about the joys of the marriage bed? Might you not regret sampling those?"

She gave a disdainful sniff. "If what I have just seen is an example of those 'joys,' perhaps I am well rid of them."

His fingers tightened in her hair. "You didn't enjoy watching me fuck your maid?"

Sara gaped at him.

His smile widened. He extended his index finger and gently closed her mouth. "Not only are you a prude, Miss Harrison, but you are also a liar."

Heat flooded her cheeks. Sara wanted to cross her arms over her breasts. She trembled when he stepped back and studied her.

"Your skin is flushed, and I can see your nipples through your nightgown. If I slid my hand between your legs, I wager you'd be wet and ready for me."

Sara's fingers twitched in an instinctive impulse to slap his handsome face. She waited for a rush of anger to fuel her courage, but nothing happened. Only a strange sense of waiting, of tension, of need—as if her body knew something her mind hadn't yet understood. She let him look at her, tempted to take his hand and press it to her breast. Somehow she knew he would assuage the pulsing ache that flooded her senses.

As if he'd read her thoughts, he reached out and circled the tight bud of her nipple. Sara closed her eyes as a pang of need shot straight to her womb.

"Sara. . . ."

His low voice broke the spell. She covered herself with her shawl and backed away. As soon as she managed to wrench the door open, she ran. His laughter pursued her down the stairwell.

Valentin stared after Sara Harrison as his shaft thickened and grew against his unbuttoned breeches. He absentmindedly set himself to rights and considered her reaction to him. She needed a man inside her whether she realized it or not. Perhaps he should reconsider his plan to marry the young and oh-so-biddable Charlotte.

His smile faded as he followed Sara down the stairs. John Harrison had a special bond with his eldest daughter. Knowing Valentin's sordid history, would John allow him to marry his favorite child? It was interesting that she hadn't been offered to him as a potential bride to begin with.

He strolled down one flight of stairs and made his way back along the darkened corridor to his bedroom. There was no sign of Sara.

Valentin surveyed his empty bed and imagined Sara lying naked in the center, her long black hair spread on the pillows, her arms open wide to welcome him. He frowned as his cock throbbed with need. Sara Harrison would not be a complacent wife. To lay the ghosts of his past, he needed to settle down with a conventional woman who would present him with children and leave him to his own devices.

Before leaving town, he'd spent an uproarious evening with

his friends and current mistress, composing a list of the qualities a man required in a society wife. One of her sisters would definitely be a better choice. He suspected Sara would be a challenge.

Her frank curiosity stirred his senses. He'd wanted to part her lips and take her mouth to see how she tasted. He'd forgotten how erotic a first kiss could be, having moved onto more interesting territory a long time ago. Her innocence and underlying sensuality deserved to be explored. Wasn't that what he truly craved?

He stripped off his clothes and let them drop to the floor. The meager fire had gone out, and coldness crept through the ill-fitting windows and door. At least he had a few days' grace before he needed to make his decision. John Harrison was not due to return to his family until Friday night. Valentin climbed into bed. His brief, interrupted tryst with the enthusiastic Daisy had done little to slake his desire.

Valentin tried to ignore the unpleasant smell of damp and mildewed sheets as he closed his fist around his erection and stroked himself toward a climax. Imagining it was Sara who touched him made him want to come quickly. He didn't allow her image to destroy the sensual buildup of sexual anticipation that burned through his aroused body.

He pictured her startled face as she'd watched him fuck Daisy. Had she wanted to touch him herself? The thought made him shudder. His body jerked as he climaxed. He closed his eyes, and a vision of Sara's passionate face flooded his senses.

His last thought as sleep claimed him was of her coming under him as he took his release deep inside her again and again.